P9-CEF-256

MOMENT OF TRUTH

Cupping Diana's chin, Jared gently raised her face. His dark gaze held a glow that both frightened and delighted her, something flamelike and dangerous. Diana shivered, mesmerized by that light.

Jared bent his head. His lips brushed her cheek with butterfly softness, and from the deepest part of her, an unexpected response surged forth.

With the last of her will power, she turned her head away.

"No!" she whispered, "Please, no!"

"But, we are betrothed," he laughed softly . . . *and though there was no truth to their troth, there was no pretense in his passion. . . .*

ANNE BARBOUR developed an affection for the Regency period while living in England. She now lives in the Black Hills of South Dakota with her husband, a retired lieutenant colonel. She is the mother of six children, all grown, and she loves to boast of her five grandchildren.

SIGNET REGENCY ROMANCE
COMING IN DECEMBER 1992

Margaret Evans Porter
Road To Ruin

Melinda McRae
The Highland Lord

Mary Balogh
A Christmas Promise

AT YOUR LOCAL BOOKSTORE
OR ORDER DIRECTLY
FROM THE PUBLISHER
WITH VISA OR MASTERCARD
1-800-253-6476

A PRESSING ENGAGEMENT

by

Anne Barbour

A SIGNET BOOK

SIGNET
Published by the Penguin Group
Penguin Books USA Inc., 375 Hudson Street
New York, New York 10014, U.S.A.
Penguin Books Ltd, 27 Wrights Lane,
London W8 5TZ, England
Penguin Books Australia Ltd, Ringwood,
Victoria, Australia
Penguin Books Canada Ltd, 10 Alcorn Avenue,
Toronto, Ontario, Canada M4V 3B2
Penguin Books (N.Z.) Ltd, 182-190 Wairau Road,
Auckland 10, New Zealand

Penguin Books Ltd, Registered Offices:
Harmondsworth, Middlesex, England

First published by Signet, an imprint of New American Library,
a division of Penguin Books USA Inc.

First Printing, November, 1992
10 9 8 7 6 5 4 3 2 1

Copyright © Barbara Yirka, 1992
All rights reserved

REGISTERED TRADEMARK—MARCA REGISTRADA

Printed in the United States of America

Without limiting the rights under copyright reserved above, no part of this
publication may be reproduced, stored in or introduced into a retrieval system,
or transmitted, in any form, or by any means (electronic, mechanical,
photocopying, recording, or otherwise), without the prior written permission
of both the copyright owner and the above publisher of this book.

BOOKS ARE AVAILABLE AT QUANTITY DISCOUNTS WHEN USED TO PROMOTE
PRODUCTS OR SERVICES. FOR INFORMATION PLEASE WRITE TO PREMIUM
MARKETING DIVISION, PENGUIN BOOKS USA INC., 375 HUDSON STREET, NEW
YORK, NEW YORK 10014

If you purchased this book without a cover you should be aware that this book
is stolen property. It was reported as ''unsold and destroyed'' to the publisher
and neither the author nor the publisher has received any payment for this
''stripped book.''

Prologue

The young woman stepped from the village church and breathed in the cool morning air. She glanced over her shoulder to where her husband still stood in the interior shadows of the building, engaged in conversation with the vicar and his wife.

Her husband. How strange the words sounded. And what a strange turn her life had taken. She glanced at the little ring encircling the third finger of her left hand. It was, William had told her, a talisman ring, and had been in his family for many generations. It was never to be worn by any other than a family member.

She turned her hand, idly examining the strange symbols etched into the silver circlet. She was a family member now, and wouldn't the old man howl to heaven if he were to hear of it? She curled her fingers into fists at the thought. Well, he never would. He would never hear anything again from his son and the wife he had taken.

Her husband emerged from the church and paused to stand beside her.

"Is it done, then?" she asked quietly.

"Aye." He nodded, a lock of fair hair falling over his forehead. "All right and tight, with our names in the record and the stipend paid to the vicar. We can be on our way."

Observing her expression of almost blank bewilderment, he drew her to him and laid his cheek against her hair.

"It will be all right, my dearest. You won't be sorry."

The woman turned her head to gaze up into his face.

"Oh, no, William, never sorry."

He took her hand in his and ran his fingers lightly over the talisman ring. His laugh was warm, if somewhat shaky.

"I'll buy you another when we are settled. A gold ring to proclaim to the world that you are wed to a man of substance."

Following his gaze, she reflected that there was little chance of a gold ring for her. They would be lucky to scratch together enough substance to keep them fed and clothed.

She covered William's hand with her own.

"No!" she said fiercely. "I do not want a ring of gold. I want the one you have given me out of the love in your heart. This is my wedding ring, and my treasure. Besides," she added in an effort to lighten the moment, "I have quite enough gold jewelry, thank you."

She lifted a hand to touch the small pendant that hung from her neck. He had given it to her less than an hour ago, just before they had knocked on the vicarage door to wake its inhabitants. She knew whence the necklet had come, and knew what it meant to William.

He turned to her once more.

"Oh, love, I know we have done the right thing, but I wish . . ." He halted, his eyes wide and dark in his pale face.

Inexplicably, the young woman's heart lifted, and she threw her arms around her husband.

"Yes!" she laughed, the joy she felt so strong that she thought she might burst with it. "Yes, we have, William. Come!" She grasped his hand and ran down the steps to where a small gig awaited them. "We must be on our way. Our new life awaits us, my husband!"

Catching her mood, the young man grasped her around the waist and swung her off the ground in an exultant pirouette before depositing her with great ceremony into the gig. Then he mounted the vehicle and set the horses trotting toward the east, where the sun's rays were beginning to tinge the world in a blaze of pink and gold.

As they clattered across the little humpbacked bridge that marked the limits of town, the young woman swung to face her husband.

"William, I do not even know the name of this place."

"Bythorne, love. You may tell your children you were married in Bythorne."

1

Dusk was falling on an evening in early spring as a curricle and four bowled along the Dover Road at a shocking pace. Its sole occupant, aided by the light of the rising moon, appeared oblivious to the danger he presented to himself or to any other travelers whom he might encounter. Indeed Jared Talent, Earl of Burnleigh, seemed wholly preoccupied by his own grim thoughts, sparing not a glance for the shadowed landscape flashing past the hooves of his matched bays.

Suddenly, the smooth stride of the horses faltered, and the curricle veered uncertainly. Swearing softly, Jared pulled the team to a halt and, with an impatient exclamation, dismounted from his vehicle. He bent to examine the hooves of his inside horse; then, growling a second, richer oath, he straightened and looked about him.

What a time for the wretched animal to cast a shoe. He was not five miles from his destination. Well, there was no help for it, he'd have to stop and have the damned horse shod. At least the Green Man was close. The lights from the small establishment, less than half a mile distant, cast a welcoming glow into the twilight.

The earl's luck held, for the ostler at the Green Man, no doubt encouraged by the promise of largesse from a member of the area's most notable family, reported that the shoe replacement could be accomplished at once. Pulling vigorously at his forelock, he promised a speedy resolution to the problem, and Jared repaired to the interior of the inn to wait.

A glimpse inside the taproom showed it to be full as it could hold with thirsty locals and coach passengers. Jared made his way to a small but comfortable coffee room. This, too, was crowded, the inn being located halfway between London and Canterbury on Kent's major artery, and the only vacant seat appeared to be one at a table occupied by a woman eating alone. She was of an indeterminate age, and swathed in a gown of dark bombazine. A voluminous and heavily veiled bonnet concealed her features, and she picked at her food daintily, in prim isolation. Sighing, Jared made his way toward her, but was relieved to spot another table, unoccupied, a few feet away.

He waved away the waiter's dinner offerings and ordered a simple repast of bread and cheese and ale. When it arrived, he simply stared at it in frowning abstraction, his thoughts occupied with events transpiring at his home nearby.

Damnation, it was hard to believe the summons that had arrived at his lodgings in London some five hours ago. Grandfather on his deathbed? Impossible. He had left the old man in roaring health not two weeks previous. They had parted after one of their familiar brangles on the subject of the Talent succession, when Grandfather had bellowed at some length on Jared's unreasonable insistence on remaining a bachelor. Oh, yes, the old gentleman had been in fine form. Surely, nothing as trivial as a cold in the head could have brought him to—

An odd sound interrupted his thoughts, and he turned to observe the solitary female in bombazine. She had uttered a small murmur of what might have been puzzlement, and now put a hand to her head, knocking askew the dismal structure that was her bonnet. Glimpsing her profile, Jared realized that she was younger than he had first surmised, and a good deal more attractive. As he watched, her fingers came to her mouth to cover the hiccup that escaped her softly curved lips. The motion of her hand caused the cup in front of her to spill its contents, and she dabbed ineffectually at the spreading tea stain. Jared realized with amused surprise that this figure of apparently unrelieved propriety was obviously tipsy.

A man entered the room and made his way to her table. He greeted her affectionately as he seated himself and pulled his chair close to her. The woman said nothing, but she giggled and swayed toward him, settling into the arm he placed around her in a familiar manner.

To be sure, Jared thought with a cynical shrug of his

shoulders, a creature like that would be bound to have a protector, though judging from the leer on the fellow's face, protection was the last thing on his mind.

He turned his attention to the meal before him, but he found he could not attempt the bread and cheese. He downed a few swallows of ale, then brought the tankard down on the table with an impatient thud. He pushed himself away and rose to make his way to the cloak rack.

While he shrugged into his caped driving coat, the couple he had been watching also left their table, the woman requiring some assistance to get to her feet. The man drew her to him, guiding her faltering steps to the room's exit.

As they passed Jared the woman stumbled against him, and he was aware of a full bosom pressing into his chest. Her head jerked up, and Jared was obliged to thrust his hands out to prevent her from falling. Huge gray eyes slewed up at him in a blank stare, and her slack mouth was slightly open. With a feeling of distaste, Jared backed away. Her escort steadied her to a more or less upright position, and then turned to bestow an awkward pat on Jared's shoulder, straightening the earl's disarranged coat as he did so.

"Sorry about that, guv'nor. She never could hold 'er liquor. But then—" his eyelid drooped in a suggestive wink, "she's got other talents."

The man's hand dropped from the woman's waist to rest for a lingering moment on her enticingly curved derriere. Then the two moved on, making their uncertain way through the outside door and into the stable yard.

Jared arrived there a few moments later in time to watch a traveling carriage speeding smartly through the gates onto the main road. Through the window he caught a glimpse of the woman and her companion, and as he watched, a third face appeared, though he could not perceive whether the additional passenger was male or female. A moment later, the carriage rattled out of sight into the darkness.

Shrugging, Jared entered the stable, where he found the ostler busy at work. It was another twenty minutes, however, before the team was again harnesed to the curricle. The ostler hovered in a hopeful manner, and Jared reached into his pocket for the purse he kept there.

It was then that he learned he had been robbed.

His enraged thoughts at once swung to the female in the coffee room. No—she had been much too drunk to have picked his pocket. But she was, he concluded furiously, capable of obeying orders to fall against him so that her lover would have the opportunity to do so himself.

His first instinct was to pursue them. He had observed the direction the coach had taken, and his well-designed curricle stood an excellent chance of catching up with the heavier vehicle. It would give him a great deal of pleasure to haul that gin-soaked drab out of the coach by her hair and to give her gentleman friend the thrashing of his life. A moment's reflection, however, decided him against this appealing course of action. The amount he had been carrying was small, due to the haste with which he had left London, and he did not wish to spare the time it would take to bring the thieves to justice.

The landlord was most understanding. But what an unfortunate occurrence to have taken place at his inn! He hoped Lord Burnleigh would not hold it against him personally, and of course he was more than happy to accept his lordship's note for payment at a later date—at his lordship's convenience, naturally. He accompanied the earl into the inn yard to bid him farewell, and was still engaged in his obsequious handwashing as the curricle clattered through the gates.

Soon Jared's anger faded, overshadowed by the far more pressing concern over the reason for his journey. By the time he had turned off the main highway, his thoughts had resumed their preoccupation with the well-being of his grandfather, the man who had raised him.

Why had Aunt Amabelle not notified him sooner of the old man's illness? He could guess the answer. The Marquess of Chamford would no doubt have forbidden his household to create any sort of fuss over what he would have termed a passing indisposition. At seventy-two, he ruled his domain with the vigor of a young man, and his word was not to be brooked. It was difficult to believe that a mere cold could wreak havoc on such a man, but—

Once again Jared's unpleasant ruminations were cut short. A sharp crack sounded through the night. Good

God, was that a shot? Slackening his pace slightly, he peered into the darkness ahead of him, and perceived a figure running toward him on the shoulder of the road—a woman, by the look of it. He pulled up shortly, and by the time his feet hit the ground, she had nearly reached him. Her arms were outstretched, and her hair floated behind her like a pale banner.

Behind her, two more figures could be seen in the moonlight. They were some distance away, traveling across the fields toward the road, but Jared saw a flash as another shot was fired. The woman flinched, and uttered a gasping cry.

The earl pulled his traveling pistol from one capacious pocket and ran up the embankment toward the figures. He could not make out their features, but one was a tall man. The other was short and squat, and when he raised his arm, it could be seen that he held a pistol. Taking quick aim, Jared fired. He produced no visible results, but both men drew to an abrupt halt. Swiftly rotating the gun barrel, Jared fired once more, and the two shadowy figures scrambled away into the darkness. In an instant they were lost to sight.

Jared prepared to follow, but another cry from the woman caught his attention. She was running toward him, her eyes wide and staring. When she hurtled herself against him, Jared found himself clutching an armful of bombazine.

With an oath, he grasped the girl by the shoulders.

"You!" he growled. "What have you done with my money? And where have your friends loped off to?"

She gave no answer, but stared back at him, uncomprehending. He shook her ungently, and her head lolled on her shoulders. She mumbled something under her breath, but when he bent his head to listen, Jared could catch only the words, "No, no, no!" repeated over and over.

As he stared at her in bemusement, her gaze widened. For a moment, a glimmer of horrified awareness shone in her eyes; then they closed, and she slipped from his grasp to slide in an unconscious mound at his feet.

A cursory examination showed that the woman—although on further inspection she seemed scarcely more than a girl—was unharmed, at least physically. His ef-

forts to return her to consciousness resulted only in a
sobbing moan from her soft, pale lips.

Whether she was in shock, or merely an alcoholic stupor, he could not tell. She must have been drinking gin,
for he could smell no evidence of her inebriation. Now
what the hell was he to do? He was loath to delay his
journey any further, but he could not leave her in a heap
by the side of the road, even if she richly deserved whatever fate might befall her. Of course, her sort usually
managed to land on their feet—after first having spent a
profitable length of time on their backs. But no, he would
have to get help for her.

The question was, where? He knew this portion of the
road well enough to be aware that he would find no inn
or farmhouse nearby. The closest habitation was Stonefield Court.

He sighed. There was no help for it.

He bundled the woman's inert form into the curricle
and cheering himself with the thought that in bringing
this sodden little doxie to his home, he at least stood a
chance of recouping the money stolen from him. And
then there were her companions.

He looked forward with pleasure to learning the iden-
tities and whereabouts of those gentlemen.

As he set his vehicle in motion, he glanced down at
the slender figure curled beside him in an attitude of almost childlike oblivion.

"May angels of mercy sing thee to thy rest, little tart,"
he murmured, "for you will find no mercy in me."

The girl woke to a sense of deep unease; her eyes flew
open and then widened. Shafts of early-morning sunlight
revealed a small chamber, sparsely furnished. The quilt-
covered bed on which she lay was narrow and none too
comfortable.

She sat up abruptly and winced. Her hands went to her
throbbing head. Good heavens, what had happened to
her? She gave her head a tentative shake, and her hair,
the color of old gold, tumbled in heavy waves over her
shoulders.

The room was strange to her, and the household noises
sounding faintly from below were unfamiliar. She looked

down at the cotton nightdress in which she was clothed, then sank back into the pillows.

"I have gone mad," she said aloud, though there was no one to hear her. As if in answer, a light knock sounded at the door, immediately followed by the appearance of a young woman dressed in the garb of a housemaid.

"Ah, ye're awake, then," she said breathlessly. "I'm t'tell ye that his lordship wishes t'see ye in the library as soon as ye're dressed. My name is Kate, and I'll come back in a few minutes t'take ye down."

She whirled about, and the next moment she was gone.

The girl rubbed her forehead, and glanced about the room before sliding from the bed. She moved to a tiny mirror that hung over a wobbly dressing table, and stared, mesmerized, at her reflection.

"What has happened to me?" she whispered again. "Dear God, what *is* this place?"

She surveyed the room once more, and for the first time saw the clothing that had been laid out, apparently for her. She contemplated the simple woolen gown, and felt suspended in a nightmare.

Pressing her fingers to her temples, she tried to arrange her whirling thoughts into some sort of order. The events of the previous evening swam before her, jumbled and confused. Images floated in elusive fragments.

The last thing she remembered clearly was partaking of a meager dinner at the coaching inn. After that, everything was a blur. There had been a man—two men—and a dark, musty carriage—and running along a road—and shots! Another man—tall, powerful—grasping her, hurting her. She covered her face with trembling fingers and moaned in confusion.

She turned again to the girl in the glass, and stiffened at the sight of the weeping creature who stood before her.

"No!" she thought fiercely. "I am *not* such a poor, whimpering rabbit!"

Drawing a deep breath, she straightened her shoulders.

"I am *not* mad. There has to be an explanation for this absurd situation."

"My name is Diana." She spoke the words aloud, her thoughts clear for the first time. "My name is Diana St. Aubin, and I do not live in this house."

But why am I here? How did I get here? And where is here?"

The questions spun in her mind and then tumbled into chaos. If only she could remember!

She thought again of the maid, Kate. She had seemed friendly enough. Perhaps she could help.

Diana pulled on the woolen gown, and swept her hair into a makeshift bun on her neck with hairpins she found scattered on the dressing table. When Kate returned in a few minutes, she greeted the little maid with a smile.

"I'm sorry to have been such a sleepyhead when you came in before," she said, choosing her words with care. "You see, I'm a little lost. I—I'm not quite familiar with the house."

"Well, mercy, how could you be?" chuckled Kate. "You being brought in at the dead of night. You've been having your troubles, sure enough, haven't you?"

Diana remained silent, nodding warily, but Kate had nothing more to say. Instead, she opened the door for Diana to pass into the hallway outside.

"We'd best hurry. Lord Burnleigh doesn't like to be kept waiting."

She led the way through several corridors and down narrow flights of stairs before they reached what was apparently the main house. Diana found herself somewhat intimidated by the size and grandeur of the rooms through which she passed, and her curiosity about the unknown Lord Burnleigh mounted. He must be a powerful personage indeed to be the owner of such magnificence. Surreptitiously, she smoothed her skirt, and patted tendrils of hair that had escaped the bun.

When the maid paused at last before a pair of paneled doors, Diana gathered her courage and allowed herself to be ushered into a spacious chamber. She was aware that the room was lined with books, and furnished in the first stare of elegance, but her attention was absorbed by the room's sole occupant.

Standing before the fireplace was a tall man, dark of countenance and harsh-featured, who appeared to be about thirty years of age. One shining top boot rested casually on the fender. His coat of blue superfine indicated the finest tailoring, though he could by no means be called a dandy. Fawn-colored pantaloons fit superbly about a trim waist and muscular thighs. His dark hair was cropped shorter than the current style, and his physique spoke of hours spent in athletic pursuits.

All this was absorbed by Diana with some interest in a matter of seconds, but as her eyes traveled to his face, a wave of terror nearly overcame her.

"You!" she whispered hoarsely. "It's—last night—you are the man in the curricle!"

2

Jared made no move to approach the girl, controlling with difficulty his astonishment at her appearance. Was this splendid creature the stumbling tart who had set him up for robbery the night before? He observed her huge gray eyes, fringed with smoky lashes, her straight nose, and the wide, generous mouth set over a rather decided chin. His gaze moved along the slender column of her throat, noting the pulse that beat wildly at its base, and the rapid rise and fall of her breasts. The thought sprang unbidden in his mind that her waist would feel supple and slender in his hands. For a surprised instant he felt an urge to pull her to him, to feel her slender length along his, the gold satin of her hair soft against his chin. He returned hastily to the purpose at hand.

"I see you recall our encounter." His voice was cold.

Our encounter! Diana fought for composure. She would not stand trembling before this arrogant stranger.

"I fear," he continued, a sneer lifting the corners of his firm mouth, "that circumstances last night did not permit a formal introduction. I am Jared Talent, Earl of Burnleigh, and you have spent the night in my home, Stonefield Court."

"Your home?" she repeated in a shaking voice.

"Yes. I trust you are fully recovered from your—indisposition?"

Diana made no response to this, but went directly to the concern uppermost in her mind.

"What am I doing here? How did I get here?"

"Events a little hazy, are they, pet?" Cynical amusement flashed in the earl's eyes. "You have my sympathy, for I have experienced the same unpleasantness myself after a night on the tiles."

"A night on the . . . ? I don't understand, my lord."

Jared frowned.

"Are you saying you remember nothing?"

"Only vaguely." Diana lifted a hand to her head. "My head aches abominably."

"Yes, I should imagine it does, but you will forgive my indifference to your problem. Very well, I shall explain why you were brought here—it's very simple. I want my money back, and I want the names of your confederates."

"My confederates!"

"Yes. Surely, after what happened, you can feel no loyalty to them. You will soon be going to jail, my lovely, and I'm giving you the opportunity to bring down with you the men who tried to kill you."

The feeling of nightmarish unreality returned to Diana, and though she had not been invited to be seated, she sank into a convenient armchair of cherry-striped silk.

"What are you talking about?" she asked, desperation in her tone.

A hint of impatience touched Jared's frown.

"I am talking about the episode that occurred last night at the Green Man, where you and your confederate contrived to rob me of fifty pounds."

"*What!*" Diana leapt to her feet, stiff with outrage.

"By the by," continued the earl without pause, "whatever did you do to change your lover from the ardent swain I saw at the Green Man into an infuriated assassin?"

"I think you must be mad!" Diana gasped. "I insist that you tell me why you brought me here, and—and that you release me this instant."

"Oh, very well done," drawled Jared. He raised his quizzing glass, allowing his gaze to travel from tear-filled eyes to heaving bosom. "Quite the picture of persecuted innocence. However, I am in no mood at the moment for histrionics, my sweet. I—what *is* your name? I cannot continue addressing you in nauseating endearments."

Diana felt the blood rush to her cheeks.

"Your endearments are no more repugnant to you than they are to me, my lord," she snapped. "My name is Diana St. Aubin, and I know nothing of robberies or confederates—or—or lovers."

"You are beginning to try my patience, Miss, er, St. Aubin. Please believe me, you have nothing to gain from these protestations of ignorance. I had thought my fifty pounds gone forever, like a lover's promises in the light of day, but since circumstances have delivered you into my hands, I see no reason not to pursue the matter."

Diana's forehead wrinkled in concentration. Her memory of last night's events was sketchy at best, but the images that flashed before her mind's eye gave credence to the accusations of this insufferable man. Before she was taken from the Green Man she must certainly have presented the appearance of a—well, a drunken slut. She blushed hotly. As for the robbery . . .

She whirled to face Lord Burnleigh, whose stony expression remained unchanged.

"My lord," she began, "I don't know precisely what happened last night, but I am willing to admit that you have grounds for your suspicions." She ignored the muffled snort emanating from the earl. "However, if you will let me explain, I'm sure you will be convinced of my innocence."

Jared sighed. He would have to make it clear to this clever adventuress that he was not the man to be cozened by a lovely face—too many had tried before. The appeal in her smoky eyes was undeniable, however, and the earl admitted to a certain curiosity as to what she could possibly say in extenuation of her actions.

He sat down on a settee near the fireplace and gestured Diana to one opposite.

"Pray go on. I'm sure your tale will prove entertaining, if not particularly instructive."

Restraining an urge to respond in kind, Diana seated herself and clasped her hands together in an effort to concentrate.

"To begin with, I am a French citizen. I live in Paris."

She essayed a smile at the earl, who returned it with a stare of undiminished skepticism.

"In that case," he said with a sardonic smile, "I must congratulate you on your grasp of the English tongue. You speak with no trace of an accent."

Diana raised her hand to her forehead.

"Please, my lord. I was born in France to English parents. My father died when I was very young, and my mother took care that I should not forget my heritage. She spoke only English to my brother and me in our home.

"My brother," she repeated slowly. She sat very still, her expression intent. "I remember now. That's what the man wanted!"

"The man?" asked the earl in a puzzled voice.

"The man in the carriage—the one who waited there when I was forced inside. He kept asking me about some papers—family papers, and when I did not understand, he wanted to know where he could find my brother! 'Where is Marcus?' he asked—over and over. 'Come now, missy, you'd better tell me!' He knew my brother's name. How—"

The cool voice interjected once more. "I must compliment you again on your seemingly endless powers of invention. The introduction of a brother in mortal danger lends a certain piquancy to the tale—but I wonder if we could return to the, er, main thread."

Diana whirled to face the earl.

"But you don't understand! I must warn Marcus. . . ."

Observing Lord Burnleigh's implacable expression, she abandoned this line of argument. She sank back once more into her chair.

"I am the English mistress in a seminary for young ladies in Paris, and that is where I live. Marcus is two years younger than I, and with the cessation of the war, he came to England several months ago to seek employment. He is a poor correspondent, but a week ago I received a rather garbled note from him telling me that it was imperative that I join him here. He told me to travel to the town of Aylesford, where he would meet me.

"Such was the urgency of his letter that I complied at once. I set sail from Calais two days ago. I disembarked at Dover, and was en route to Aylesford by stage. The coach made a stop at the Green Man for dinner, and I ordered a meal of cutlets and peas, and a pot of tea. I recall the tea took an unconscionable time to arrive—I had nearly finished eating—and it tasted odd, as though it had been highly spiced. I had taken only a few sips when I began to feel very odd. Then—"

She broke off, aware that the earl had begun to drum

his fingers on the polished surface of the small table beside the settee, and was glancing with undisguised boredom at the ormolu clock on the mantelpiece.

Diana flushed, and experienced a strong desire to slap that arrogant face.

"I trust I am not boring you, my lord. Perhaps I may be excused for placing a certain degree of importance on the event."

The earl stifled a yawn, and rose. He moved leisurely to seat himself behind the desk.

"And I trust," he murmured, "that I may be permitted a certain degree of skepticism concerning this entire farrago. You have neglected to provide a reason for this dastardly kidnapping. Are you, perchance, the heiress of a wealthy *citoyen?* Ah, but no, that would not jibe with the schoolmistress story, would it?"

Diana clamped her lips together. How could she convince this wretched man that she was not lying?

The earl continued in an uninterested tone.

"Could we get on with it, please? Time grows short, as does my patience. I suppose you are going to tell me that your tea was drugged."

Diana sprang to her feet and strode to the desk.

"Yes," she replied in a gritty voice. "I believe that is what happened, because it is from that point that my memory is blurred. All I know is that I seemed to be incapable of coherent thought. I remember a man—I remember he—touched me, as though . . ." Her eyes dropped, and her cheeks flamed. "But none of it seemed to register. It was as though I had no control over my actions or my mind."

She stole a glance into the eyes glaring into hers, but the earl's only response was a noticeable hardening of his already forbidding expression.

Diana shivered, but she continued in haste.

"By the time I began to come out of—whatever it was, I realized that I was in a coach. There were two men with me, one of whom was the one who had—approached me in the Green Man. I never did get a good look at the other. I know only that he was short and squat, and powerfully built.

"I began to struggle, but to no avail. The two men kept questioning me." She put her hands to her forehead, as once more the images of last night's ordeal began dissolving into a kaleidoscope of terror. "If only I could remember!"

Observing the unpromising expression on his lordship's face, she dropped her gaze once more and continued on.

"I slumped in my seat, pretending to have fallen back into a stupor in order to avoid their incessant queries. It was a difficult pretense, to be sure, since the coach was traveling so fast that I found myself bouncing around like an India-rubber ball. The powerfully built man kept urging the coachman to go even faster. But then the coach slowed. The two men shouted at the coachman, but we slowed even more, and at last came to a stop. The man was apparently lost. My captors climbed out of the carriage, and I could hear the three of them cursing and shouting.

"I think they both believed me incapable of movement—or perhaps they forgot about me altogether, because they moved to the front of the vehicle, where they huddled in the lamplight, poring over a map. I could hear them berating the coachman and deciding what to do next, with never a thought to me. I peeked out and saw their attention was wholly diverted, so I slipped through the door and ran as fast as I could. I was still dreadfully dizzy, and . . ."

She raised a hand to her head.

"I'm not sure—that is, I don't know precisely what happened then—everything is so muddled in my mind. I believe that's when I met—that is, you . . ."

Jared rose abruptly, and came around the desk to where she stood.

"My dear young woman, I am agog with admiration at your acting abilities. I must assume you earn your bread on the stage, when not otherwise, er, occupied."

Ignoring her gasp of indignation, he bent to capture one slim hand, turning it over in his own.

"You have the speech and appearance of a gentlewoman, and you have not, evidently been engaged in any ungenteel labor recently. However, gently reared ladies rarely appear unaccompanied in coaching inns, sloshed to the eyeballs."

Diana opened her mouth to retort, but Jared raised a hand.

"Nor can I recall ever seeing a lady giggling uproariously, and snuggling against supposed strangers like a cat in heat."

Diana whitened as though she had been struck.

"No!" she whispered brokenly. "I could not have acted so."

Observing her stricken expression, Jared spoke in a softer tone.

"Well, I may have overstated the case, but it is no good denying you were under the influence of drink, or that you acted with your gentleman friend to rob me. Although," he mused, ignoring the sob of protest emanating from the direction of the little settee, "I cannot imagine what a diamond of the first water like yourself was doing dressed in that wretched bombazine affair, and in the company of a third-rate Captain Sharp."

Diana leapt to her feet once more. She was unused to having her word disputed, and she was certainly unused to being accused of robbery and—other things. She faced the earl, her eyes glittering with icy indignation.

"I have told you, my lord, what I was doing in the company of that dreadful man. I was his prisoner, my lord—his victim. As for the bombazine, it was precisely to discourage the attentions of such persons that I dressed as plainly and unattractively as possible. Now, I ask that you release me. I have important family business to pursue, and I must be on my way."

Patience was not foremost among the Earl of Burnleigh's virtues, and he had exhausted his minuscule supply. Upstairs, the person who meant the most in the world to him lay fairly writhing in distress upon what appeared to be his deathbed.

If only he had listened to Grandfather's pleas that he take a wife. There was no denying he should have been wed years ago. If he had, Grandfather, while he would certainly fight to his last breath, could face death with equanimity.

And Jared had come close, not a fortnight past. He had been within Ames ace of asking Lord Brierly for the hand of his second daughter. It was only the echo of the girl's piercing giggles penetrating the paneling of her father's study that had stayed him.

Now he wished with a bleak ferocity that he had girded his loins—to say nothing of his ears—and gone ahead with the proposal. If he were at least betrothed, Grandfather would not now be kneading the coverlet in his anguish.

Jared flung up his hand.

"Look here, Miss St.—whatever," he growled, "I am not prepared to waste any more time on you. If you will not tell me what I wish to know, perhaps you will change your mind after cooling your heels for a few days in the village jail."

He moved to the bell pull, speaking over his shoulder. "Perhaps you can convince the magistrate of your innocence. With your spurious air of gentility, and your skill on the boards, you should certainly—"

He stopped, suddenly, and turned swiftly. He stood rooted for a full minute, staring at the girl before him.

Diana returned his gaze in growing bewilderment and anger.

"Sir, you must believe—"

She, too, stopped, with equal suddenness, as the earl grasped her by the shoulders and pulled her to stand before a large window, through which the morning sun streamed into the room. To Diana's fury, he turned her slowly about, examining her from head to toe.

"Now, see here . . ." she began, but his lordship thrust her from him and turned to pace the carpet.

"Be quiet! I must think."

He continued to travel the rug in ever-decreasing circles while Diana stood in fulminating silence. He stopped again, and once more came to stand before her, staring at her as though he were considering the purchase of an objet d'art.

"Please be silent and listen to me. Perhaps you may escape the roundhouse after all, for I have a proposition for you."

Diana made a choking sound, her hand lifted in a protective gesture.

Lord Burnleigh's smile was not pleasant.

"Spare me your maidenly blushes, my charming doxie, for I have no designs on your very doubtful virtue. I do not want you for a light o'love. I want you for my fiancé."

3

"Your fiancée!" Diana fairly rocked on her heels in astonishment. Was the man deranged? "My lord, I cannot have heard you correctly! What—"

The earl interrupted with a brusque gesture.

"I am not offering you a proposal of marriage, of course. What I meant was . . ."

He broke off. She was eyeing him as though he were a dangerous lunatic. He resumed in a quieter voice.

"Please. Sit down and let me explain."

Despite the seeming courtesy of his words, Diana could find only detached calculation in his face. His dark eyes commanded, and she seated herself on the edge of a chair.

"Stonefield Court," began Lord Burnleigh, "is the primary seat of Peter Talent, the Marquess of Chamford. Lord Chamford is my grandfather. Several days ago he took a spring chill, and was unable to shake it. Despite all efforts, he fell into an inflammation of the lungs, and has now passed all hope of recovery. At this moment"— here the icy voice harshened—"he lies abovestairs, dying."

"Oh!" Despite herself, Diana lifted her hand toward the earl in sympathy. The gesture seemed in no way welcome to him, and he continued as though he had not seen it.

"Perhaps I should also mention that I am Lord Chamford's heir, my father having been killed in a hunting accident some sixteen years ago. The matter of succession has been of great concern to my grandfather of late. I am unmarried, and my younger brother, Simon, is in the Army. The next in line for the title is a distant cousin, now residing in the Indies. When Simon was transferred to the Peninsula, my grandfather took a maggot into his head that Simon was sure to be carried off by a French ball. Grandfather relaxed somewhat when Napoleon was defeated, for Simon scraped through the entire war with nothing worse than a saber nick. However, when word reached us last week of the Corsican Monster's escape from Elba, all his fears returned. He now envisions Simon slain in some future battle.''

The earl turned to pace the floor, running strong fingers through his crisply curling hair. Watching him, Diana was acutely aware of the man's almost mesmerizing masculinity. She forced her attention to his words.

"To me his concern seemed unnecessary. That is— Grandfather was always so alive! It seemed as though there was plenty of time for . . .''

The earl stopped, and for the first time, Diana observed signs of uncertainty in his demeanor. He turned to face the fireplace.

"He is in torment. He tosses constantly, muttering about Stonefield passing from Talent hands . . .'' The earl swung around to face Diana.

"Do you see what I require of you?''

His voice was harsh with strain, and Diana could only stare at him in growing apprehension.

"I have failed him, failed him terribly, but I can at least ease his last hours. If he believes me to be betrothed, he will die in peace.''

Diana gasped in disbelief. First this arrogant wretch accused her of thievery and of being the veriest trollop, and now he was trying to coerce her into some sort of mad masquerade.

"You want me to—pose as . . . ? Oh, this is abominable!'' she cried. "To ask me to be a party to such a deception!''

Lord Burnleigh moved to her in a swift motion and, grasping both slender wrists, pulled her to her feet.

"You are very quick; you have apprehended my meaning precisely. Before you refuse, however, you should remember that I am in a position to cause you a great deal of unpleasantness. Have you considered what a few months in prison—or transportation—would do to your beauty? The beauty which provides you with your livelihood? On the other hand, if you agree to my—deception—

I promise you shall be well paid for your time. You will not be here above a few days.''

He surveyed her coldly, and Diana felt as though she were being stripped naked, all her vulnerability exposed to this hateful man. How was she to convince him that she had fallen in with thieves through no fault of her own? Did she truly bear the look of a lightskirt? She tried to wrench free, but her hands were still imprisoned in his. An odd sensation swept over her that her flesh would bear a permanent imprint of his fingers.

Diana raised her eyes, determined that her captor would find no fear in them. Meeting her gaze, the earl slowly released her, and she crossed the room to seat herself again. She folded her hands and gazed at him, her icy composure matching his own.

"Pray continue, sir. You have my undivided attention."

"Very well. When I brought you here last night, the only persons to see us enter were Mrs. Ingersoll, our housekeeper, and Fishperk, my grandfather's valet. They, and one housemaid, are the only persons who know of your presence here. They were told to keep this knowledge to themselves, and I believe they have done so. First of all, I shall install you in one of our best guest rooms, and find you a more suitable gown. Then . . ." He stopped, frowning.

"And then?" prompted Diana, all politeness. "And then you will explain to your grandfather—and your household—how your fiancée showed up in the dead of night, with neither abigail nor coachman—nor coach, for that matter—and was taken to an attic bedroom."

Once more, the earl ran nervous fingers through his dark thatch of hair, and once more, Diana found herself contemplating with some misgiving the sharply chiseled plains of his face.

"Yes," he said at last. "Well, that will no doubt require some explanation."

His gaze raked her once again as he moved to the bell pull.

"As soon as I have worked out the details of this, er, project, I shall send for you again. Do you have any questions?"

"Questions!" gasped Diana, her composure deserting

her. She could hardly speak for the emotions raging within her. "Sir, I think you must be mad. How can I convey to you that I am not what you think me? My birth may not be noble"—here her lip curled to indicate her contempt for the class of which the arrogant Lord Burnleigh was a member—"but I live respectably."

The earl snorted . . .

"Let us have no more of this nonsense. There is little time for preparation, and as you say, there are many details to iron out before I can present you to Grandfather as the future Countess of Burnleigh."

By this time, Diana was trembling with rage.

"I will not agree to this—this ludicrous pretense! I wish to leave this house, and I wish to leave now. You cannot—"

The earl, advancing on her once more, cupped her chin in one strong hand.

"It is not my habit to coerce helpless females into doing my bidding. But, you see, I am desperate. I will do anything necessary, up to and possibly including murder, to ease my grandfather's torment. He deserves no less. Besides," he continued, "I am not asking so very much of you. Only a few days of your time and a little exertion of your undeniably formidable acting talent. You will have very little actual contact with Grandfather—I don't propose to push my luck any further than necessary—but you will meet some of the family. There is Aunt Amabelle, of course, and my sister Felicity, who is at present visiting friends in Tunbridge Wells in the company of her governess. My brother has been notified of Grandfather's illness, but I should think it will take some days to make the trip from Toulouse, where he is currently billeted. My sister Charlotte lives in Northumberland with her husband, Lord Kelmarston, but she is expecting to be confined shortly with her third child and is thus unable to travel.

"Now then, I promise you, you will leave much richer than you came, though since you arrived penniless, I grant that is not much of an inducement. Shall we say three hundred guineas?"

"Once again, my lord," grated Diana, almost breathless in her determination, "I have no intention of lending myself to this lunacy you have concocted. One might say that your motives in fashioning such a monstrous lie are honorable, possibly the only honorable sentiment I have heard you express since our extremely unfortunate encounter, but—''

The earl's straight, dark brows lifted quizzically, and in the black depths of his eyes, Diana could swear she caught a flicker of amusement.

''I wish you would cease this ridiculous spitting and hissing. Please try to get it through your head that by accepting my offer you will not only be much better off financially at the end of the week, but you will be safe, at least temporarily, from the unkind attentions of your cohorts, who may still be scouring the countryside for you—with no good in mind.''

Diana turned to the long windows which overlooked a sweeping lawn, and she stared blindly at an ornamental lake sparkling in the distance. She had so far given little consideration to the men who had pursued her over the fields last night. Why had she been chosen as their victim? What was their purpose in abducting her? She frowned. Were they still searching for her? And what would be her fate if they found her? And what of Marcus? He was no doubt waiting for her in Aylesford, and . . .

The questions jangled in an increasing crescendo, and she shook her head in an effort to still them, or at least to arrange them in some sort of order.

Watching her, Jared was aware that he was finding it difficult to maintain his usual detachment in his dealings with the fair sex. No one knew better than he that an air of innocence and a sigh of distress could wheedle the soul from a man. Yet it was almost impossible to believe that this willow-slim creature whose silver eyes seemed honest and clear as a Madonna's tears was anything but the lady she claimed to be. Then he recalled her wanton response to the advances of her lover, and how her lush body had pressed against his in the inn's coat room. He straightened, and his voice knifed through her thoughts.

''I hate to interrupt this moment of self-communion, but I must have your answer. What is it to be, then, a pampered week in one of England's most notable piles as my fiancée, or a stay of undetermined length in some unsavory hole as a guest of the crown?''

"My lord!" Diana gazed at him beseechingly, "you would not."

My lord, his arms folded, was unmoved. "Try me."

She raised a hand in supplication.

"Lord Burnleigh, I know that the circumstances in which you discovered me can only be described as questionable." The earl uttered a sound of patent disbelief. "But what I have told you is true. I ask you once again to release me and to assist me in completing my journey to Aylesford. I must be on my way."

The earl laughed mirthlessly, and the gray eyes fastened to his grew cloudy with disappointment. Diana was dimly aware that her desire for his lordship's good opinion was not wholly connected with her predicament, and the thought did nothing to restore her equanimity.

He continued in a brittle voice.

"I applaud your ingenuity, my dear, but it simply won't fadge. I have heard too many piteous stories from too many tarts, highborn and otherwise, whose only purpose in telling them was to lighten the purses of well-breeched swells."

"Such as yourself, my lord?"

"Precisely."

Diana stood for a long moment, her gaze locked with that of the earl. Never had she felt so helpless. She was completely at the mercy of this arrogant, supercilious wretch, a virtual prisoner in his home. It would be useless to scream—she was surrounded by his minions. She was penniless, her money in the hands of her erstwhile captors, and her luggage no doubt in Aylesford, some thirty miles distant.

"I will agree," she said through gritted teeth, "to think over your proposal, if you will let me send a message to my brother. Since I have not appeared at the time and place specified in his letter, he will be expecting word from me."

The earl's glance was unreadable, but he nodded and pulled on the bell rope.

"I, too, must have time to plan the entrance of my fiancée into Grandfather's presence. I will give you an hour, Miss St. Aubin." He hesitated, then placed his hands on her shoulders. "In your meditations, you might consider the fact that by acceding to my wishes, you will be granting the last, desperate wish of a dying old man.''

Diana stepped back as though she had been struck.

"That's not fair," she murmured through stiff lips.

Jared's mobile brows flew up in surprise. His words had been spoken almost without thought, certainly without any hope of influencing the hardened adventuress before him.

He opened his mouth to reply, but was stayed by the stately entrance of Mallow, the butler.

In a few moments Diana was delivered once more into the hands of the housemaid, Kate, who escorted her with ill-disguised curiosity to a bedchamber in the upper regions of the great house. Diana gazed about her in bemused appreciation of her rapid change in status. Here, the morning sun glowed warmly on pink silk hangings and a polished rosewood cabinet. In a corner of the room stood a dainty satinwood dressing table, and a cozy blaze crackled in the fireplace.

Kate darted from the room, and returned some minutes later bearing a dimity gown of pale green. Silently she assisted Diana into the dress, which had obviously been made for someone of more diminutive stature. Then, in a few deft strokes with comb and brush, she dismantled the makeshift bun and curved Diana's guinea-gold hair into a simple but elegant Clytie knot.

When Kate had finished, she slipped from the room.

Diana's first action was to search the drawers of a small, tambour-topped writing desk set in an alcove opposite the bed. Here she found paper and pens and ink, and after some repair to the pens, she scratched a hasty note to Marcus.

She hesitated for a moment, nibbling doubtfully at the quill, then strode to the bell pull and gave it an authoritative tug. When Kate responded a few moments later, Diana handed her the paper with an airy command to see that it was delivered to the Swan Inn in Aylesford—immediately, if you please.

This done, she sank onto the luxuriously quilted feather bed and gave herself up to bewildered reflection.

4

In what seemed like a very short time, a knock sounded at the door, followed by the immediate entrance of Lord Burnleigh. He seated himself in a small armchair near the fireplace. With a brusque gesture, he waved Diana to another and began speaking without preamble.

"My first act on leaving you was to go to Grandfather. Even in his weakened state, he gave me a prompt dressing down. 'Didn't I tell you, lad? Didn't I tell you? And now you've left it till too late.' "

Once again the earl's brittle composure wavered, but he continued stiffly.

"It was then that I told him I have brought home my affianced bride."

"You are very sure of yourself, my lord," Diana interrupted icily. "I have not agreed to this insane proposal."

She may as well not have spoken.

"My announcement," continued Lord Burnleigh, "had the desired effect. He was overjoyed, and within minutes was breathing easier. I then let his valet, Fishperk, in on the deception, since he is one of the few household members who witnessed your entrance last night. I can trust his discretion. When I left, Grandfather had lapsed into a peaceful sleep, the first, I am told, since he fell ill.

"I next went to my Aunt Amabelle. She is a widow, and has been our chatelaine since my mother died seventeen years ago, giving birth to my sister. My aunt is not a strong person, and my grandfather's illness has driven her to a state of near prostration. When I told her what I had done, I was afraid for a moment that she, too, might succumb. However, once her sensibilities were soothed, she realized that since I had already set the plan in motion, there was no choice but to carry it through.''

Diana reflected that the occasions must be rare when those involved in his lordship's plans failed to carry them through.

"We put our heads together and came up with a coherent story—more or less.''

The earl paced the floor in concentration.

"I have maintained for years a desultory correspondence with my mother's old friend Helen, Lady Bavister. She is a widow, and has been living in seclusion in Wales since the death of her husband, an Army general, some fifteen years ago. So far, this is all quite true. Grandfather was acquainted with her, having met her in London, and I believe he knew the general slightly. However, here the fiction begins. Grandfather now believes that I visited Lady Bavister some time ago, while on a walking tour, and there I met her wholly fictitious daughter, whom I have named, in the interest of simplicity, Diana.''

"Of course," murmured Diana.

"In the years since, through further correspondence, Diana and I discovered a mutual attraction, and when you wrote that you and your mother were obliged to travel to Canterbury on family business, I extended an invitation to stay on in Kent for a visit to Stonefield. My invitation, of course, was promptly accepted.''

"Of course," repeated Diana.

"I beg your pardon?''

"Nothing, my lord. Please continue. Your fabrication is so far quite fascinating.''

"Thank you," his lordship said drily. "At the last minute, Lady Bavister became ill and was unable to travel. Such was the urgency of your business that you were forced to make the trip without her, with the understanding that she would join you as soon as she was able.

"Unfortunately, you met with a coaching accident just outside London, in which both your abigail and footman were severely injured. Since I am the only person in the entire metropolis with whom you are acquainted, it was only natural that you would turn to me in your hour of need. Rather neat, that, don't you agree?''

"Quite, except for the fact that I would sooner turn to Attila the Hun in my hour of need. But do go on."

The earl's lips twitched, but he continued as though he had not heard.

"These are the details that are now being circulated among the household. Kate has been told that it was only through a mix-up in communication, the circumstances of your arrival being somewhat chaotic, that you were lodged last night in the servants' quarters." A small, rueful smile appeared on his lips in response to Diana's lifted eyebrows. "Yes, I know that part is a little shaky. But I believe I can rely on our housekeeper's iron hand to squelch any untoward supposition on the part of the staff.

"Of course," he continued, "the version presented to Grandfather implied that I have already spoken to you of marriage, and your response was amenable. I told him that I had so far withheld the glad news from him because I wished him to meet you first. After Grandfather . . ." The earl bowed his head as though a burden had settled on him. Again, hardening his voice, he continued. "Afterwards, you will resume your supposed journey to Canterbury. You will leave Stonefield much wealthier than when you arrived, you will have my promise not to turn you over to the unkind mercies of the law, and our paths, I most devoutly trust, need never cross again."

The earl rose from his chair, and moved to stand over her.

"I must have your answer, Miss St. Aubin."

There was little in his aspect to suggest outright menace, but Diana was intensely aware of the air of authority that surrounded the man as naturally as a comfortable cloak. She, too, rose to her feet, and faced him squarely.

"You must surely be aware, my lord, that in making the announcement to your grandfather, you have made my acquiescence a *fait accompli*. Much as I resent your high-handed action, I am not the cold-hearted monster you think me, and I will not destroy the fiction that evidently means so much to him. However—" she raised a hand to halt the smile of triumph that appeared on the earl's harsh features—"this scene will be played out on my terms, not yours."

Lord Burnleigh stood motionless, an expression of

blank astonishment on his face. Diana felt a knot gather in her stomach, but she proceeded coolly.

"You will pay me, not three hundred, but five hundred guineas. You will provide me with a suitable wardrobe, and when I leave, I want the use of one of your carriages; I want an abigail, a footman, and a coachman to drive me to my meeting with Marcus."

The earl stood staring at her and then he took a deep breath, evidently curbing his temper with some difficulty.

"You insolent jade!" he grated. "What makes you think you are in a position to dictate conditions?"

"Do but consider, sir," returned Diana with venomous sweetness. "Your grandfather is expecting you momentarily, with a fiancée in tow. Do you not think you will find yourself in some difficulty if, at that point, the blushing bride-to-be is hauled away in chains to the roundhouse?"

The earl stood as though turned to stone. He bore the look of a man who has brought home a starving kitten, only to see it transformed before his eyes into a snarling tigress.

Good, thought Diana. *You arrogant bully! You think me a hardened trollop? You may as well think of me as a self-possessed trollop, with intelligence to match your own; not one to be threatened and browbeaten by the likes of you.*

For a moment, Jared glared at Diana.

"Supposing I agree to this ridiculous demand, how do I know that once you have the money in your greedy little fist you won't hare off on me? I can't very well lock you in your room."

"Because," Diana replied haughtily, "I give you my word that I shall abide by our bargain." Catching the expression on the earl's face, she added, "And if you utter one syllable about the word of a trollop being worthless, I—I shall strike you!"

For the first time, Jared's face lit with genuine laughter, and Diana was astonished at the transformation. Why, he was not nearly as old as she had first supposed, and his features, though too roughly chiseled to be called handsome, were heart-catchingly attractive.

The laughter ceased as quickly as it had begun. As though ashamed of having unbent, even for a moment,

Jared turned stiffly and crossed to the bell pull, giving it a vicious tug. This action apparently restored his control, for his face once again wore an expression of cold detachment. He moved to the fireplace and, picking up a poker, began stirring and rearranging the burning logs, apparently having forgotten Diana's existence.

Diana strode to the window and gazed intently at a sweep of velvety lawn as though it held her complete attention.

In a few moments a tall figure dressed in footman's livery entered the room, and the earl ordered the removal of the sum that Diana had specified from the estate safe. The man bowed as though he saw nothing untoward in this extremely odd direction, or in the fact that his master was closeted alone with a female guest in her boudoir, and exited sedately from the room.

"I will see that the money is brought to you. Will that be satisfactory, Miss St. Aubin?"

"Quite, my lord."

"Very well, then, let us get on with it. My aunt awaits us in her chambers." He rose and walked to the door.

Diana knew a sudden moment of panic.

"No!" she cried. "It is too soon. I—I must freshen my appearance. I cannot . . ."

The earl paused in the doorway.

"You look charming. Come."

Upstairs Amabelle, Lady Teague, stood at the window of her sitting room, distractedly fingering the amber beads about her neck. She was short and plump, and her somewhat protuberant brown eyes gave her an appearance of youthful naiveté, belied by the sprinkling of gray in her brown hair.

What could I have been thinking of? And what was I thinking of to have agreed to this lunacy? To allow a female of that sort here!

On the other hand, she had to admit the old gentleman was resting easier. He was very weak, but determined to see the young woman and give his blessing to their union.

But, good heavens, I never thought to see the day when I would welcome a—a lightskirt into this house.

How could Jared hope to pass off such a creature to his grandfather as a lady of quality? Papa might be on his deathbed, but he had not lost a whit of his considerable powers of observation.

At any rate, the die was cast, and one could only—

Her jumbled reverie was interrupted by a light tap at the door. A moment later, the tall figure of her nephew entered the room, accompanied by a young woman.

Lady Teague's gaze swept from the crown of golden hair to the tips of borrowed kid shoes. She looked into wide gray eyes, and read there an odd mixture of determination, shame, anger, and bewilderment.

"But," blurted Lady Teague, her glance flying to her nephew's face, "she is a lady!"

She stretched her hand to Diana and drew her into the room, her natural goodness of heart touched. "A lady— and yet so troubled. My dear, are you sure you want to do as my nephew has asked? We do not wish to force you."

At these words, the first kindness she had been shown since leaving her home in what seemed like years ago, Diana's eyes brimmed with unexpected tears, and she fought the urge to sink to her knees before this comfortable little woman, and beg for help.

"Not, I fear, a lady, Aunt Amabelle, but a reasonable imitation of one."

The words, spoken in that familiar hateful voice, served to bring an abrupt end to Diana's moment of weakness.

"Thank you, ma'am," she said huskily, "but I have given my promise to carry out Lord Burnleigh's project. Though," she continued, glaring at the earl, "I cannot help but express the opinion that this is an absolutely outrageous scheme, and I already regret becoming a part of it."

Lady Amabelle clicked her tongue in distress.

"I must say that I agree with you, my dear, but Jared has apparently taken the matter out of our hands. I am sorry to hear that he has plunged you pell-mell into such a situation. Perhaps before you leave us . . ."

Jared observed this exchange in some astonishment.

"My dear Aunt, I believe you must have taken leave of your senses! Did you perhaps not understand me when I told you how I met Miss St. Aubin? I will regale you later with the tale she spun for me of how she came to

find herself—all through no fault of her own, you understand—in the company of a pair of ruthless sharpers."

Jared stopped abruptly, and continued in a quieter tone.

"However, there is no time for further discussion. With
your permission, I will now escort my affianced bride to
Grandfather's rooms."

Lady Teague nodded, albeit unwillingly, and stood
aside.

"I wish you well," she said as she saw them out of
the room. Her words were directed at Diana rather than
her nephew.

The marquess's rooms were in another wing of the
Court, and in the time it took Jared and Diana to make
their way through the seemingly endless network of corridors, the earl maintained a steady stream of instruction,
relating the life history of his supposed fiancée. He drew
a deep breath.

"Do you thoroughly understand the situation?" He did
not wait for an answer. "All you have to do is curtsey
when you are introduced to him. Say 'yes' or 'no' as required. Otherwise, keep quiet. Do you think you can remember that? Just don't speak any more than you have
to."

"My lord." The cool voice at his side effectively
stemmed the flow. "I may be a trollop and a thief, but I
am not stupid, and I have given my word. I will do nothing to disabuse your grandfather of the notion that you
are about to provide the House of Talent with a bride."

At this, the earl seemed bereft of speech. He remained
silent until they reached a heavily paneled doorway on an
upper floor. Here he paused, and turned to grip Diana's
shoulders.

"You have chosen wisely, which is not surprising in
one of so practical a nature. Should your resolve fail,
keep before you the thought of the handsome reward you
are earning by your efforts. I have only one more request.
Since we are supposed to be betrothed, I would like you
to address me as Jared rather than 'my lord.' "

Giving her no chance to deliver herself of a reply, he
tapped lightly on the oak paneling. The door was opened
immediately by a small, elderly man, dressed in the con-
servative garb of a gentleman's gentleman. He bestowed
upon Diana a glance of surprised approval, then ushered

her into a cavernous bedchamber. Lord Burnleigh followed close behind.

The focal point of the room was an enormous canopied bed, surmounted by griffins and flying dragons, and hung with curtains of crimson damask. It was bolstered with a welter of pillows and quilts, and surrounded by candelabra. The only sound came from the painful breathing of the man who lay there. Diana was drawn to the bed's occupant, and without urging she approached him.

Lord Chamford was obviously not the strapping figure of a man he once had been, but evidence of his former strength could be seen in the size of the frame that lay wasted beneath the covers. Piercing eyes, set over an imposing nose, surveyed Diana sharply as she drew near.

"Hah!" This to Jared, in a voice that was weak, but authoritative nonetheless. "You've brought her to me, then. Splendid! Come here, my dear, and let me look at you. No. Closer. Sit here, by my hand."

Lord Chamford rested his gaze on Diana's face, surveying her keenly. His eyes, as dark and deep-set as those of his grandson, bored into hers, but Diana found she was able to return his gaze unflinchingly.

The old gentleman sighed and sank back into his pillows, as though satisfied by what he had seen.

"Jared tells me you have resided in some godforsaken corner of—Wales, is it?—for many years."

"Yes, sir. My mother and I have lived for some time in Dhu-Rydd."

"Dhu-Rydd." He repeated the name in a hoarse whisper. "I believe I visited there many years ago. Old Fensborough had a place nearby. Nothing but rocks and mountains."

Diana replied in a prim voice, "Yes, indeed, my lord. Dhu-Rydd is, of course, situated at the foot of Mount Snowdon, the highest elevation in Britain." Behind her, she heard the sound of an indrawn breath. That last bit had come from her fund of schoolmistress's knowledge, not from Jared's hurried biography.

"Shooting wasn't much good that year, either," rumbled the marquess, apparently still lost in memory. But then . . . "Ah, never mind all that. Tell me about yourself, my dear."

Diana breathed a prayer.

"There is little to tell, my lord. My father died—many years ago. My mother's health was never strong, and we have lived in virtual seclusion. I have seen little of the world."

His lordship gave a tremulous bark of laughter.

"No Season for you, eh?" He added with a shrewd twinkle, "The dibs not in tune? Well, so much the better. We Talents, don'tcher know, can choose beauty and breeding above wealth in our brides."

Diana's cheeks flamed, and the old man laughed again.

"You're even more charming with your flags flying. Hah! I always did have a weakness for a yaller head, and yours is true gold. Odd shade, too." He frowned. "I've seen it somewhere before—can't remember—but, by God—" he gave a rasping laugh—"if I were fifty years younger, demmed if I wouldn't cut out that grandson of mine."

Diana chuckled, strongly attracted to this fierce old man.

"And I'll wager you were just the handsome rogue who could do it."

"Aye." His laugh was a coarse bark. "You have the right of it there, m'dear." Visions of long ago smiled in his eyes. "But I shan't sully your young ears with my wicked past. Tell me, how do you like your new home? Has Jared shown you about yet?"

The earl spoke.

"There has not been time for the Grand Tour, Grandfather. That will come later. In the meantime, you have tired yourself. We will leave you to rest now."

"Rest now, is it?" gasped the marquess. "I haven't cocked up my toes yet, y'young jackanapes. Right now I've a mind for some conversation with your bride-to-be. Tell me, then." He turned once more to Diana. His breathing was becoming more labored, and the lines on his face were deep. "It's been many years since I met your father. Only saw him once, I think. How did he die? How long has your mother been a widow?

Diana knew a moment of panic. She had exhausted her fund of false information, and she sensed that Jared had all but stopped breathing. She opened her mouth and cast her hopes in Providence.

5

"My father died some years ago, sir." Diana engaged in some rapid arithmetic. "He was in the Army, as you know. He, um, served in America during the Colonial war. His—his horse was shot out from under him in battle, and he took a bayonet in the lungs. His health was always weak after that, and he died when I was only, ah, seven years old."

From behind her came a faint, ragged sigh of relief. Lord Chamford smiled at her once again, but then gestured weakly.

"Ah, well, then—mayhap it's up with me this time." He gazed into Diana's face once more, then turned his eyes to Jared.

"I know you've come to me for a blessing, lad—but it's you who've given me one. It's fretted me for so long— you clinging to your bachelorhood, and Simon over there in the thick of the fighting. Who knows what will happen, now that Bonaparte has escaped his cage? Aye," he grated, in response to Jared's gesture of protest. "I know you think I've a maggot in my head, but it can happen, you know. Look at the troubles at Silverwell!

"She's a right one, sure enough, lad. You've made a wise choice." And then, to Diana, "He's a good man, m'dear—a trifle headstrong, but he will make you a good husband and a good father to your children, and Stonefield will be safe in Talent hands."

The earl stood close behind Diana. He ran his fingers lightly along the side of her cheek, and Diana had the sensation of a trail of effervescent heat tingling in her nerve endings. He bent his head, and as she turned to search his face, she was caught unaware by a look of such warmth and tenderness that somewhere deep inside her a response stirred. The thought flashed through her mind: *This is how he will look at the woman he loves.* Then: *You fool, this man is your enemy. His eyes lie for his grandfather's benefit.*

Still, when Jared withdrew his gaze, she experienced a sharp sense of loss, knowing that she would never again find that expression in his eyes.

Fool! Jared berated himself. Why did the nearness of this woman move him so? Her cheek, so deliciously curved, and soft as crushed flowers—and those eyes . . . A man might drown in their misty depths. *But never forget,* he reminded himself harshly, *she is an artful siren, and in those silvery pools a man could run aground on the rocks of greed and cruelty.* No one knew better than he the treachery to be found in the limpid innocence of a woman's gaze.

Suddenly, Lord Chamford released Diana's hand. She turned to find that his eyes were closed, his face whiter than the pillows upon which he had sunk. His breathing had become labored again, and Jared turned Diana toward the door. Fishperk, the valet, hurried forward, exchanging a meaningful glance with the earl as he saw the two from the room.

In the corridor, Diana leaned against the wall, pale and shaken. Her glance caught that of the earl, and she surprised a flash of respect in his eyes.

"A formidable performance," he acknowledged.

"Yes," she replied bitterly, "I believe I was satisfactory. Between the two of us, we have successfully hoodwinked that wonderful old man."

Despite herself, tears welled in her eyes.

"Please have done, madam," sighed Jared. "Spare me your false expressions of pity. You have nothing further to gain from them, you know."

Diana's breath came fast in indignation.

"Do you not think I have human feelings?" she cried.

"Possibly," he returned. "However, your tears would be much more convincing had you not bargained quite so cleverly before inducing them. No, do not fly up at me." He grinned sourly as Diana's eyes flashed. "I will not permit you to assault me in my own home. Please try to conduct yourself . . ."

They had been moving toward the staircase, but Jared stopped suddenly at the sound of voices rising from the great hall below. One of them, clear and youthful, could be heard distinctly.

"Yes, we did make good time. But never mind that now, Mallow. Quickly—take my pelisse, and here is my hat. I must go directly to Grandpapa."

The voice of the butler could be heard in ineffectual remonstrance.

"But of course I'm going up. He will want to see me—I know."

Now the voice grew closer. Jared stiffened, and cursed under his breath. He grasped Diana's arm in an attempt to draw her away from the staircase, but it was too late.

In a flurry of gauze and flying ribbons, the owner of the voice came into view around the curve of the staircase. She appeared to be about seventeen years old, and was quite astonishingly beautiful. A tumble of brunette curls framed an enchanting little face, with dark, sparkling eyes, a small, straight nose, and an adorable pink bow for a mouth. Her figure was small and slender, her movements graceful, and she gave the impression of floating, fairylike, up the stairs. On catching sight of the earl, she launched into hurried speech.

"Jared! We started as soon as the message came. I thought we'd never get here. Mallow says I'm not to see Grandpapa, but that's—"

She stopped short as she caught sight of Diana, standing a little behind Jared at the top of the stairs.

"Oh!" she exclaimed, her delicate brows arching in surprise.

Then she took in the borrowed dimity gown. Her mouth formed a small pink O of astonishment as she shot a questioning glance at Jared.

The earl, with creditable aplomb, turned to Diana.

"Miss Bavister, may I present my sister Felicity?" Then, to the younger girl, "Lissa, this is Miss Diana Bavister. She is the daughter of a dear friend of our mother, and she has come all the way from Wales to visit us."

Lissa, her eyes still on the gown, bobbed a dubious curtsey and murmured a greeting.

Diana took Lissa's proffered hand, concealing her trepidation. She had hoped for more time to recover from the interview with Lord Chamford before embarking on an encounter with another member of the family, particularly since this enchanting beauty was obviously the owner of the pale green dimity.

"How do you do, Lady Felicity? You must think me a strange visitor, indeed, to have pilfered your wardrobe. When you hear my sad story, I hope you will forgive me."

She then, with appropriate interjections from Jared, related the tale of the overturned coach. Lissa was all concern.

"What a dreadful thing to have happen!" she exclaimed. "Please call me Lissa. And, of course, you are welcome to anything I have. But," she continued, not to be deterred from her purpose, "right now I must go to Grandpapa. Oh, Jared," she choked, "is he really. . . . ?

"I'm afraid so, my dear. He is very weak, and cannot see anyone just now."

"But that's nonsense!" cried Lissa mutinously. "I know he will want to see me immediately!"

"Absolutely impossible. Now, go to your room, and I will call you as soon as Grandfather has rested."

In his voice Diana caught the sound of nerves rasped raw, and as a look of battle flashed in Lissa's eyes, she spoke without thinking.

"But, Lord Burnleigh, you have not explained the situation to your sister. Lissa, I'm afraid this is all my doing."

Two pairs of dark eyes swung toward her, and she placed her hand on the young girl's arm.

"As you can imagine, when your grandpapa heard there was a strange female in the house, nothing would do but that I be brought to attend him at once. We talked at some length, which I fear cost his lordship a great deal. He was indeed very weak when we left him just a few minutes ago."

Lissa appeared to digest this with a tolerable degree of acceptance, but opened her mouth to deliver what promised to be a strong caveat. Diana continued quietly, "If the decision to see him were yours alone, which do you think would be the best course?"

Once again she was the recipient of a thunderous scowl from the earl. Lissa did not reply, but remained still for a moment, her head bowed. Then she spoke in a subdued voice.

"I did not perfectly understand. Of course, I'll wait until Grandpapa is able to see me." To Jared she said, "You will tell him as soon as he is awake that I am here?"

Jared appeared dumbstruck as he observed the unaccustomed expression of gravity on his sister's willful young face.

"You know I will, Lissa," he said, his voice softer. "As soon as he awakens. And now," he continued, "I wonder if I might impose on you to accompany Miss Bavister to her room. We have put her in the rose bedchamber. Aunt Amabelle has had her women sewing since early this morning, and by now should have a gown ready for her."

Diana glanced at Jared in blank bewilderment.

"Ah, Miss Bavister," said the earl with a smile, a glint of pure mischief in his eyes, "my aunt prides herself on her efficient household. Did her maid not tell you that measurements were taken from the ruined gown in which you arrived, and that one or two garments would be ready by late this morning?"

Diana, her improvisational abilities deserting her, responded with a strangled gasp. Lissa took her hand.

"Of course she will need a guide. Grandpapa always says this place is such a barracks one needs bearers and a batman to get from the hall to the scullery."

Diana contented herself with a speaking glance at his lordship and allowed herself to be drawn along the corridor.

Jared watched the two figures disappear from view, and turning away, he mused for a moment in brief self-congratulation. He had chosen his tool well, he thought crudely, and so far all was going according to plan. The female had performed beyond his hopes; Grandfather was at peace.

He was not particularly surprised that the manners of a lady could be successfully counterfeited by a woman of the streets. Her sort could be found in discreet little *pieds-à-terre* all over London, the mistresses of wealthy men. Not, he thought wryly, that their morals were much different from those of the noble ladies they emulated.

An image of the lovely Cleanthe flashed into his mind. He was startled by the vision, for he had not thought of that high-born beauty in years. He was grimly pleased that the memory of her cornflower-blue eyes no longer had the power to twist his insides into knots of hurt and humiliation. If anything, he mused, he was grateful to her for teaching him the eminently practical lesson that the heart of a noble lady could be as wanton and rapacious as that of the lowest street drab.

Armed with this invaluable knowledge, he had for many years sought his pleasures not only from among the muslin company, but in the softly lit boudoirs of accommodating peeresses whose husbands attended to pressing affairs elsewhere.

He sighed, his thoughts turning back to his present predicament. Why had he for so long put off choosing a bride? Despite his grandfather's urging, he had avoided parson's mousetrap with great care, and had for many Seasons remained the most determined of bachelors, eluding the myriad lures cast by hopeful mamas of the *ton* and their dutiful daughters.

What—or who—was he looking for? he wondered. Would marriage to one of the dutiful daughters be so terrible? Surely, it would not necessitate a change in his pleasant life-style. After all, men of his station wed for advantage, and they joined with women who married for the same reason. That was the way of the world. His world, at any rate. The bride of his choice would be an ornament to his family and their name. He would support her in magnificent style, provide her with clothes and jewels, and assure her of a place in the highest ranks of the *haut ton*. She, in turn, would maintain his home, bear his children, and conduct her own affairs with discretion. It was certainly not to be expected that she would interfere in his pleasures. All in all, he could look forward to a most comfortable existence as a married man.

Why the prospect of such a union filled him with only the most profound depression he could not say.

He snorted contemptuously at his jaded maunderings, and turned back toward his grandfather's chambers.

6

As advertised, Diana discovered two gowns awaiting her in the little dressing room adjacent to her bedchamber. She presented them for Lissa's inspection.

"I must say," she exclaimed, "the hospitality in your grandfather's establishment apparently knows no bounds. I could sink with embarrassment at being found in such a predicament, but I am prepared to accept with gratitude his charity to a castaway. What shall it be, then—the gray or the lavender?"

Lissa sat curled up in an armchair of cherry-striped silk.

"Nonsense," she responded, with a magnanimous wave of her hand. "We are more than happy to render whatever assistance we can. The gray, I think. With your hair, you'll look just stunning. Or, at least . . ." She trailed off, surveying again the sober round gown, unadorned by so much as a ribbon or a flounce. "I wonder what Aunt was thinking? One would suppose you were applying for a post as governess."

"No! How can you say so?" retorted Diana, her eyes twinkling. "I'll wager this was your brother's idea. In my short acquaintance with him, I find that he seems to have an inordinate penchant for respectability."

"Jared?" Lissa exclaimed. "Respectable? That's just about the last word any of his friends would use to describe him, if one can believe half the *on-dits* that have been spread about him. . . ."

Any interesting revelations about to be made by Lord Burnleigh's undutiful sister were left unreported. The maid, Kate, entered, announcing breathlessly, "Lady Teague sent me, Lady Felicity. She said to tell you to bring Miss Bavister down for luncheon now, please. It will be served a little early, as the doctor is expected soon.''

At these words, Diana realized that she was quite hollow with hunger. By her recollection, she had eaten nothing since last night's ill-fated cutlets and peas at the Green Man.

With Kate's help, she shrugged into the gray gown, and glanced in the mirror to adjust her collar. Suddenly, her eyes widened, and she uttered a soft cry of dismay.

"Why, what is it, Diana?" asked Lissa. "Whatever is the matter?"

"I was wearing a small pendant," whispered Diana, her hand at her throat. "I hadn't realized till now—I must have lost it when . . .'' She caught herself, and forced a smile to her lips. "It—it's nothing important." She patted a curl into place.

But her hand crept once more to her collar as she followed Lissa from the room and hastened in her wake through yet another maze of corridors.

Eventually the two reached the family dining parlor, a spacious chamber paneled in oak and hung with straw-colored brocade. Lady Teague was already seated at the long mahogany table. Gracing the board were two additional females, the first of whom was well into middle age, and thin to the point of emaciation. She put Diana strongly in mind of a worried mouse, with frightened eyes and a pink-tipped nose. In contrast, the second lady could only be described as massive. Three chins trembled over a broad reef of bosom, and two pale eyes peered at Diana unwinkingly, like mushrooms in a bowl of cream soup.

Lady Teague waved the young women to their places.

"Lissa, dearest! I had not thought to see you returned in such good time, and I see you have already met our guest. Jared will not be joining us—he is with Papa, of course. I do apologize, my dear," she said to Diana, "for the skimble-skamble manner in which we have treated you since your arrival. It's just that everything is so—so . . .'' She finished her thought with a flutter of her beringed hands. Her bracelets clinked an accompaniment.

"I understand, my lady," Diana replied soothingly.

"It is I who should apologize for intruding into your household at such a time."

"No, no—er, Diana—nothing of the kind, of course. We're most pleased to have—um . . ." Again her words trickled away, and, with the air of one grasping a lifeline, she turned to introduce the other two women.

"This—" she gestured to the large lady—"is Mrs. Lydia Sample, my cousin, and this"—she indicated the mouse—"is Miss Bledsoe, Lissa's governess."

Feeling a pang of sympathy for this frightened little person, obviously the product of years of living on the sufferance of wealthy families, Diana gave her nod of encouragement. Receiving no response beyond a quick, nervous bob of the head, Diana turned to the proffered dishes.

Regretfully, this was only a small luncheon. Cook, familiar with the eating habits of the females of the establishment, had provided a scanty selection of cold meat, salad, and fruit. To this, Diana addressed herself with enthusiasm, under the mildly astonished eyes of the others.

The talk was of Lord Chamford and his illness.

"I am simply saying, Amabelle," intoned Mrs. Sample, with the air of one who had been simply saying this for some days, "that if his lordship had taken my advice when he first came in from his day out in the wet fields, he would not now be in this sad state. Goose grease. Hot goose grease and flannel. It never fails."

"Yes, Lydia," replied Aunt Amabelle, a touch of impatience in her voice. "That's very true, no doubt, but you know how it is with Papa. At the merest suggestion of interference in his affairs—particularly from a female—he flies up in the boughs. I don't know how many times I have endeavored to guide him in matters of his health and well-being, only to be rebuffed in the most unseemly terms."

"As well I know, my dear," Mrs. Sample interposed with a sigh. "I recall the occasion upon which you recommended a series of galvanizing treatments for his gout. I myself would not have suggested a regimen so sadly out of date, but there was really no excuse for the tongue-lashing he gave you."

"And just a few weeks ago," continued Lady Amabelle tearfully, "when I mentioned that if he persisted in consuming such quantities of port after dinner he should balance the effect with a dose of Dr. James's Powders, I thought he would go off in a fit of apoplexy right on the spot."

"Well, I'm sure it's no wonder!" interjected Lissa, her black eyes snapping. "Galvanizing! Goose grease! I never heard such fustian as your everlasting quacking, Aunt. Between you and Cousin Lydia, it's enough to try the patience of a saint. Which," she added fair-mindedly, "Grandpapa is a long way from being."

At the commencement of this short diatribe, Miss Bledsoe had begun an ineffectual twitter of protest, which was reinforced by a gasp of indignation from Lady Teague.

"Lissa, that will do! Will you never learn to mind your tongue?"

Miss Bledsoe continued twittering, and Mrs. Sample rumbled.

"Indeed, Lissa, most unbecoming," the latter said, "A young lady. . . ."

Lissa, her eyes flashing, opened her mouth, but was interrupted in her spirited rejoinder by the entrance of Mallow, who bore the intelligence that the doctor had come and gone, and Lord Chamford was at last requesting Lissa's presence.

The girl sprang to her feet, and, contenting herself with a darkling glance at her preceptresses, hurried from the room.

Lady Teague was the first to speak.

"I really don't know what we're going to do about that girl. She gets more and more unmanageable every day." She cast a look of reproach at Miss Bledsoe, who squeaked even more agitatedly, and plaited the fringe of her shawl with trembling fingers.

"One must be fair, Amabelle," said Mrs. Sample judiciously. "Lissa has been a rare handful since the day she was born, and with the cosseting she has received from Lord Chamford, to say nothing of the indulgences heaped on her by her two older brothers, it's simply not to be expected that she can be controlled by a governess or anyone else short of one of those Greek women."

"Greek women?" came the surprised query, in unison, from the others at the table.

"Well, I think they were Greek. Big, strapping wenches—used to hunt and shoot, and they poked at people with spears."

At this, Diana choked on a bit of cold chicken.

"I believe they were called Amazons, Mrs. Sample," she said when she had recovered. "They weren't real. That is, they are from classical mythology."

"You don't say," said Aunt Amabelle, obviously much impressed with Diana's erudition. "Just as well, no doubt. They do not seem at all the sort of female one would want running tame in one's household."

"No, indeed, ma'am," agreed Diana, with barely a quiver in her voice.

"At any rate," continued her ladyship, "something must be done about Lissa."

"She is certainly one of the loveliest young girls I have ever seen," said Diana, "and I do think—" Here she broke off, embarrassed that her instincts as a schoolmistress had overridden her social sense. "I beg your pardon, ma'am. I have no business offering an opinion of a member of your family."

"Nothing of the sort, my dear."

"Good heavens," added Mrs. Sample. "I'm sure the opinion of a well-bred young woman such as yourself could not help but be welcome."

Now it was Aunt Amabelle's turn to choke. Red-faced and spluttering, she turned away offers of assistance from Mrs. Sample. Fortifying herself with a sip of water, she motioned Diana to continue.

"Thank you, ma'am. You're very kind. Well—I do think her liveliness of manner springs from an overabundance of sensibility rather than from an ungenerous spirit. She is at present very concerned, as are all of you, with her grandfather's health, which must naturally lead to a certain agitation of nerves. She seems to be most generous in nature."

"Oh, yes," Miss Bledsoe interjected unexpectedly, "she really is a lovely girl—so kind—and vivacious. And very quick in her lessons as well."

Aunt Amabelle sighed.

"Yes, that's true. When she is in spirits, there is no

one more affable and kindhearted. The thing is, she has
all the Talent wildness and stubbornness, which is difficult enough in the sons of the family. In a female, it
simply won't do.''

On this note, Lady Teague rose, signifying that the
meal was at an end. Diana hoped the others would not
notice that she had emptied every serving dish on the
table.

As the ladies left the dining parlor, her ladyship announced her intention of returning to her father's bedchamber.

''Although,'' she admitted with a disconsolate sniff,
''my presence does nothing toward his improvement.''

She turned toward the stairs, only to halt abruptly as
she absorbed for the first time the full impact of Diana's
gown.

''Good heavens, child! That cannot be one of the
gowns made up by my woman.'' At Diana's affirmative
nod, she gasped in horror. ''But it's absolutely dreadful.
I can't think how this came about. My dear, I shall see
to it at once. You know, we have several wardrobes full
of clothes left behind by Charlotte—Jared's older sister—
when she married. You and she are nearly of a size—just
the merest alteration is needed—and a few touches to
bring the gowns up to style. I promise, you will have
something suitable to wear to dinner.''

Then, after suggesting several means by which Diana
could occupy herself for the remainder of the afternoon,
she hurried away, with Mrs. Sample treading sedately in
her wake. Since Diana did not desire to take a nap, or
improve herself with a religious tract, of which Lady
Teague evidently possessed an extensive collection, she
accepted Miss Bledsoe's offer to accompany her on a walk
toward the neighboring village.

Shortly thereafter Diana, bearing a borrowed parasol,
found herself strolling along a charming country lane,
the estimable Miss Bledsoe at her side. This lady, away
from the environs of the Court, became much more
cheerful, and she regaled Diana with all the information
at her disposal on the Talent family.

Her recital did not take long, since Miss Bledsoe had
arrived less than a month ago to take up her position.

Apparently, this constituted a fairly long tenure for one of the willful Lady Lissa's governesses.

"She really is a sweet girl—underneath," Miss Bledsoe concluded. "It's just that when she gets her back up, which I'm afraid happens all too often, there's no doing anything with her."

Miss Bledsoe sighed.

"I have endeavored to give satisfaction, but it is so very difficult to instruct a young girl in the art of needlework, and the pianoforte, and all the other accomplishments so necessary to a lady of quality, when the lady in question says, 'What stuff!' The next one sees of her, she is racing along the downs on horseback with her hat hanging down her back.

"And the family is so kind. As you saw, I have been invited to take my meals with them, and Lady Teague is in everything most agreeable."

"And Lord Burnleigh?" Diana assured herself that she had no real interest in the wretched earl, but it would be useful to learn as much about her adversary as possible.

Regrettably, Miss Bledsoe proved to be a bent reed on the subject of his lordship.

"No, indeed, Miss Bavister. This is only the second time I have had the pleasure of seeing him. He spends most of his time in London." She simpered, and an unbecoming blush spread over her thin cheeks. "Perhaps that is just as well. From what one hears of him, no lady of virtue would wish to be very long in his company."

Encountering Diana's look of cool inquiry, Miss Bledsoe colored even more deeply, and she continued in some haste.

"That is to say, I have never heard him say anything beyond the most proper, but—well, everyone knows of his carryings on in Town. My dear, he is a Corinthian!"

The word meant nothing to Diana, and her brows rose. Miss Bledsoe smiled, as one in the know imparting wisdom to the uninitiated.

"No doubt, living in seclusion as you do, Miss Bavister, you are unaccustomed to the wild ways of our young blades, if you will excuse the vulgarity. 'Corinthian' is the epithet applied to the very wildest. This set is addicted to every form of sport, and they associate with all manner of the lower orders, sometimes speaking in the most appalling cant. To be a Corinthian, one must be a top-of-the-trees, a prime go, if you please. As for female companionship—well, that is better left unsaid,'' she finished repressively.

Overcoming her scruples, however, she plunged on with what could only be described as a certain degree of relish.

''I have seen those women—bold as brass in their expensive carriages, taking the air in Hyde Park—to the manner born, indeed!''

Her voice dropped to a whisper.

''I have heard Lady Teague on the subject of Lord Burnleigh and his 'Paphians,' as she calls them. The amount of money he squanders on them is rather a sore point. When her ladyship, quite tactfully of course, once brought up the subject to his lordship, he only said, ever so gently, 'But Aunt, it is my blunt, after all.' Did you ever hear the like?''

Diana agreed that she had never heard the like. By now, her better self had surfaced, and she was experiencing a strong distaste for the intimate nature of Miss Bledsoe's gleanings. She turned the conversation, admiring the beauty of the Kent countryside.

''It is lovely, isn't it?'' The governess smiled. ''Now that spring is here, all the orchards are coming into bloom. Such a charming panorama. See how the golden daffodils beckon to us with their nodding.''

Quite caught up in her flight of poesy, she hastened toward a grassy bank to pluck one of the graceful flowers, but was stayed by the sight of an approaching phaeton and pair.

''Why, it is Lord Stedford!'' She explained hurriedly, ''The Viscount Stedford, that is. His Christian name is Ninian, I believe. His estate, Silverwell, marches with Stonefield. He is such a gentleman, Miss Bavister! So handsome, with such an air. That is his man, Augustus Churte, with him.''

She hurried forward. ''Good afternoon, Lord Stedford. Such a perfect afternoon for a drive in the countryside, is it not?''

The phaeton drew abreast of the ladies, and Diana lifted her head to gaze into eyes of a clear and startling blue.

7

Ninian, the Viscount Stedford, glanced indifferently at the plainly dressed females standing by the road. He slowed his phaeton, and bestowed upon them the nod of condescension he reserved for persons of the lower orders.

Then Diana straightened. A stray breeze swept the round gown against her inviting curves, and caused tendrils of silken hair to play about her cheeks. The viscount reined in abruptly, causing the rather bulky gentleman seated beside him to skew sideways in his seat.

"What a happy surprise, my lord," said Miss Bledsoe in a breathless quaver. "Are you and Mr. Churte out to take the air?"

Lord Stedford slid his brilliant blue gaze to Miss Bledsoe's unprepossessing countenance and smiled.

"It is indeed a very fine spring day, Miss Bledsoe."

He turned to face Diana once again, his eyes traveling over her form in a familiar manner. Diana felt the blood rise to her cheeks, and lifting her chin, she returned his stare with affronted dignity.

Miss Bledsoe tittered uncertainly.

"My lord, you must allow me to present Miss Diana Bavister. Miss Bavister is a guest at the Court—all the way from Wales. She is the daughter of an old friend of the family."

His lordship's manner underwent a marked transformation. His smile broadened, and he doffed his curly-crowned beaver hat, revealing a fair head of pomaded curls. If he considered it odd in a guest of the Court to be jauntering about the countryside with no other companion than a governess, dressed in a gown a scullery maid would scorn, no sign of this showed in his expression.

He sprang from the phaeton, thus exposing the full magnificence of his raiment. His coat of dove-gray superfine was cut in a mode that might be considered somewhat showy for the country, but no fault could be found in the elegance with which it fitted his slender form. His cravat was carefully arranged in a cascade of precise folds, and his collar was starched into stiletto points. Several fobs dangled from a waistcoat of embroidered Turkish silk, and yellow pantaloons clung to his well-formed limbs.

"But what an auspicious encounter!" he cried with engaging ebullience. "Churte, be a good fellow and walk the grays while I make the acquaintance of this fair visitor to our neighborhood. Churte! What ails you, man?"

Indeed, Lord Stedford's man looked unwell. He still sat askew on his perch, and his eyes were fixed on Diana in an unfocused stare. As the viscount called his name again, he passed a shaking hand over his forehead, then seemed to come to himself. With a murmur of apology, he straightened and tipped his hat to the ladies.

Casting a brief, puzzled glance after his manservant, Lord Stedford bent his attention to Diana.

"Please, ma'am, allow me to introduce my humble self—but perhaps Miss Bledsoe has already made my name known to you?"

Diana smiled and acknowledged that this was so.

"Splendid! Then we are already old friends. Tell me, Miss Diana—if I may make bold of your name?" Taking her acquiescence for granted, he smiled roguishly. "How long do you intend to make your stay here?"

Diana, feeling herself on shaky ground, attempted a noncommittal answer.

"I really don't know, sir—just a week or so. I shall be leaving shortly to continue my journey. That is—I must travel to Canterbury—on family business."

"But that is absurd. Surely you cannot expect your new friends to let you go so soon. You must inform Lady Teague that you plan to stay much longer—till Christmas, at least."

Diana was unimpressed by this display of boyish enthusiasm, but she smiled as she shook her head. "I'm afraid I have already imposed on her hospitality quite long enough."

"But how is this?" asked his lordship. "Surely my lady can only be pleased to have the family manse graced with such loveliness."

Sighing inwardly, Diana embarked once more on the tale of the overturned coach. When she had concluded her story, the viscount's face took on an expression of sympathy.

"Well, well, such an adventure. So Burnleigh is at home, is he? Interesting. But tell me, if I may be so bold, when may I come to call on you at the Court?"

Diana hesitated. The prospect of a visit from the dashing Lord Stedford to herself, the supposed bit of muslin, under the outraged nose of the insufferable earl, was appealing. She sighed again and suppressed the ignoble impulse.

"I don't think that will be possible, sir. Perhaps you have not heard, the marquess is very ill. I don't believe the family is receiving."

"No! That is too bad," replied the viscount, a pout on his full lips. "I did hear that he had taken a chill, but I had no idea he was in such a bad case." He brightened. "We shall just have to contrive something else. Would you care to accompany me tomorrow morning on a drive through the neighborhood? There's no end to the sights around here. The village has a fine Norman church, and within a very few miles are some Roman ruins. Most enjoyable for you, I'm sure."

Diana was torn between disapproval of the gentleman's cavalier dismissal of Lord Chamford's condition and amusement at his childish efforts to win her approval. A chuckle escaped her.

"Roman ruins are certainly an inducement, but I'll have to ascertain any plans that Lady Teague may have."

"Of course," the viscount agreed smoothly. "Perhaps Lady Teague, and Lady Felicity, as well, would like to take the air. An outing would do them much good, do you not agree?"

Feeling that circumstances were proceeding much too fast, Diana contented herself with a smile and a "Perhaps." She then announced that she and Miss Bledsoe really must be getting back to Stonefield.

With another bow and yet another brilliant smile, Lord Stedford leapt into his phaeton. He took the reins from

Mr. Churte, who now seemed completely recovered from his indisposition. As the elegant equipage drew away, Lord Stedford turned for a final wave of his hand. Miss Bledsoe murmured a faint good-bye, but it was quite evident that for the viscount, the little governess had ceased to exist some time ago.

"Well!" breathed that lady. "I believe you have made a conquest, Miss Bavister." She looked back at the receding vehicle. "My goodness, he is still looking at you, and Mr. Churte gabbling at him a mile a minute!"

Suppressing an impulse to glance over her shoulder, Diana turned back toward Stonefield Court.

She set a brisk pace, and the two ladies soon arrived at their starting point, the manor's great stone portico. Here they were met by the odd sight of an aged farm cart standing before the massive center doors. From the rear of this vehicle a footman, under the direction of Mallow, was removing a portmanteau, while on the front stairs Lord Burnleigh clutched a tall, young stranger in a laughing embrace. Lissa danced around the pair excitedly, and Aunt Amabelle, in the background, was fairly wringing her hands.

Indeed, from the number of persons clustered in the vicinity, it appeared that most of the household had turned out to welcome this personable youth.

As Diana and Miss Bledsoe approached, they were observed by Lissa, who hurried to meet them.

"Diana, I'm so glad you are returned! Just see who has come. Simon! My brother Simon, all the way from France. He has come for . . ."

In sudden recollection, a shadow fell on Lissa's face. Almost in unison, the others gathered seemed to feel the same heaviness settle over the homecoming. Jared sighed, and with an arm still flung around his brother, made his way inside the house. Diana entered the hall in time to catch Simon's words.

"Yes, I was lucky. I set out as soon as I received your letter, and made excellent connections. At least until I debarked from the stage at the Pig and Whistle, in the village. There wasn't a vehicle or animal to be had there for hire. Fortunately, I spotted old Suggs on his way home from market, and caught a ride with him."

He glanced at the faces surrounding him, and his own grew serious. "Am—am I in time, Jared?"

"You've come in good time, Simon. We must get you up to see him right away. I have just come from his rooms, and he is awake, but very weak. It will do him good just to know you have come."

With a tired smile, he began to lead Simon toward the central staircase, but on catching sight of Diana, standing diffidently aside, he paused.

"Oh, but wait, Simon. You must meet our guest." He drew Simon toward her. "Allow me to present Miss Diana Bavister. She is an unexpected visitor, but a welcome one, nonetheless."

In the brief moment she was given to study this additional member of the Talent family, Diana's impression was of an open, even-featured face, with eyes of a clear and inquiring brown. Simon kissed her hand with an air of natural gallantry, but his manner was distracted as he murmured the usual courtesies. Diana responded briefly in kind, and Jared whisked his younger brother away.

Lady Teague, in a nervous flutter, hurried off in the company of Mrs. Sample to see to the readying of Simon's bedchamber.

"Thank goodness the linens have been kept aired, but we must get the dust covers removed—and, of course, flowers . . ." were the last words Diana heard as Aunt Amabelle bustled out of sight.

Diana turned to the stairs, declaring her intention of retiring to her bedchamber for a rest before dinner. She was not fatigued, but felt the urgent need for a period of reflection. The day was barely half over, but Diana felt as though she had lived through a lifetime of misadventure in a few short hours.

Declining an escort, she reached her chambers after only a few wrong turnings. There she found resting upon the satinwood dressing table a fat little packet, upon which her name (or, rather, that of the nonexistent Diana Bavister) had been written in a bold scrawl. It contained a roll of notes, which she counted with care. Yes, it was all there. Five hundred guineas. She sank into one of the pretty little chairs set by the fireplace, and gave herself up to thought.

She had the money with which to make her way to

Aylesford and, after she met with Marcus, back to Paris. When her bargain with the odious Lord Burnleigh had been fulfilled, she could look forward to a comfortable journey, provided with all the accoutrements of genteel travel.

She meditated on the earl, and became prey to wildly mixed emotions. On one hand, she was filled with indignation at his ruthless treatment of her. On the other, she wished that she had met him under different circumstances. But again, in what other circumstances would she be likely to encounter someone of his elevated standing?

"And—" a small voice made itself heard—"even if you were to meet under different circumstances, what possible interest could the Earl of Burnleigh be expected to take in a virtual nonentity from a ladies' seminary?"

Diana had no difficulty in recognizing the voice. It belonged to the Schoolmistress, of course, that prim and practical personage who emerged from the recesses of her mind every now and then to deliver instructive lectures when Diana's thoughts were in danger of taking a frivolous turn.

"None at all," was her instant retort. "Nor have I any interest in him beyond a desire to leave his influence at the earliest opportunity. After all, I am not an emptyheaded widgeon, falling into a swoon over deep-set eyes and a pair of broad shoulders."

"Quite," sniffed the Schoolmistress repressively.

In a distant wing of the Court, in Simon's chambers, Jared was deep in conversation with his brother. The two had just come from the marquess's chambers, and were in a somber mood. Jared briefly scrutinized the younger man. At their first meeting, in the hall below, Simon had appeared relatively unchanged from the hey-go-mad youth who had ridden off some three years ago to go adventuring in the Army. Brown hair waved just as luxuriantly over a broad brow, above eyes that were still clear and laughter-lit. But war had marked him in subtle ways—a slight harshening of regular, almost classic features, and the hardening of an already determined jawline.

"I can't believe how he has changed," Simon was

saying. "He seems to have aged ten years since I've been gone. And he is so thin! God, Jared, he's really dying, isn't he?"

"So say his doctors," agreed his brother with a grimace. "I'm glad you were able to be here for him."

"I'll only be able to stay for a few days," said Simon. "The news that Boney has slipped his leash didn't get out until I was already on my way home, or I might not have been granted leave at all. But what's this about your betrothal? Grandfather was very full of your news. Are you actually about to become leg-shackled? To a nobody from the depths of Wales? Not your style, I would have thought, though she is a rare beauty. That, of course, is very much your style."

Jared uttered a long drawn-out sound, half sigh and half groan.

"Sit down, Simon. It's a long story, and at the end of it, you may be ready to have me committed to Bedlam."

The tale was not so long in the telling, after all, but when Jared had finished, his brother indeed looked as though he believed him to have taken leave of his senses.

"That regal creature? A lightskirt? And she was able to fool Grandfather? This is—incredible, Jared. And Aunt Amabelle is part of the scheme? I begin to believe you're both candidates for the loony bin!"

Jared flung up a hand.

"Peccavi, brother. Enough. I know the plan is dangerous. All right, foolhardy, if you will. But, Simon, if you had seen him, worrying and fretting. . . . I would have done anything to bring him peace. And let us have a little less of the moral outrage, my lad. This little project is a drive in the park compared to some of the crack-brained schemes I've seen you through over the years."

Simon had the grace to blush. "But—"

Jared continued, ignoring the interruption. "Besides, the thing is working. So far, at least. As you saw, Grandfather is happy. To give the adventuress her due, she is a consummate actress, and has convinced not only the old gentleman, but Aunt Amabelle and the entire household, of her gentility."

"All but you, that is."

"Indeed. I wish you could have heard her story, Simon. Well, perhaps it is better you did not. Her tears are

most effective, and her voice, soft as summer rain. Of
course, it's a tale guaranteed to touch the hardest of
hearts.''

"But not yours, I take it.''

Jared laughed shortly.

"I think you know better than that. It's been a good
many years since I allowed my purse to be lightened by
a sad story and a pair of appealing eyes.''

"Ah, yes, the lovely Cleanthe. Jared, are you still
smarting over that? Good God, that was over ten years
ago! I was just a sprout at the time, but I can still remember you glumping about the place as though you
meant to put a period to your existence at any moment.''

"Was I that bad?'' Jared's mouth curved in a rueful
smile. "No, little brother, I am not smarting over it. I've
enjoyed as many enjoyable connections since then as the
next man, I should imagine. I am, of course, always willing to pay handsomely for services rendered, but I have
become a little harder to fool than the next man.''

"Yes, and just a bit more reluctant to fall in love.''

"Nonsense. I just told you—''

"I don't mean agreeable connections, Jared. I mean
love—as in marriage and children.''

"Good God,'' exclaimed the earl, "who looks for love
in marriage? And who in their right mind would wish for
that wretched condition of petty jealousies and whining
recriminations? But to answer your question, yes, I shall
marry. Having been brought to the realization of my der-
eliction, I have promised myself to make an offer within
the next few weeks.''

"Ah. Who is the lucky candidate? Anyone I know?''

"Don't be an ass. I don't know. Sally Westerby,
perhaps.''

"She squints, don't she?''

"Well, Eleanor Forbes-Lacey, then.''

"Oh, yes—the Incomparable. Has her temper improved any?''

A touch of impatience crept into Jared's voice.

"All right, what about Catherine Ponsonby, or what's-
her-name, Framlingham's youngest daughter? The point
I am trying to make is that there are any number of 'candidates,' all well-bred, dutiful, and noticeably anxious to
wed the heir to a noble fortune.''

"And you really don't care which of them you marry?" asked Simon curiously.

"No. Not since the days when I burned with passion for the exquisite Cleanthe, and had visions of installing her as Countess of Burnleigh, have I considered marriage anything more than an extended tour of duty. Lord, what callow dreams those were!"

"What . . ." Simon hesitated. "What did happen, Jared, with Cleanthe?"

"Did I never tell you? No, I suppose not; you were just a stripling then." Jared sighed again. "I, of course, was a sophisticate of nineteen. I thought she was my soul mate, and I lost my heart in the beguiling depths of those pansy-blue eyes. I loved her to distraction, and was fairly dazzled when she swore that she loved only me. I showered her with bad verses and expensive trinkets." Jared's lips curved in a tight smile. "And then—I can still remember the night she came to me, her pink little mouth trembling in despair. She needed, she explained, oh, ever so much money. Her brother, you see, had gambled unluckily, and was about to plunge headlong into the River Tick. Father would disown him, family dishonored. 'Oh, Jared, what am I to *do*?'

"She left my house that night with a roll of soft she could not even fit into her reticule. I learned shortly thereafter that the gambling debt had been incurred not by her brother, but by her lover, of whose existence, needless to say, I had heretofore been unaware. I was crushed, to understate the matter. You see, I was so very young. Ah, well." He laughed softly. "It was a long time ago. And even at that, sad to say, I failed to learn my lesson, for my next *chère amie* was pretty Patsy Fordham. She was a viscountess, whose doting husband was wealthy enough to buy a small country. When she bestowed her favors on me, I was vastly set up in my own estimation, but she was the greediest baggage imaginable. You can understand how lowering it was for me to discover that she was merely using me as a source for whatever jewelry she desired that the viscount had neglected to purchase for her.

"It was at that point, I'm pleased to say, the lesson sank in. Suffice it to say that the time is past when I can be duped by a touching story no matter how lovely the teller of the tale.

"Which brings us back to Mademoiselle St. Aubin. We have come to a business arrangement, and so far she has lived up to her part of the bargain admirably. She has more or less abandoned her 'damsel in distress' position, so things will no doubt proceed smoothly."

"Oho," chuckled Simon. "Another agreeable connection in the offing?"

Jared was startled by the question, and made oddly uncomfortable by it, but he replied lightly.

"I think it unlikely. She seems to have taken me in an unaccountable dislike. And with that I will leave you, for it is time to dress for dinner. I trust you brought appropriate attire."

"Yes, if you mean knee breeches. I assume the old standards still prevail? I thought so. Have no fear, I shall dazzle the assembled company. Now be off with you."

In her chambers, Diana was made aware of the approaching dinner hour by the advent of Kate, bearing another addition to her wardrobe. It was evident that Lady Amabelle had made good her promise, for this time the ensemble was suitable for evening wear. The lustering gown, of palest lime, was not precisely in the first stare of fashion, but the low neckline was trimmed in French ruching, and there were two flounces around the hem.

Having buttoned and tucked Diana into the gown, Kate was all admiration, declaring herself obliged to create a hair style that would do the raiment justice. The result was a becoming swirl of curls perched atop Diana's head. A few ringlets were allowed to escape, framing her face in an enchanting filigree of antique gold.

Surveying herself with guilty pleasure, Diana discovered the age-old feminine truth that almost any trouble can be lightened by the knowledge that one looks one's best.

As Kate led her once more through endless passages to the drawing room, she made another discovery. Her heart was pounding in an alarming manner in anticipation of another confrontation with Lord Burnleigh!

8

Upon entering the pleasant chamber that served as the drawing room, Diana found the other members of the household already assembled. Lady Teague, Jared, and Simon were seated in earnest conversation on a settee of straw-colored silk. Mrs. Sample and Miss Bledsoe carried on their own exchange by the fire, while Lissa sat some distance away, stabbing with her embroidery needle at a tambour frame.

At Diana's entrance, Jared rose and escorted her to a comfortable armchair near the settee.

"Ah, Miss Bavister. So pleased you could join us." This with a satirical lift of his eyebrows. "I understand Miss Bledsoe has been showing you a little of the countryside. Very charming this time of year."

"Yes, indeed, my lord," contributed the governess in a tremulous voice. "And in our travels we met Lord Stedford, out to take the air, you know. He seemed quite taken with our guest," she simpered.

"Umph," was the earl's only response.

"You do not like the viscount, my lord?" inquired Diana, managing to convey in her tone that the world seemed inordinately full of persons who did not meet with Lord Burnleigh's approval.

Jared frowned.

"I barely know the fellow. My impression is that he's a rum touch if ever I met one, but then, as I'm sure you will agree, Miss Bavister, first impressions can so often be misleading."

Diana felt herself flushing, but she lifted her chin as she replied. "You are so right, my lord. It is refreshing to hear such a sentiment upon your lips."

Here Lady Teague took issue.

"I do not know what you can mean, Jared. The circumstances of his coming to Silverwell are, of course, unfortunate, but the viscount is a very nice young man.''

Diana interrupted diffidently.

''Excuse me, my lady, but Lord Chamford mentioned something about the trouble at Silverwell. I—I would not like to say something untoward to Lord Stedford out of ignorance . . .'' She finished her sentence with a questioning lift of her brows.

''Oh, not trouble, really—that is, not precisely,'' said Lady Teague.

She launched into a somewhat disjointed explanation.

''You see, the old viscount—Charles—was a great friend of Papa's. He had three sons. The youngest became estranged from the family many years ago and ran away to America. He died there not long after. He was always a sickly lad, and, of course, the climate in the Colonies is notoriously unhealthy. His lordship's wife passed away not long afterwards.''

Lady Teague's eyes filled with easy tears.

''He felt her loss keenly. Then, a few years ago, the two remaining sons and their families perished in a boating accident. The old viscount was devastated. He never did regain his health, and he passed away last fall. With all his sons gone, the title and the estate—which was considerable, Lord Stedford being a very warm man, as they say—went to his great-nephew, Ninian. Papa took the whole thing very badly. I don't think he has yet received the poor boy. It's really too bad. I mean, it's not the young man's fault if—well . . .''

She broke off and twisted to face the earl.

''I don't care what you say, Jared, Lord Stedford is in everything unexceptionable. His manner, his bearing . . .''

''Yes, Aunt, one would have to agree that he is charming, handsome, and dresses with extreme, er, elan.''

Lissa sat up very straight at that.

''I think he is dashing!'' she said abruptly.

''Throwing down the gauntlet, Lissa?'' Jared smiled. ''I am quite ready to admit that he is the fulfillment of a schoolgirl's dream.''

Lissa pouted.

''But not, I trust,'' continued Jared, a slight edge to his voice, ''the fulfillment of your particular dreams.''

Lissa's cheeks flamed, and she tossed her head.

"I have outgrown schoolgirl fantasies," she sniffed.

"I'm pleased to hear that," her brother retorted. "I hope, then, that we will not have a repeat of your disgraceful behavior at Tunbridge Wells. I understand that you embarked on a desperate flirtation with at least three of the military men stationed there."

"Well, really, Jared!" Lissa fairly leaped from her chair in indignation, and she shot an accusing glance at Miss Bledsoe. "You have no right to interfere in my— that is, are you implying I would . . . ?"

"I imply nothing. Merely placing a word where it will do the most good."

Lissa set her lovely mouth, and Diana instinctively moved to spread oil on these turbulent waters.

"Lissa, how did you find your grandfather when you went to him this afternoon?"

This served to divert the girl's thoughts, and she sighed.

"Very badly. I could not believe the change that has taken place in such a short time. His mind seemed to be wandering and—and he could scarcely speak."

Jared moved to her and put his arm about her shoulders. Brother and sister stood silently for a moment, differences forgotten in their common pain.

Simon spoke then.

"I was with him until just a few minutes ago. He was sleeping deeply when I left, and Fishperk will send to us immediately if there is any change."

Since no one was expected to sit down to the table with a hearty appetite on this somber evening, a simple meal had been set out on the snowy table covers. To Diana, however, accustomed to thrifty boarding school fare, the array of dishes seemed positively sumptuous. A raised mutton pie was accompanied by Hessian soup and cucumber prawns in a wax basket. Next appeared a neat's tongue with cauliflowers, and a variety of vegetable dishes, served with appropriate sauces. Jellies and creams and cakes were offered as a remove, including a Gateau Mellifleur.

Conversation was desultory, consisting mainly of talk between Jared and Simon of the probable outcome of Napoleon's march to Paris.

When the last covers had been removed, the gentlemen waved aside the brandy and port, declaring their intention of looking in on Lord Chamford, and promising to join the ladies in a few moments. Aunt Amabelle rose and led the ladies from the room.

"What a magnificent piano!" were Diana's first words on entering the music room behind her ladyship. She crossed to the instrument, which occupied one corner of the room in lordly splendor.

"Yes, it's quite beautiful, isn't it?" replied Lady Teague. "Papa had it installed several years ago, when Lissa began her lessons."

"And I absolutely trembled in awe the first time I sat down at it," Lissa said with a laugh. "The sheer grandeur of the thing still makes me feel totally inadequate."

"Nonsense, my dear," said Aunt Amabelle. "Your playing is delightful, I'm sure. Why don't you favor us with a little something?"

Sighing, Lissa sat down at the keyboard and launched into a lively sarabande. She played with great spirit but little technical prowess, giving evidence to Miss Bledsoe's comments on her lack of application.

After only a few bars she gave up, splaying her fingers across the keys in a dissonant jangle of chords.

"But dear Lissa," murmured her governess nervously, "that is our new piece. Perhaps if you try one of the others that we have mastered—more or less . . ."

"Well, I shan't," cried Lissa. "I can't think about the stupid music when Grandpapa is . . ." She pushed back the piano bench and stood with a mutinous flounce.

Diana also rose, and moved toward the piano as though drawn. Under Lissa's wondering eyes, she sat down before the instrument and raised her hands. She held them suspended for a few moments over the keys, then, with a little choke, dropped them into her lap.

"Do you play, Miss Bavister?" asked Mrs. Sample brightly.

"Yes, a little."

"But how delightful," intoned Mrs. Sample, "You must treat us to a tune."

"Yes, Miss Bavister, please favor us with a selection. I've been told you have a gift for the pianoforte."

Diana whirled in her seat. Jared had entered the room

quietly, and stood leaning against the door jamb, the familiar, hateful smile curling his lips.

Diana shivered, and felt the fingers twined in her lap stiffen into kindling wood. She vacated the piano bench precipitously, and fled to the sanctuary of a huge wing chair.

"No, no, really I would rather not, my lord. Besides, I'm sure your family wishes to know how Lord Chamford goes on."

"Yes, Jared," Lissa urged. "Tell us, has there been any change?"

All in the room turned to him.

"I'm afraid not. At least, not a change for the better. Grandfather is growing weaker, I fear. He is still sleeping. The doctor looked in while I was there, but could do nothing beyond shaking his head. Simon is still with him." He looked around. "I suggest we make an early night of it. Tomorrow may be a difficult day for all of us."

Lissa made no reply, but ran from the room in tears. Lady Teague left the room with Mrs. Sample, the two ladies murmuring words of comfort to one another. Miss Bledsoe followed silently.

Jared watched Diana as she rose and prepared to leave the room. Perhaps, he mused, it had been unfair of him to embarrass her in the matter of her skill at the pianoforte. However, it had been uncharacteristically foolish of her to make a claim that could so easily be disproved.

Nonetheless, he was irritated to discover that he was faintly disappointed. There was, of course, not the slightest possibility that this golden-haired beauty was anything but a tart. Why should he find himself wishing she had managed to squeeze an étude or two from those slender fingers?

Stifling this unwelcome line of thought, he hastened from the room, following the path taken by the ladies.

"Miss Bavister," he called peremptorily, "would you come with me, please? I have something for you."

Without waiting to see if Diana followed, he turned and proceeded to the library, a few steps down the corridor.

He went to the handsome Sheraton desk, and from one of its drawers produced a small pendant, hung on a slim golden chain. He turned to Diana, who had entered the room behind him.

"Turlock, our head coachman, brought this to me just before dinner. He found it behind the squabs of my curricle. It does not belong to me, so I must assume it is yours."

He held the pendant up for Diana to examine. On a small drop of carnelian, the letters "A.L." were carved in decorative script. The stone was set in gold, worked in a simple, old-fashioned design.

"Oh, yes!" Diana cried, reaching for it. "It is mine. I thought I had lost it. I have worn it most of my life, and it means a great deal to me."

Jared maintained his hold on the little necklet.

"How touching. Most of your life, you say? And I had rather assumed it must be a token of your erstwhile lover's devotion. 'A.L.' Can it be that you have given me a false name? Such perfidy, my pet! Or, perhaps, your protector stole the jewel from someone else? From his looks, I would not put highway thievery beyond him. It's a pretty little bauble, to be sure, but not of great value, I think."

Diana, determined to avoid any more brangles with his lordship this evening, swallowed her anger at his words, but she watched in growing fury as he held up the pendant, idly examining it. He paused, an attentive expression on his face.

"That's odd. I could swear I have seen this before. Umph. Most probably it is a copy of a more famous piece. At any rate, you may keep it with my blessing. Allow me."

Jared bent to secure the chain around Diana's neck. His hand hesitated, and his fingers brushed warmly against the back of her neck. Diana looked at him, startled, but found no softening of the granite in his gaze.

"By the by," he continued, "speaking of devotion, I shall take this opportunity to inform you that while I realize it behooves you to lose no time in finding a new source of feathers for your nest, I will not permit any dalliance with Lord Stedford while you are a guest in my home. A word to the wise will suffice, I am sure, for a woman of such eminent practicality as yourself."

Diana simply stared at him. Was there no limit to the man's incredibly insulting behavior? She was swept by a gust of rage that seemed almost physical in its force. Her hands clenched into fists, and in a voice shaking with fury, she cried, "By God, sir, what a contemptible cur you are! If I were a man, I would run you through. *Dalliance!* A *guest* in your house! Tell me, does it feed your overweening masculine pride to humiliate one who has not the means to defend herself? Or are you merely the kind of wretch who cannot feel himself a man unless he has some unfortunate victim to browbeat? I did not ask to be brought here; I only asked for my freedom. I had not thought anyone could be so hard as to take advantage of someone in trouble, but you have no difficulty in doing so. Indeed, it apparently gives you great pleasure to have another human being, no matter how insignificant, at your mercy. You sicken me. You are wealthy and elegant and privileged, and you call yourself a gentleman, but you are nothing but a swaggering bully!"

Diana stopped only because she had no more breath with which to infuse her tirade. With a scathing glance, she swept past a white-faced and speechless Jared. Once in the corridor, she fled blindly toward the staircase. Somewhere, she thought wrathfully, in the upper regions of this glorified rabbit warren, was her bedchamber, a temporary haven in which she could cry the furious tears welling hotly in her eyes.

As she passed the music room, however, she came to an abrupt halt. She entered the chamber and strode directly to the huge piano. Seating herself, she raised her hands high and brought them down upon the keys with a crash, launching herself into a thunderous passage of wild beauty. The stormy melody echoed through the lower passages of the Court, sounding in a crescendo of brilliance. The music swelled in a passionate expression of rage and anguish until, long minutes later, Diana lifted her hands, and the final majestic chords died away.

She drew a shuddering breath. Rising from the bench, she walked to the door, where she encountered the earl. Observing his almost ludicrous expression of astonishment, she nodded regally.

"Ludwig van Beethoven, Sonata in C-sharp Minor, Third Movement. Thank you for the use of your piano. I enjoyed that immensely."

So saying, she continued without pause on her march down the corridor. Jared made no move to stop her as she swept up the staircase, but behind her, Diana thought she heard a faint, ''Good God!''

9

The next morning, when the sun again glowed pink against the bed hangings, Diana woke unrefreshed. Sleep had come only after hours of fruitless reflection. The words she had hurled at Lord Burnleigh the night before rang in her ears like a prelude to disaster. He had richly deserved them all, but what would his response be? She had given him no chance to reply to her harangue, but what retribution would he exact today?

What if she had enraged him to the point where he would demand the return of the plump little packet which was now tucked under her pillow? True, they had struck a bargain, more or less, and an English gentleman was bound by his word. However, she placed no reliance on the Earl of Burnleigh's sense of honor. Without the money, she would be unable to continue her journey.

And where was Marcus? Surely he must have received her note by now. Why had she received no answer?

Diana pondered again, as she had done so often in the past week, on the hurried message she had received from her brother. Her relief in hearing from him after his long silence had been overshadowed by his tone of urgency. She did not sense that he was in any danger, but he was certainly up in the boughs about something. Blast the boy! Why couldn't he simply have told her what had caused his excitement instead of penning a mysterious missive bidding her to come to him with all haste? She sighed. It was ever his way. He loved adventure, and everything he undertook must be imbued with high drama.

Squinting against the early-morning sun that assaulted her eyes, Diana pushed aside the bedclothes. She moved to the window and opened the curtains. Fresh air. That's what was needed. She surveyed the exquisite rose garden beneath her window. Still bare in the early-spring chill, it seemed the perfect place for a brisk, head-clearing walk.

Resolutely she strode to the wardrobe. There were now five gowns hanging there, and from among them she chose a becoming morning dress of apricot sarcenet, made up to the throat, with a treble pleating of lace falling off around the neck. Remembering her role as a pampered member of the *ton,* she rang for Kate.

When the little maid appeared a few moments later, she bore a tray on which were set cup and saucer and a pot of chocolate. Arranging this on a small table near the bed, she turned to Diana and began a breathless recitation.

"Mallow says t'tell you, miss, that the messenger y'sent to Aylesford returned very late last night, and he says the young man you was inquirin' about was at the Swan, but now he's gone."

Diana drew in a quick breath of dismay.

"But not t' worry yerself, miss. The young man left a message for a Diana Stubbins, which Henry—the footman who took yer note—figured must be you, though how the simpleton at the Swan could make Bavister into Stubbins, I'm sure I don't know."

Stubbins?

Diana wrinkled her forehead in puzzlement. Then, after a moment's thought, she realized that to English ears the name St. Aubin must sound very much like Stubbins.

"We are, um, distant cousins," improvised Diana. The thought flashed through her mind that she had told more lies in the past few days than she had in the entire course of her life previously. "We don't really know each other. Stubbins was—was my mother's name, and possibly he thought it was mine."

"Oh." Kate paused, evidently assimilating this with some difficulty. "Anyway, the young man said he'd be back. Henry left yer message, anyway, so maybe it will all work out."

I doubt it, groaned Diana inwardly.

"And," continued Kate, her forehead wrinkling in concentration, "there is luggage waitin' for you at the Swan."

She paused, her expression puzzled, and Diana, wishing to forestall any more awkward questions, indicated that she wished to dress.

She was soon garbed in the apricot sarcenet, her hair brushed and curved into a shining sculpture.

She declined Kate's offer of guide service to the rose garden, accepting detailed instructions instead. After several turnings into elegantly furnished dead ends, however, she was forced to admit defeat. She was about to seek assistance from one of the Court's ubiquitous footmen when a distant clamor of feminine voices reached her ears. Sure that she recognized one of them, she followed the sound, and soon found herself at the open door of a charming sitting room, hung in palest blue. There she was met by the startling sight of Lissa, engaged in spirited verbal conflict with her own maid. The contretemps was rendered all the more chaotic by the fact that it was being conducted in two languages. The maid, slight and wiry, wore her linen round gown with an air that proclaimed her to be a French lady's maid of the first stare. Gallic imprecations streamed from her lips in wrathful bubbles. Neither of the combatants so much as glanced toward Diana, and the pitch of battle seemed to be gaining in intensity.

Without thinking, Diana strode upon the scene and addressed the maid sternly.

"Tiens!"

This had the desired effect. The woman broke off her impassioned diatribe and swung toward Diana. She flung her hands skyward, and cried out in the voice of one whose patience has been frayed to breaking point, *"On ne peut pas faire deux choses à la fois!"*

Resting her case, she stood panting, her black, snapping eyes fastening on Diana's in an insolent manner.

Diana responded calmly.

"Of course your mistress realizes that you cannot do two things at once. I suggest you apologize to her ladyship for your outburst, and leave her to recover herself. She will ring for you later."

The young Frenchwoman opened her mouth, but apparently thought better of relieving her feelings any further. She bobbed an unrepentant curtsey, flung a staccato, *"Je regret, madame,"* which sounded more like a parting salvo than an apology, and hurried from the room.

Drawing a deep breath, Diana turned to Lissa, who stood gazing at her in astonishment. Only then did she realize that she had conducted her entire conversation with the maid in French.

"In Dhu-Rydd," she began carefully, "my closest playmates were the children of a family of émigrés. I learned to speak their language—better, I think, than they learned to speak mine."

She noted with relief that Lissa appeared to find this entirely reasonable. Indeed, that volatile young lady seemed unprepared to spare the slightest attention from her domestic difficulties.

"That wretched creature!" she cried, in mingled tones of fury and indignation. "I cannot think why I put up with her impudence and her perfectly lamentable laziness!"

Diana, soothing the distraught damsel with word and gesture, managed to restore her to relative calm. As Lissa's temper subsided, so did her sense of injury, and it was not long before she returned Diana's look of inquiry with a rueful chuckle.

"Yes, I can see you believe the whole imbroglio to be of my own making, and I daresay you're perfectly right. But she is absolutely infuriating. Grandpapa hired her for me several months ago right out from under the nose of Lady Biddlesley. Her name is Odile, and she is frightfully high in the instep. She as much as told me that the only reason she agreed to come here was because I shall be going to London soon for my come-out, and she feels I shall be a great credit to her." Lissa related this last with naive pleasure, adding, "She does turn me out in style. If only she weren't so excitable."

"Odile is obviously a real treasure," agreed Diana, smiling. "But as you say, her volatility is unfortunate. I believe it is considered a national attribute of the French. So unlike we phlegmatic English, who never allow ourselves to fly up into the boughs."

At this, Lissa colored faintly, then sighed.

"Yes, I suppose that is the problem. Every time she gives me one of those disdainful shrugs, I simply lose control." She laid her hand on Diana's, her eyes laughing in self-mockery. "Very well, *Madame la Préceptrice.*

From now on, I shall remain calm with Odile. I shall be firm but fair, and I will *not* allow her to bully me.''

"Magnifique!" applauded Diana. "Behold the perfect mistress!"

Lissa giggled, then launched into another topic.

"Diana! You must help me choose a morning dress. Jared says I may go up to see Grandpapa after I have had my breakfast, and I wish to wear something very gay and cheerful.''

She bustled to her wardrobe and removed, in rapid succession, several gowns which she spread out for Diana's inspection.

"I wish I did not always have to wear such insipid pastels. When I am older, I intend to wear nothing but brilliant reds and yellows and absolutely shocking blues. Here.'' Lissa proffered a frothy confection in pale pink. "What about this one?''

"It's lovely,'' replied Diana appreciatively. Really, the child could wear a nankeen smock and still appear perfectly ravishing. "But what about that primrose muslin? Perhaps with the string of amber beads I see spilling out from your jewel case.''

Diana assisted Lissa into the gown, and accomplished the necessary buttoning and tucking.

"There—perfect! You look like a burst of May sunshine. And, if you will allow me, *mademoiselle*, these ribbons through your hair. *Zut alors—très ravissante!''* She stood back to admire her handiwork.

"Merci bien," responded Lissa. "And, may I say, *ma'm'selle,* you are looking *très—um—très élégante* yourself? Apricot does become you. Oh! I have just had a thought!''

The girl whirled to a large wardrobe, and after some searching, produced an exquisite shawl of pale gold silk. This she draped over Diana's shoulders in a carefully casual fashion, and stood back to exclaim in admiration.

"There! If that isn't just the very thing. I bought it months ago—it's Norwich silk, you know—and when I wore it, Jared rang such a peal over me, just because I spent over a week's pin money on it. So I don't wear it anymore. But see how well it goes with your own gown. Please take it.''

"So that your brother can ring a peal over me?" Diana said smilingly.

"Of course he won't." Lissa giggled. "You're a guest, and he wouldn't dare. Besides, he will think I am being ever so noble in giving it up to a stranded traveler, don't you think?"

"And so you are," replied Diana, much struck.

"Actually, the real reason I don't wear it is because when I got it home, I realized it makes me look quite sallow, but one hates to admit when one makes expensive mistakes. So you will really be doing me a great favor by accepting it. Please?"

Touched by the young girl's unself-conscious generosity, Diana accepted the gift with simple thanks, and the two ladies set out sedately for the breakfast parlor.

As they made their way downstairs, Diana regaled Lissa with the tale of her failed attempt to find her way about.

"When, for the third time, I found myself at a standstill in yet another gallery, I was tempted to tear a strip from my petticoat, scrawl a note on it, and toss it out the window in the hope that a passerby might find it and come to my rescue!"

"Poor Miss Bavister. Is it always to be your misfortune to depend on strangers?"

At the sound of the quiet, deep voice behind her, Diana stiffened. Arranging her face in a cordial smile, she turned.

"Why, good morning, Lord Burnleigh." As she spoke, she searched the earl's face in an effort to read his mood. "How you do creep up on one! I believe there must be some Red Indian blood in the ancient Talent lineage."

Jared's only response was a thin smile. He was dressed for riding, and there was no gainsaying that buckskin breeches and a buff coat set off his athletic form admirably. He turned to address Lissa.

"On your way to breakfast, Puss? I'll join you. I have just come from Grandfather."

Lissa fastened her wide eyes to those of her brother.

"Oh, Jared! How did he pass the night?"

"In deep sleep. There seems to be little change, but if you still wish to go to him, I cannot see the harm."

The girl would have turned away in a rush, but Jared stayed her.

"Best eat something first. Grandfather is still asleep; when he wakes, Fishperk will notify me immediately. I know Grandfather will enjoy seeing you in that very fetching ensemble."

Lissa laughed engagingly.

"Diana helped me to choose it. And have you no compliment for *her* very fetching ensemble?"

A slight flush spread over Jared's bronzed cheeks.

"Of course. How remiss of me. A charming gown, Miss Bavister. I see my aunt's women have been busy, but I did not realize any of them was possessed of such talent. And that shawl—very, er . . ."

"Elegant, is, I am sure, the word for which you are searching, my lord. And I have your sister to thank. She was kind enough to bestow it upon me, and I must say I feel complete to a shade wearing it."

"Yes." Jared frowned slightly. "I seem to recall. The infamous Norwich silk, is it not?" he asked, turning to Lissa. "Purchased at Madame Toinette's very modish and extremely expensive establishment last fall."

Lissa's eyes sparkled dangerously.

"Why is it you always remember precisely what one wishes you wouldn't, and why must you always be bringing it up?"

"The peculiarities of the male mind, my dear," put in Diana before Jared could form an answer. "It is my belief they do it just to be irritating."

Lissa drew her close in an impetuous hug.

"Oh, Diana," she chuckled. "I'm so glad you have come to us. I just knew we would deal famously!"

Diana, glancing at the earl, surprised an almost comical expression of puzzled suspicion in his eyes.

They had by now reached their destination, and Jared ushered the ladies into an informal breakfast parlor. He led Diana to a chair at a small table near a pair of French doors.

Breakfast was a casual affair, with only the three of them at table. Lady Teague, it appeared, was an early riser, and preferred to take a light meal in her chambers, as did Mrs. Sample. Miss Bledsoe's whereabouts were unknown.

"She's probably up in the schoolroom concocting French declensions for me," muttered Lissa with foreboding.

"But speaking of French," she added, turning to Jared, "I wish you had been present abovestairs a few minutes ago. You remember Odile? And the problems I've had with her? Yes, I know it's mostly my fault, but what I mean to tell you is that just now Diana came to my room in the middle of one of our brangles, and absolutely stopped Odile in mid-spate. Jared," she continued in an awed voice. "Diana spoke to her in French. Fluent French. Odile simply folded her tent and crept off meek as a nun's hen, if you can believe it."

Lissa beamed at Diana in simple pride, as though it were she herself who had been responsible for Diana's miracle.

Jared's expression as he absorbed this information was unreadable. To Diana he said only, "I am indeed impressed, both at your linguistic fluency and your triumph over the notorious Odile. May I serve you, Miss Bavister?" He indicated the laden buffet table standing nearby.

With what she hoped was a patrician nod, she accepted from his lordship's hands eggs, toast, and several generous slices of York ham. The food was proffered with an exaggerated air of solicitude that went unnoticed by Lissa, but was enough to set Diana's teeth on edge with annoyance.

Suppressing a desire to empty the steaming silver coffeepot into Jared's lap, she maintained a flow of small talk as servants threaded their way among the diners, filling cups and replenishing plates. Midway through the meal Mallow entered, bearing a salver upon which rested the day's post. This he placed before Lord Burnleigh.

"Anything for me?" asked Lissa idly, sifting through the assorted missives. "Ooh, what's this?" She selected a note of pale pink, and waved it delightedly in the air. "Why, it's addressed to you, Jared, and—" she drew it slowly under her small nose, sniffing noisily—"what an exotic scent. And lavender ink, in such a flowing hand. She must be a very *special* friend."

Jared reached peremptorily for the letter.

"Merely an acquaintance," he replied curtly, and then turned with obvious relief as Mallow indicated he had an additional message for his lordship. Lord Chamford was awake, and asking for Lady Felicity.

"Go along, Lissa," said Jared. "Go be Grandfather's tonic."

"I will," replied Lissa stoutly. "I can always cheer Grandpapa out of the dismals."

She hurried from the room enveloped in sunshine and sprig muslin.

10

Silence fell heavily on the two remaining breakfasters, and Diana's glance flicked to the letter looming on the salver like an exotic flower.

"Would you not like to attend to your correspondence, my lord?" she inquired in dulcet tones.

"There is nothing here that requires my immediate attention," the earl replied stiffly. His face relaxed in a slight smile as he continued. "At the moment, I would like to hear about this marvelous fluency in French."

"Why, my lord," Diana answered tartly, "surely you must know that any adventuress worthy of the name must become proficient in a foreign language. It's one of the first things they teach us in Trollop School."

She rose with an indignant rustle of silken skirts to pace the room.

Jared watched her, his eyes warming with an irrepressible amusement. The moment passed quickly, and he sobered.

He, too, had passed a restless night, caused not only by concern for his grandfather, but by the image of luminous gray eyes meeting him with annoying frequency in the corridors of his thoughts.

Her impassioned words had threaded in and out of his dreams through the long watches of the night. There could be no doubting her anguished sincerity last night, particularly after her virtuoso performance on the piano. Lissa said she spoke fluent French, and she certainly seemed to have a knack for handling high-strung young girls.

He sighed. The woman was obviously who she said she was, and being so, he had behaved unforgivably.

She was unlikely, of course, to be any less rapacious than any other woman of his acquaintance. The brazen manner in which she had coerced him into raising the fee for her services was proof of that. Still, he would be careful in the future not to wound her sensibilities any further.

"*Touché,*" he said now with a laugh, and Diana was once again struck by the transformation in his features. The harshness to which she had become accustomed was gone, and she was drawn against her will to the dark eyes lit with genuine amusement.

"And do they also," continued Jared, "at Trollop School, provide instruction in the pianoforte?"

At this, Diana raised her eyes to his face. She felt the blood rush to her cheeks, and took a deep breath.

"About last night," she began, "I must apologize for my outburst."

Jared's brows rose in surprise.

"Apologize? I did not think to hear that word on your lips, Miss St. Aubin. But you were rather harsh."

Her clear gaze met the earl's unflinchingly.

"I will admit that I meant my words to sting."

"Sting! My dear young woman, I went to bed feeling as though an entire hornet's nest had been loosed on me."

Diana colored.

"My lord, you deserved every word. But," she added hastily, "I am sorry to have behaved so intemperately."

"As an apology," responded the earl with the faintest of smiles, "I feel your little speech leaves much to be desired, but I suppose when the hornet withdraws its stinger, even temporarily, one must be grateful.

"In any event," he continued, "your talent at the pianoforte is most impressive. I hope you will take the opportunity, while you are here, to make use of the instrument in the music room, or any of the others in the house. Perhaps you would like to try your hand at the pipe organ in the ballroom. And now, to change the subject, what are your plans for the day, Miss St. Aubin?"

"You must know, my lord," she replied stiffly, disappointed that the earl had offered no apology for his own inexcusable behavior, "that I have no plans, either for this day or for the ones hereafter. Except, of course," she added coldly, "to do your bidding, as does every other unfortunate soul in this house."

"Submission becomes you, my dear, although I feel I

would be deluding myself to grow accustomed to it. But, as for this day, Grandfather has given me express orders that I escort you on a tour of the Court. Since we have several hours before luncheon, we should be able to cover at least the main wings.''

"Lord Burnleigh," Diana began, "I have no desire to spend even so much as one hour in your company, and the prospect of an escorted tour of this grotesque monument to the feudal system is repugnant. Please do not—"

Jared interrupted.

"What happened to 'doing your bidding, my lord'? As I said, this is not my idea, but my grandfather's, and be assured, if he should summon you again, he will want a full accounting of the expedition."

Without waiting for a reply, he turned to the door. Diana, swallowing a number of scathing responses, followed.

Some time later, she was obliged to admit that she was enjoying herself. Stonefield Court was a magnificent old pile, dating from medieval times. The original building had formed a large square, but as the Talent fortunes prospered, more wings had been added, and the present edifice was comprised of a harmonious hodgepodge of courts and passageways and galleries.

"Most of which," explained Jared, "are closed off. Now the family makes do with twelve saloons, twenty bedrooms, not including the state suites, a mere three dining rooms, and various parlors, service rooms, and, of course, the library. When we entertain on any scale, we scrape through by opening up the west wing—the original portion of the manor—and using the old Great Hall as a ballroom."

Despite Jared's casual attitude toward the home of his ancestors, his love for it was obvious. Starting in the old hall, with its suits of armor and a fireplace into which, Diana was told, entire trees were flung, the tour led through innumerable rooms and corridors. Everywhere, centuries of care and attention were evident. Brasses glistened, marble gleamed, and wooden floors, paneling, and balustrades glowed with fragrant waxes.

Wide-eyed, Diana listened to histories of linenfold paneling, Gothic archways, Chinese hangings, and Restoration staircases. It was not until they had reached the oldest of the state suites, supposedly constructed for a visit by Queen Elizabeth, that she sank down on a brocade sidechair, embellished with Tudor roses, and pled for mercy.

"But you have not seen the Jacobean suite yet," pointed out the earl. "Nor the muniments room, which contains records going back, I daresay, to the days of Ethelred the Unready."

"Perhaps we could postpone that treat until another day?" asked Diana in a failing voice. "You must have many other demands on your time, my lord."

"Not at all," disclaimed the earl smoothly. "I am completely at your disposal. Perhaps we could have a picnic lunch sent up, thus allowing the entire afternoon for the northernmost sections. They have been closed off for as much as a century, I should imagine, and are now used mainly for the storage of abandoned belongings. A fascinating glimpse of the Talent family through the ages may be obtained through their perusal. I beg your pardon?"

"That was a groan," replied Diana. "Lord Burnleigh, my interest in your family history borders, of course, on the breathless, but I simply cannot take another step. If you will not guide me back through the trackless wastes, I shall have to find my own way."

"Nonsense, my dear Miss St. Aubin—but did we not agree on first names at the inception of our, er, agreement?" He continued without waiting for an answer. "If you set off on your own, we would find you months hence, white-haired and witless in some closet in the nether regions. I have one more area I wish to show you before I return you to civilization, Diana. I believe you will find it of interest."

As Jared turned aside to allow Diana to precede him through the doorway, her toe caught on the fringe of the fragile old carpet. She stumbled and would have fallen, but the earl grasped her to him and held her until she was righted.

At his sudden closeness she stiffened. She was intensely conscious of his solid masculine strength, and, for an instant, felt the beat of his heart against her own.

With an incoherent murmur, she thrust herself away and
fled into the corridor.

Diana did not allow herself to glance at the earl, thus
she could not perceive any discomfiture he might have
felt at the encounter. Indeed, he had little to say until,
after several turnings, they found themselves in a long
gallery. The walls were hung with portraits of stiffly
posed personages.

"The family gallery," announced Jared. "We begin
with the first of our line to make his mark on the world,
Henry Talent, the third Earl of Burnleigh, and the first
Marquess of Chamford. By all accounts an opportunist
of the first order, he found favor with Henry the Eighth.
He must have been an accomplished fence-sitter, not to
say the most appalling toadeater, as he continued to pros-
per mightily through the reigns of both Catholic Mary
and Protestant Elizabeth."

"Whatever do you think he would say if he knew of
the monumental hoax his umpty-great grandson is per-
petrating on the unsuspecting head of the family?"

Jared smiled.

"I suspect old Henry was not above a little embroidery
of the truth to advance his ends."

"I can well believe it. He has the close-set eyes of the
born deceiver, a trait obviously nurtured and handed
down through the generations."

The earl turned away, unscathed.

"Ah, but look over here at my lord Harold. If you are
searching for nobility of soul on canvas, here is your
example. He perished at Agincourt, or was it Crécy? You
would have to ask Simon. He's the military historian of
the family."

Diana peered at the likeness of a warrior, dressed in a
hundredweight of armor, leaning negligently against his
horse. He gazed heavenward with a pious expression on
his face, while the battle raged behind him in wooly puffs
of cannon smoke.

"I am sure it's not surprising that he succumbed,"
remarked Diana, "if he spent his time on the battlefield
striking poses. And who is this?" she inquired, turning
to a voluptuous beauty whose beribboned charms were
almost totally exposed in an alarming décolletage.

"Ah. That would be Lucy, wife of Robert, the fourth

marquess. Word is, he tumbled head over heels for her while she was a lady-in-waiting to Charles the Second's queen. Word also is that Robert snatched her from under the king's wandering eye. Just in the nick of time, I should imagine,'' he added, leveling his quizzing glass at the lady's most noteworthy assets.

Stifling a gasp of amusement, Diana hurried toward the end of the gallery. She stopped short at a small group portrait hung low on the wall. A mother and three children were portrayed in a charming garden setting. Diana gazed intently at a thin, wiry boy, who stared gravely at the world from under dark, straight brows. She turned questioningly to Jared.

"Yes," he responded. "That is my mother and all of us brats, done by Hoppner when I was eleven. The rather autocratic young miss seated next to me is Charlotte. She was thirteen then. And Simon—what a limb of Satan he was, even at six—is seated on Mother's lap. Lissa was not yet on the scene. In fact, this was done less than a year before her birth. Within a few months of this sitting my father was dead, and in a year my mother, too, had left us.''

"Poor little babies," murmured Diana. "Left alone so young.''

Jared's crack of laughter startled her, and sounded harsh in her ears.

"Save your pity, Diana. We were scarcely alone. Never, I warrant, was a group of youngsters nurtured with such care and attention. Don't forget, we were in the care of our grandfather.'' His voice softened perceptibly. "If there were such a thing as a father hen, that was he. Not only did he hire the most highly qualified nursemaids, governesses, and tutors, he was beside them every step of the way. He was at my heels when I played tag with the footmen, and he tossed me onto my first pony. I can recall venturing into Charlotte's room one day to find him haranguing an unfortunate female who was endeavoring to teach her the rudiments of needlework. 'Progress, my good woman! I see no progress from the seam she showed me yesterday to the unutterable mess she's struggling with today!' ''

Jared's voice was warm with memory. "I wonder we were able to keep any staff at all.''

Meeting Diana's eyes, he seemed to recollect himself, and continued in a more prosaic vein. ''Well, that's the lot, and now, if we hurry, we shall return in time for luncheon, thus escaping a scold from Aunt Amabelle. I'll show you a shortcut.''

He led Diana through more turnings and down a narrow servants' staircase, emerging at last into the corridor leading to the now familiar small dining parlor.

Lissa came running from the opposite end of the hall to meet them. Her wide eyes and pale countenance betrayed her urgency even before she spoke.

''Jared!'' she gasped. ''We have been looking for you everywhere. It's Grandpapa. . . . You must come quickly!''

11

Diana stood at the French doors that gave out from the music room to a broad terrace. Her ears strained for the slightest sound indicating the approach of Jared or any of the other family members.

It had been over two hours since the earl hurried away with his sister in the direction of Lord Chamford's bedchamber. Since then, Diana had engaged herself in various aimless activities in an effort to still the churning sensation in the pit of her stomach. Despite her most optimistic surmise, she could only conclude that Lissa's frantic summons indicated the marquess's imminent passing. The intensity of the sadness she felt at the prospect of the death of this elderly autocrat surprised her. In the few minutes she had spent in his company, the old gentleman had wrought a profound effect on her, and she grieved that she would never see him again.

Diana gradually became aware that her deepest sympathy was reserved for the grief that Jared must now be experiencing. Despite the apparent coldness of his character, it was obvious that his love for his grandfather was true and deep.

"But his feelings are nothing to me," she murmured as she stepped through the French doors. "Absolutely nothing," she repeated. The demise of the Marquess of Chamford, she reminded herself, meant to her only that her bargain with the odious Earl of Burnleigh had been fulfilled and she would be free at last to track down her peripatetic brother. By this time tomorrow, she might be on her way to Aylesford. She was surprised, and somewhat dismayed, to discover that the thought did not fill her with the delight it should have.

Giving herself a little shake, she stepped from the terrace onto a broad sweep of lawn. She sniffed appreciatively at the fresh country breeze, and paced the green-sward with measured tread, as befitted her surroundings. How many generations of Talents, she mused, had taken the air here, promenading in hooped brocades and pan-niered satins, or ruffs and doublet and hose.

When she reached the farthest boundary of the lawn, Diana was provided with a view of the Court's rear gardens. Emerging into one of these from a service entrance was a squat figure, dressed in black. Seen at a distance, it was impossible to make out his features, but his form was nonetheless familiar. Wasn't it . . . ? Yes, she was sure it was the man she had seen yesterday with Lord Stedford. What could his business be at the Court? she wondered idly. A message to be delivered, perhaps, or a visit to a friend in service here.

Dismissing the incident, Diana turned and made her way back to the music room. Seating herself at the great piano, she allowed her fingers to drift into a pensive Bach fugue, and was thus occupied when Lord Burnleigh strode into the room.

Rising to greet him, she observed a look of dazed incomprehension on his face, and her heart sank. Instinctively, she put out her hand.

"Your grandfather—is he . . . ?"

"I thought I'd find you here," he replied. Suddenly, his face lit with a blinding smile. "Grandfather is apparently on the road to recovery!"

As though his legs would no longer support him, he sank onto a brocade settee and, grasping Diana's hand, pulled her down beside him. His voice was shaky as he continued.

"It's the most amazing thing. When Lissa went up from the breakfast table, he had just waked from his long sleep through the night. His fever was gone, and he was calling for breakfast. The doctor arrived some time after that, and he reports that Grandfather's lungs are much clearer now. He is by no means out of the woods, but all the signs indicate a return to health."

Jared laughed. It was a sound of pure exuberance and release, and Diana found herself smiling in response.

"That is marvelous news, my lord. I am truly happy for you and your family."

"The rest will be down soon, I daresay. When I left

Grandfather, he was brangling with Aunt Amabelle over whether he should be allowed to get up. Out of the question, of course, for several days yet, but lord, it was good to hear him back in form.''

Jared rose, as though finding relief for his emotions in movement, and strode to the window. He turned to face Diana.

"I wish Simon could remain longer. He has only a day or two before he must return to his post. As for yourself . . .''

Yes, indeed, thought Diana, suddenly struck by this new complication in her situation. As for herself, what?

She raised her eyes to find that Jared was gazing at her in a measuring way that she did not care for. She rushed in to take the offensive.

"As for myself,'' she began briskly, "how fortunate that you will no longer require the presence of a fiancée. If you will be so kind as to fulfill the rest of our bargain—the coach and the abigail and footman—I shall prepare to make my departure at the earliest opportunity.''

The earl's response was as she had feared.

"Don't be absurd. The news of my betrothal is no doubt what pulled Grandfather out of his sickness. In his present state the unexplained departure of my betrothed would be extremely detrimental to his health. You must remain here until he regains his strength.''

Diana was silent. The man was insufferable in his peremptory demands, but he was right. She remembered the marquess's eyes, filled with tears of gratitude. To leave now would be equivalent to signing his death warrant. As for her search for Marcus, she could not plead that as an excuse, since there was little she could do at the moment but wait for his promised return to the Swan.

"Very well, I will stay.''

"Thank you.''

"I am not remaining in order to oblige you, my lord. I am thinking only of Lord Chamford.''

Jared nodded, his dark eyes unreadable.

"However,'' continued Diana, "you must see that this situation cannot go on for long. To begin with, I am not prepared to maintain this masquerade indefinitely. Nor, I should think are you. You must see—''

Jared flung up a hand in protest.

"To coin a phrase, my dear, I may be a swaggering bully, but I am not stupid."

Diana's lips tightened.

"I am well aware," he continued, "that a betrothal usually culminates in a wedding. Since I am not prepared to sacrifice myself to that degree, even for Grandfather, I promise you that I will take immediate steps to acquire a bona fide fiancée."

"But, of course," Diana returned, unaccountably stung by this statement, "you need only to snap your fingers in order to command the adoring attention of every maiden on the marriage mart."

The earl's smile was cold.

"Bluntly put, but accurate nonetheless. I could very well be ninety years old, with a wen the size of a cabbage on my nose, but as long as I remain heir to the Marquess of Chamford, and refrain from gambling away the family fortune, I believe it is safe to say that I can choose where I may for a bride."

Diana could only stare at him. Unbidden, the memory of the child in the portrait flashed through her mind. How sad that that vulnerable, appealing little boy should have grown into this utterly cynical, flint-hearted man.

Jared continued in a flat voice. "At this moment, I can think of half a dozen obedient maidens who would receive my offer with breathless acquiescence. I shall make a choice within the week, and wrap the thing up within two. At that point, you, Miss St. Aubin-Bavister, will decide that we do not suit, after all. You may then pack your bags and depart—groom, abigail, coach, and all. Before Grandfather has a chance to absorb the fact that his wayward heir is once more unencumbered, I shall have a new candidate to present to him. I trust that this arrangement meets with your satisfaction."

Diana received this statement with such a tumultuous mixture of emotions that for a moment she could not speak. To her annoyance, she was prevented from venting even one of the furious replies that sprang to her lips by the whirlwind entrance of Lissa.

"Diana! There you are. Has Jared told you the news? Isn't it wonderful? Oh, I just know Grandpapa will get better and better. Jared, Aunt Amabelle sent me to find you. She wishes to meet with you and Simon in the

Crimson Saloon for a moment. Something about the papers you wanted to discuss with the bailiff tomorrow.''

All through this speech, Lissa danced about the room like a joyful sprite. Jared, rather than trying to stem her excited chatter, merely nodded to both ladies and exited the room, leaving Diana to contain her fury.

Lissa, unnoticing, continued her happy burbling.

''Diana, I have a famous notion. Come with me to the church. The vicar will wish to know of Grandpapa's recovery. He's an absolute lamb, and his daughter, Patience, is a particular friend of mine. The family knows how worried we have been. Besides, they have the most beautiful lilac hedge in the county, and I wish to pick simply armfuls for Grandpapa's bedchamber. He does so love their scent. I sent Odile to tell Aunt that we will be back in time for tea. Come, let's go right now.'' She moved to the door, then stopped abruptly and turned back to Diana, her eyes very wide.

''Oh, I almost forgot. What is all this about you and Jared? Grandpapa says you are betrothed.''

Diana grew still. That Lord Chamford would tell others in his household of the ''betrothal'' was an eventuality Jared had discussed with her. Now it was time to bring out the simple denial that the earl had assured her would suffice. She fluttered her eyes in maidenly confusion.

''Oh, Lissa, did he tell you that? I don't know how he got the idea in his head, but he has come to believe that your brother and I are engaged to be married. He is quite wrong, of course.''

Diana searched Lissa's face for a response, but the dainty features displayed only a waiting curiosity. Diana continued firmly.

''Lord Burnleigh and I are barely acquainted, of course, and his—his invitation was merely a courtesy extended to an old friend of your mother's.''

Diana limped along for another few sentences, but observing Lissa's blank expression, she felt that on the whole, the simple denial was not meeting with a great deal of success. She hurried on in a brisk tone.

''So, since his health is still in a precarious state, we have not disabused him of the idea as yet. Later, of course, we will put Lord Chamford in possession of the facts.''

Lissa stared, unwinking, for a moment, but she said nothing more. To Diana's relief, the girl's grasshopper mind leapt back to its former preoccupation.

''Come!'' she cried. ''We'd best be on our way. We can take the willow walk to the vicarage, rather than go the long way by the road. It will be just a hop and a skip!''

She ran from the room, scarcely waiting for Diana's acquiescence, and Diana, nothing loath to escape even momentarily from the Court's confines, flung the Norwich silk shawl over her shoulders and hurried after her.

Reverend Smalley was as lamblike as advertised. The bespectacled cleric explained that his wife, lamentably, was away from home, but he and his daughter, a shy brunette of the same age as Lissa, were highly gratified at the news of Lord Chamford's turn for the better. The vicar said that, of course, dearest Lissa and her friend were welcome to all the lilacs they could carry. First, however, would Miss Bavister like to look at the church, while Lissa and Patience enjoyed a comfortable coze?

This program found immediate favor with Lissa. Now that her worries over her grandfather had lifted, her recent visit to Tunbridge Wells had taken precedence in her mind, and she was big with news to relate to her friend. She was sure Diana would simply adore an inspection of the little Norman church, and she promised she would not be above a few minutes in conversation with Patience.

Diana suspected that a large part of Lissa's revelations would concern certain red-coated gentlemen stationed near the Wells, but she agreed that a visit to the church was what she would most like at the moment. With courteous attention, she trod the path from the vicarage on the cleric's arm. They had scarcely begun their tour, however, when the vicar glanced from the transept door and exclaimed, ''Why, there is Squire Delaney's footman riding up to the kitchen door. He's come for a book I promised his master. Will you mind waiting for just a moment, my dear?''

''Not at all, sir,'' said Diana. ''The spring sun is so

delightful that I shall wait for you in the little orchard I spied just around the side of the building.''

The vicar hurried back to the house while Diana, turning in the opposite direction, was soon drawing deep breaths of the fragrant blossoms just beginning to bud on the gnarled old trees. Beyond the orchard, against a crumbling wall, she saw the beginning of the famous lilac hedge, and moved toward it.

She did not observe the figure waiting there.

As Diana drew abreast of the wall, the man leapt at her from behind. In an instant he had flung a cloak over her head and borne her to the ground.

Diana's senses reeled in shocked disbelief. This could not be happening again! Determined that her captor would not be successful a second time, she struggled violently, and managed to free her mouth from the folds of the coarse cloth. She screamed once, but her outcry was quickly silenced by a glancing blow to the side of her head. She heard approaching voices, and fought the darkness that threatened to overpower her. In the distance, Lissa's inquiring treble could be heard, while nearby sounded a masculine shout and the pounding of horses' hooves. With a snarled curse, her assailant thrust Diana from him, and the beat of his running feet could be heard fading in the distance.

"Here! I say—what the devil—Hi! You, there! Stop! After him, Churte!''

Diana, sick and dizzy, fought her way clear of the cloak, and the first sight to meet her eyes was the Viscount Stedford's face bending over her. His blue eyes crinkled in concern as he assisted her to her feet.

"Why, it's Miss Diana. My dear girl, are you all right? I cannot believe what just took place! Here.'' He led her to a seat under a tree. "Rest here a moment. Churte has run after the fellow. I caught only a glimpse of him as he ran off into the spinney yonder.''

Lissa rushed up just then, accompanied by the vicar and Patience, as well as what appeared to be the entire vicarage staff. To a chorus of shocked inquiry, Diana responded as calmly as she could.

"I am quite well, thank you. I really don't know what happened. I was just . . .'' Her eyes widened as she caught sight of the cloak, still lying on the ground, and she shivered in sick fright.

Reverend Smalley sat down beside her, patting her hand ineffectually.

"Diana!" exclaimed Lissa. "You are so white. Are you sure you're all right? I know! You must have a cold cloth for your poor head. Come, Patience, let us fetch one immediately."

In a burst of nervous energy, she ran off toward the rectory, towing Patience in a fierce grip.

Lord Stedford, having inspected the almost iridescent splendor of his waistcoat, and satisfied that it remained undamaged, seated himself beside Diana. He availed himself of the hand not being patted by the vicar, and stroked it tenderly. One of the maids offered to procure some burnt feathers.

"Really, I am quite well," protested Diana. "I am sorry to be the cause of such a disturbance. No, thank you, I do not require burnt feathers, and no, I do not wish to lie down. Oh, thank you—so thoughtful," as Lissa returned and hastily placed a dripping dishrag on entirely the wrong spot. "However, I would like to return to Stonefield now."

Lord Stedford declared himself to be in support of this plan.

"And I shall drive you there myself, Miss Diana. How fortunate that we came out in the barouche, so that you may be comfortable in a closed carriage. We'll have you all right and tight before the cat can lick her ear!" he cried gaily. "Ah, here comes Churte. Perhaps he can tell us something of your attacker."

But when Mr. Churte drew up to the group, puffing and sweating, he had nothing to report.

"Caught just a glimpse of him as he flashed through the trees," panted the thickset valet. "Wore some sort of homespuns. But then he disappeared—couldn't find hide nor hair of him."

"Hah!" said the viscount, taking charge. "No more to be done on that score, then. Now to get you home, Miss Diana. Churte, you assist Lady Lissa. I shall lift Miss Bavister into the vehicle."

Despite Diana's protests that she was able to walk unaided, he placed his arm about her waist and led her with exaggerated care to the waiting carriage. Lissa followed, still chirping distressfully. As Lord Stedford lifted Diana to a seat, a sudden thought struck her, and she twisted in his grasp.

"The cloak! I wish to take the cloak with me, please."

His lordship thought little of this notion.

"Now, why would you want that nasty thing? Churte will dispose of it. No need to worry your pretty head, my dear."

But Diana was insistent, and with a moué of distaste, Ninian ordered Churte to place the garment in the carriage. Then he tenderly deposited Diana in a seat next to Lissa, while he took the one opposite. Further orders were issued, and the comfortable vehicle moved off, leaving the vicar and his household discussing in wild surmise this disaster on their very doorstep.

12

On the drive back to Stonefield, Ninian was all solicitous concern.

"Are you sure you're quite the thing, Miss Diana? No, of course you are not. Just rest and do not try to talk, as our journey will be quite a short one. Tell me," he continued, ignoring his own instructions, "did you see the man at all? Will you be able to give a description of him?"

Diana shook her head, wincing at the pain the movement caused her. She lifted her hand to the bruise, and encountered the little pendant, which she had tucked inside her collar that morning, but which now had worked its way into view. She hastily adjusted it, and noted a startled expression on the viscount's face as he observed her activity. She smiled inwardly. Really, the man was such a fop, to notice at such a time the clash between the carnelian necklet and her apricot gown.

"No," she replied to Ninian's question. "I saw nothing. It was very sudden, you know."

The viscount watched her closely for a moment, his wide blue eyes oddly opaque. Then he sank against the cushion, smoothing his glossy curls, apparently disappointed that she could tell him no more.

It was late afternoon when the little party reached the Court, and its inhabitants were already gathered for tea in one of the saloons that opened directly off the entrance hall. As the carriage rattled into the portico, the viscount called peremptorily to the attending footmen. This brought the family members on the scene, whereupon Lissa launched into an excited and highly colored version of the abduction attempt.

"And if Lord Stedford had not happened by at the

moment, why heaven only knows what might have happened!'' she finished breathlessly.

The viscount shrugged in affecting modesty, but did not disclaim his part in the rescue of the fair damsel. He turned to assist Diana from the carriage.

''Gently now, Miss Diana. I am here. Perhaps I should carry you inside. Do you think if you rest your weight on my—''

Here Diana, who was growing more embarrassed by the moment at the attention of the ever-increasing group clustered around the carriage, protested.

''No, my lord. Thank you.'' She stepped down from the carriage unassisted. ''You are very kind, but as you can see, I am completely recovered.''

No sooner had she expressed this assurance than everything before her blurred in a sickening fashion, and her knees gave way. The viscount stretched out his arm to her, but found himself shouldered out of the way by Lord Burnleigh, who had just emerged from the house. White-faced, Diana slumped against him, and he swept her into his arms. At once she grew so dizzy that she was obliged to let her head sink onto Jared's shoulder.

Calling for a glass of wine to be brought immediately, he carried her to a thickly cushioned settee in the hall. With surprising gentleness, he brushed fine golden tendrils from her forehead, and when she winced at his touch, his fingers stilled.

''What is it? Are you in pain?''

''He struck me—there. I'm sorry to be such a baby,'' she gasped shakily, ''but it does hurt so.''

With infinite care, Jared probed and examined the area, until the whole ugly bruise was exposed. He stiffened, and in a colorless voice said, ''I should imagine it is extremely painful indeed. Fortunately, Dr. Meering is still abovestairs with Grandfather.''

He silently signaled a nearby servant.

''Oh, no,'' protested Diana in a weak voice. ''I'm sure it is not serious. I shall probably have a nasty headache, and that will be the end of it. I was not rendered unconscious by the blow, and—''

''Your medical opinion is of no interest to me,'' interrupted the earl brusquely. ''A doctor is what you need, and a doctor is what you shall have.''

Disinclined to argue further, Diana sank back into the cushions and closed her eyes. His fingers still moved on her hair with the lightest of strokes, and his touch sent delicious ripples all along her body, until it seemed to her that her very toes tingled.

A harassed Dr. Meering arrived in a few moments, and was joined by Lady Teague, approaching from the direction of the kitchens, bearing in her hands a cold compress.

"Ah, dear lady, always in the right of it. That's just what's needed. Skin not broken—no concussion. Wise to keep the compress on until the swelling goes down. That's the checker!"

Rubbing his hands together, he bustled off again, much in the manner of a conjuror who, having successfully worked his wonders, disappears in a puff of smoke. Lady Teague, with her own hands, carefully applied the compress, and bound it with a napkin. Diana gratefully acknowledged the relief its coolness brought to her throbbing head.

She sat up cautiously, and feeling no ill effects, thanked the assembled household for their assistance. Lord Stedford, who had withdrawn gracefully to the background, received a particularly glowing smile.

"Sir, I am most grateful for your assistance. If it were not for your timely arrival, I fear I should have been in sad case."

"What I want to know," interposed Simon, ignoring the viscount's modest murmurings, "is who's responsible for this outrage. Stedford, can't your man tell us anything?"

"Yes, I, too, would like some answers." Jared spoke with quiet authority. "Where is Churte, Stedford? I wish to question him myself."

"Oh, but Jared," broke in Lady Teague, "that can surely wait, can it not? Tea has been waiting for this half hour and more. Do go and sit down to it, and I will escort Diana to her bedchamber." She bent to assist the girl to her feet. "My dear, I shall have a tray sent up to you."

Diana smiled into the kind, plump face.

"I think I have been quite enough trouble to your staff for one afternoon, my lady. If you don't mind my rather rumpled condition, I would much prefer to take tea with all of you."

"Very well, then, if you are sure you are feeling the thing. . . ."

Aunt Amabelle, gathering Mrs. Sample in her wake, made her way toward the Crimson Saloon, turning to the viscount as she did so.

"You will join us, Lord Stedford, will you not? We have not had the chance to thank you properly for rescuing our dear Diana."

The viscount smiled boyishly. "No thanks are required, dear lady, but I should be most pleased to join you." He made a slight adjustment to the magnificence of his cravat, nodded with a genial swagger to Jared and Simon, and joined the little procession trooping into the Crimson Saloon.

Over the cups, the conversation was still of Diana and her near-disastrous encounter.

"To think," said Mrs. Sample portentously, "that such a thing could happen right in our midst, for all intents and purposes. And in broad daylight. Jared, the authorities must be notified at once."

The viscount uttered a small sound that was taken as agreement.

"The authorities?" gasped Lissa. "Here? But how exciting! Can you imagine such goings on in our quiet little corner of the world? Will the authorities really come here, Jared?"

"Sparing no effort to provide you with an afternoon's entertainment, I have already sent for Simmons—our bailiff," he added, for Ninian's edification. "I shall dispatch him to the nearest magistrate, who is, I believe, a Mr. John Brandon, residing some forty miles distant. I should not imagine he can arrive before tomorrow afternoon at the earliest. I should also imagine that the first persons to whom he will wish to speak are Stedford and his man."

The viscount seemed surprised and somewhat discomfited.

"Me? Why—well, of course, I shall be glad to be of any assistance, but I really don't see that I have any information of value—or Churte either, for that matter."

"But, my dear fellow," queried Simon, "were you not the first to arrive on the scene?"

"Indeed he was!" interposed Lissa. "Ooh! I wish *I* had observed the monster. We heard Diana's piteous call for help, but by the time we arrived, all that could be seen was Mr. Churte pelting toward the woods. I shudder to think what might have happened if Lord Stedford had not arrived when he did."

"Most fortuitous," agreed Jared. "That is just my point. You must have seen the ruffian, Stedford. What did he look like?"

The assemblage waited with interest for the viscount's reply. He frowned in concentration.

"Ah, well then. I really didn't get a good look at him. He was, as Churte said, dressed in homespuns, and—he wore a large hat, with, um—a sort of floppy brim, don't you know. It completely hid his face. But he was a big, burly fellow. Now that I think of it, he was surprisingly quick on his feet for one so large."

He looked at the faces around him.

"I'm sorry, that is all I can tell you. I fear the magistrate will have a trip for naught, because I don't believe Churte has any additional information."

He drained his cup abruptly and stood.

"And now, if you will excuse me, I must leave this delightful gathering. I had not intended to be gone from my home for such an extended time, and there are matters which require my attention."

He kissed the hands of the ladies with a practiced flourish, and nodded a courteous farewell to the gentlemen. Aunt Amabelle and Lissa rose to see him out, and the three passed from the room.

Jared turned to Diana. "And now, Miss Bavister, I really must insist that you retire to your room for a rest. It cannot be good—what is it?"

Diana had uttered a small cry of dismay. She rose hastily, to the imminent peril of the compress wound round her head.

"The cloak! Lord Stedford must have forgotten—it's still in his carriage!"

Her sudden movement caused a return of the dizziness she had suffered earlier, and Jared moved to her. Simon, with a gesture to his brother, hurried out of the room and returned a few minutes later with the cloak. He raised his eyebrows questioningly at Diana, who stood in the steadying circle of Jared's arm.

"Yes," she responded, with an involuntary shudder. "He threw it over my head. But I still don't know why. I must find out the reason behind—" She caught her breath and broke off.

"You are quite right, Miss Bavister," Jared said smoothly, receiving the cloak from Simon. "Perhaps this unsavory piece of clothing will provide some answers when we present it to the magistrate tomorrow."

He glanced keenly at Diana's pale countenance. "In the meantime, I am sure that what you most desire at the moment is some rest. Ah, here is Lissa returned from bidding a fond farewell to the splendid viscount. She will escort you to your bedchamber."

With a bow, Jared left the room with Simon, the soiled cloak draped over his arm.

Diana was left to Lissa's solicitude. What she really desired most in the world right now was a conversation alone with his infuriating lordship. As she followed Lissa up the wide staircase, questions about the identity of the persons who seemed to wish her such ill tumbled in her brain with renewed insistence. When she had arrived at the Green Man, she did not know a soul in England. Who was the "Captain Sharp" who had abducted her, and the other, whom she had come to call the "dark man"? And why were they so interested in Marcus? Surely, he could not have made such a virulent enemy in the short time he had been in this country. Could he?

It was in a decidedly unsettled state of mind that Diana passed the rest of the afternoon. Aunt Amabelle had left some reading material for her perusal, but an improving tract by Hannah More, the noted ornament of the Clapham Sect, entitled *Practical Piety,* failed to hold her attention. When, some hours later, Kate tapped at her door to assist her in dressing for dinner, she welcomed the little maid like a long-lost relative.

Arrayed in a gown of deep red, of the same shade as the little carnelian pendant that lay on her breast, Diana joined the family members assembled in the drawing room. To her disappointment, Jared was not among them.

"He'll be down later," explained Simon in response

to her carefully casual question. "He is with Grandfather, and will have a tray sent up. I'll take my turn later."

The chef, in honor of Simon's homecoming, had prepared his favorite dishes, with the result that the board fairly groaned under a staggering array of brimming platters and bowls. Diana dutifully sampled the haunch of venison, the collop of beef, and an ox cheek with dumplings, along with a vegetable pudding, a preserve of olives, and a plum pudding. She was obliged, however, to turn away the pork cutlets with Robert sauce, the tenderones of veal, the cheesecakes and a perfect avalanche of creams, jellies, syllabubs, and trifles. Simon, after the deprivations of camp life, addressed himself with enthusiasm to each dish as it was offered to him, declaring that his stomach must think he had died and gone to heaven. All the while, the young captain regaled the ladies with anecdotes of his service in Spain. These tales, which Diana was sure were strongly expurgated, were of ludicrous incidents in which he featured himself as rather a figure of fun.

"Now, Simon," Aunt Amabelle gently chided, "we know you better. You cannot tell me that you spent hours crouched under some farmer's front porch while the battle raged around you."

" 'Pon my honor, Aunt!" Simon laughed. "Three of us had cleverly managed to cut ourselves off from our lines, and here came the entire Frog cavalry galloping cross-country. Had to wait 'em out!"

"Where was this, Captain?" inquired Diana, her fingers clenching in her lap at the contemptuous dismissal of the "Frog cavalry."

"At Salamanca." Simon's young face grew hard. "That was a bad time. Too many good lads gave their lives there. And many more so badly hurt, in body and soul, that they will never be the same."

"As did the French," interposed Diana in a quiet voice. "Thirteen thousand French soldiers died there."

At this, Simon glanced at her sharply. "Have you Bonapartist sympathies, ma'am? If so, I fear you are in thin company."

"I have sympathy for anyone who dies in battle, no matter on which side they fight. As for Bonaparte—"

She broke off, aware that Simon was watching her with

a sardonic glint in his eye. At once, she realized that Jared must have told him of the circumstances of their meeting. She flushed, continuing with an effort.

"As for Bonaparte, I believe the French bestowed their loyalty upon him mistakenly. When Napoleon first came to power, I thought he was the savior of that bleeding nation. But he became greedy, and drew the country into disaster."

These words were greeted by a variety of reactions, ranging from incomprehension on the part of young Lissa, startled agreement from Aunt Amabelle and Mrs. Sample, and a flash of respect from Simon.

He laughed softly. "That certainly is the long view. I wish all the *citoyens français* had felt the same way. A great deal of bloodshed could have been avoided."

The conversation turned then to matters of less import, and Diana sat silently, absorbing the easy chatter of these English, her countrymen of whom she knew so little. She was French by nationality, but she was English by birth and blood, and though she had lived all her life in Paris, she felt comfortable here, as though she had come home. This could not be, of course. Her home was a cozy set of rooms in Justine du Vrai's *pensionnat*. She sighed. What a tragedy it was that the two countries, both so close to her heart, had been torn by such violent hatred for one another. Perhaps, when "the Corsican Monster" was again defeated as surely he must be—she and Marcus would have the opportunity to learn more about the land of their ancestors.

She returned to her surroundings with a start to realize that the last covers were being removed, and the other ladies were rising to leave Simon in solitary state with the brandy decanter.

"I think not," he said with a laugh, as he stood to join them. "I am not that fond of my own company. I had better go and spell Jared now, and perhaps later the two of us can settle down for a comfortable snifter or two."

Jared, entering the room at that moment, seconded the idea. He waved Simon off along the corridor and shepherded the ladies into the music room, where he promptly invited Diana to favor the group with a piano selection. This time she seated herself without hesitation at the great instrument. She chose a short series of Haydn Variations, at the end of which she found herself the recipient of a gratifying round of applause.

"Ah, so you do play, Miss Bavister," rumbled Mrs. Sample. "It is as I thought. You were simply being miss-ish last evening."

Lissa seemed almost dazed.

"I—I never heard anything like that," she murmured. "I had no idea that music could be so, so . . ." She broke off, unable to complete her thought.

Miss Bledsoe struck while the iron was hot.

"You see, Lady Felicity, what can be accomplished through application and diligence in one's practicing?"

Lissa shot her a scornful glance.

"Fustian! I could run my fingers off in scales and chords and never come close to that perfection!"

Diana laughed. "Nonsense, Lissa. You play with a great deal of feeling. With a little technical polish, you would play beautifully. Here, for example, is a piece you could learn very easily."

Raising her hands again, she slipped into a simple yet elegantly haunting melody. When she had finished, she swung toward Lissa.

"That is called 'Für Elise,' and it was written by Mr. van Beethoven several years ago. Lovely, isn't it? And," she continued at Lissa's enthusiastic nod, "I think you could perform it very creditably within a week or two. With Miss Bledsoe's help, of course," she added, careful not to wound that lady's fragile self-esteem.

Rising from the piano, she made her way to a settee placed by the fire. As she did so, she noticed that Aunt Amabelle was gazing at her in an oddly fixed manner. As their eyes met, the older woman laughed in some confusion.

"Forgive me, my dear, I did not mean to stare. It's just that . . . Well, you see," she began in her usual distracted manner, "I was speaking to Papa just before dinner. He talked of how pleased he is that—that you have come to us, and he mentioned your lovely hair— such an unusual color—and he said he wished he could remember of whom it reminds him. Then, just now as you were playing, and the candle light caught it in such a glow . . . Well, I must say, I was struck by it as well—

and—yes, I am sure I have known someone with just such an unusual shade of hair, rather like old gold.''

She turned to Mrs. Sample, who murmured something unintelligible in corroboration.

''It reminds me rather of wild honey,'' remarked Lissa after some thought.

''It was always my impression,'' murmured Jared, who had come to sit next to Diana on the settee, ''that hornets do not produce honey.''

Diana choked on a gurgle of laughter, and her eyes flew to the earl's in a quelling glance.

The conversation continued amiably until the appearance of the tea table at eleven, after which Aunt Amabelle declared herself ready for her bed, being quite worn down with the events of the day.

''I'm much too excited to sleep a wink,'' exclaimed Lissa, suppressing a yawn as she spoke. ''This has been the most momentous day of my life,'' she added largely, as she followed her aunt and the other ladies from the room.

13

Jared glanced at Lissa in amusement, and turned to Diana.

"From one of such longevity and experience that is, of course, a portentous statement," he said smilingly.

Diana chuckled.

"She is such a darling. One never knows what she will come up with next."

"But what a handful! It comes of her being raised in such a haphazard fashion, I suppose. Aunt Amabelle is a good woman and an excellent householder, but there's no getting away from the fact that she is not a disciplinarian."

Jared paused for a moment, gazing quizzically at Diana. "I have noticed that you and she have established an extraordinary rapport in the short time you have been here. I have never seen her so amenable."

Diana smiled mischievously. "Ah, but you forget, my lord, that is my profession. I have spent many years patting and soothing and providing guidance to volatile young ladies."

She raised her eyes to his, but could find no answering smile. Instead he perused her face gravely, causing her heart to thump in an uncomfortable rhythm.

Gazing into her wide eyes, at the moment soft as moonlight on velvet, Jared again felt an involuntary stirring within him. He found himself battling with his emotions, as he had been since he'd met this slender witch, this impossible combination of silk and steel. He had known her for less than two days, yet when she had been brought home this afternoon, white-faced and shaken, his response had been one of concern bordering on the frantic. His next reaction had been one of rage at whoever had done this to her.

Jared caught himself. Handsomely over the bricks, my lad, he chided. She no doubt had plenty of experience in taking care of herself, and there was no reason to involve himself in her intrigues. Still, he felt compelled to learn more about her, to discover the woman behind those silver eyes.

Jared pulled up two small, comfortable armchairs before the fire, and he motioned Diana to one of them.

"Many years, indeed. You are not long out of the schoolroom yourself, unless I am very much mistaken."

"Well, you are! I am four and twenty, and have been with Madame du Vrai since I was nineteen."

"And before that?" he asked, seating himself opposite her. "Have you always lived in Paris?"

"Yes, as has my brother, Marcus. He is two and twenty."

"But you said your parents were English?"

"That is true. They came to France immediately after their marriage. My parents never discussed their families, so I knew nothing of them."

Diana drew a breath. This seemed as good a time as any to speak of the matter uppermost on her mind.

"My lord, I have done my part in our bargain, and I have promised to carry on your charade. Could you find it in your heart to do me one small kindness?"

Jared stiffened. Here it came, he thought. The supplication for more money, more clothes.

"Such as?" he asked warily.

"My brother. The abduction attempt on me this afternoon proves to me that the person—or persons—who are after me are very serious in their purpose. From the interrogation I underwent in the carriage after the first attempt, I must conclude that they are really after Marcus, though I cannot imagine why. In any event, I believe him to be in grave danger, or that he will be if his pursuers ever find out where he is. I must get word to him to be on his guard."

Jared felt somewhat at a loss. Was that all she wanted? Nothing for herself? He nodded.

"Very well, I will do what I can. Where is your brother now?"

"Oh, thank God," gasped Diana shakily. "I don't know his whereabouts—he is apparently engaged in some sort of romp. I do know his last address, though; it is in Lincoln."

Jared raised his brows.

"If that is where he is residing, why would he wish to meet you so far from his home? We are at almost opposite ends of the country."

Diana could only shake her head.

"Very well," continued Jared, "I shall dispatch a message to—Marcus, is it? Marcus St. Aubin, in Lincoln."

"Oh, no!" Diana exclaimed. "That would not reach him."

Surprisingly, she chuckled.

"That is the cream of the jest, you see. The reason my abductor is having such a difficult time in locating my tiresome little brother is that he is not using his own name."

"What!" The earl's eyebrows rose again.

"Let me explain, my lord." She laughed. "My brother has a very volatile personality. He is somewhat of an adventurer, you might say."

"Not a respectable sort, as is his sister," put in Jared dryly.

"Precisely," responded Diana, with a twinkle. "As the emperor's war of expansion grew more intense, the involuntary conscription of young men increased. Marcus has more than his share of courage, but was reluctant to be drawn into a situation where he would be ordered to kill Englishmen.

"He is extraordinarily athletic, and some years ago developed a skill in acrobatics. He went to Vienna, where he joined a troupe of tumblers, and no sooner had Napoleon abdicated than he traveled with them for a tour of the northern shires in this country. It is currently his ambition to come to London, perhaps, to work with the great Grimaldi. Before he left Paris, he confided in me that since Italian acrobats are considered the most skilled at their art, he planned to change his name—to Marco D'Angelini. I cannot tell you how pleased he was with this ridiculous notion. At any rate, that is the name he goes by for the present."

"An enterprising youth," murmured the earl, the corners of his mouth twitching. "I shall send one or two of my people out to make discreet inquiries as to the where-abouts of Marco D'Angelini, acrobat extraordinaire.''

Diana rose, and stood before him.

"I am grateful, my lord. I do not think he is in any trouble, at least, not so far, but you have taken a great weight off my mind.''

Jared stood also, and grasped her hands.

"As you said, I do owe you a great deal, mademoi-selle. But I thought we were going to dispense with 'my lord?' ''

The two were standing close, and the silence around them, broken only by the tick of the mantel clock and the sleepy mutter of the fire, grew thick. To Diana, the room seemed suddenly very warm, and she found she was having trouble with her breathing. She looked up into Jared's face; the dark eyes were warm now, and a dangerous light flickered in their depths.

Jared allowed his gaze to caress the curve of her cheek. It lingered on the fullness of her lips, then slid to where the carnelian pendant rested, gleaming dully, like a drop of blood, on her bosom. Diana stood still, as though mesmerized. His grasp on her wrists was light, but his touch burned into her flesh as it had before, and she could no more have moved away from him than she could have floated to the moon.

Jared moved slowly to lift the little pendant in his hand. His fingers were warm against Diana's skin, and the re-sponse that quivered within her was as new and startling as it was pleasurable.

The earl spoke huskily.

"This necklet that means so much to you—where did you get it?''

"My mother. It was a gift from my mother,'' she whispered, aware of a delicious languor creeping over her. She shook her head and abruptly stepped back, away from those questing fingers.

Jared, too, seemed to emerge from a sort of daze.

"It—it's charming. Where can I have seen it before, I wonder.''

His gaze was still fixed on the pendant, nestled in the cleft between her breasts, and Diana, in an effort to break the dangerous mood that threatened to engulf them, spoke briskly.

"My goodness, look at the time, my—Jared! I must beg your leave to retire. This has been a tiring day."

Jared stepped away from her abruptly, as though thrusting himself to safety. His breathing was ragged as he responded to her words.

"Yes, it's been a long day for all of us." He spoke slowly, like a man waking from a drugged sleep. "And tomorrow may be busy as well."

He ushered her from the room, and parted from her at the bottom of the stairs with a stiff wish for a pleasant night's rest.

Once she had blown out her bedside candle, Diana lay staring into the darkness, her eyes wide with the memory of what had just occurred. It became necessary for the Schoolmistress to deliver herself of a lengthy monologue on the inadvisability of late-night *tête à têtes* with tall, rakish noblemen whose very touch stirred heretofore sensible females to breathless delight. Just before she drifted off to sleep, her fingers touched the carnelian necklet, and she breathed a sigh that was almost a sob as she turned her face into her pillow.

As it turned out, the earl had misjudged the powerful effect of the Talent name upon the local minion of the law. It was no later than eleven o'clock on the following morning that an official-looking coach drove through the Court's entrance gate and deposited an equally official-looking personage at the great doors.

Mr. John Brandon was ushered immediately into the library, where he found Lord Burnleigh in conference with his bailiff. With what the magistrate considered a flattering degree of condescension, the earl immediately dismissed his man, and sent a footman to request Miss Bavister's immediate presence. His lordship then gestured the magistrate to a comfortable chair, and with his own hands poured him a glass of Madeira.

"A bad business, my lord," pronounced Mr. Brandon, sipping the wine appreciatively. "Things have come to a pretty pass when innocent young girls are attacked in broad daylight whilst on a country walk. And right in front of the church, too!" he added in some indignation.

The magistrate "tsk'd" portentously, and gazed about at the room's elegant furnishings, making mental notes for the interrogation he was sure to undergo from Mrs. Brandon upon his return home.

The earl nodded in grave agreement, and added a comment of his own on what things were coming to, all, no doubt, the result of the appalling laxity of today's moral standards.

The air was becoming thick with genial platitudes by the time Diana made her appearance some ten minutes later. Her demeanor was somewhat uncertain, and to her annoyance, she flushed faintly on meeting Jared's gaze. If the earl felt any discomfiture, he gave no sign, but introduced her to Mr. Brandon and settled her in a chair opposite the one taken by the magistrate.

That gentleman, observing her slight nervousness, attempted to put her at her ease.

"Now, then, miss, I'm that sorry to meet you under such circumstances, but don't fret yourself. Just tell me what happened, and we'll see if we can't catch the miscreant."

At the end of Diana's recital, however, Mr. Brandon professed himself to be at a loss.

"I'll set someone to question those in the vicinity at the time. A big feller in homespuns galloping about the countryside might well have attracted someone's attention. But," he added fatalistically, "he's most likely long gone by now."

Refusing with some regret the earl's offer of a second glass of wine, Mr. Brandon asserted that he must be on his way to Silverwell to interview Lord Stedford and his man.

"Not that I'll likely be any the wiser afterwards," he predicted with a gloomy air.

"I believe," said the earl, "that I will accompany you to Silverwell, if you have no objection."

The thought of spending further time in such exalted company evidently appealed to Mr. Brandon, for he asserted jovially that nothing would give him greater pleasure.

"In fact," continued his lordship, "we can travel in my curricle. In a small vehicle, we can avail ourselves of a shortcut I know of, and save time."

Mr. Brandon's cup ran over.

"Indeed, my lord," he said in an awe-struck whisper,

"to be driven about the country by such a notable whip as yourself would be a great honor."

Diana, observing Jared's expression of combined distaste and determined courtesy, suppressed a chuckle. Their glances met, and an involuntary smile curled Jared's lips.

The two gentlemen departed, and Diana moved to one of the long windows that overlooked the front of the house. In a few moments, the earl and his companion could be seen tooling off down the driveway at a smart pace.

Diana idly turned toward the the cases that held Stonefield's extensive collection of books, passing as she did so the Sheraton desk before which she had stood in confrontation with Jared. Was it only three days since she had arrived in such a sad state? What a turn her life had taken since then. Her lips curved in an involuntary smile and she found herself drifting into an equally involuntary daydream. Suddenly, she became aware of an oddly attractive musky scent that seemed to be filling the room. She turned to look again at the desk. Yes. Lying there, like a ripe pomegranate, was another folded sheet of pink notepaper, with my Lord Burnleigh's name and direction penned in delicate lavender script.

Her daydream disintegrated with the speed of crystal shattered by a clumsy child.

"That will teach you, my girl," snorted the Schoolmistress. "How could you forget, even for an instant, what kind of man he really is?"

Diana could find no answer for this, and after enduring a lengthy self-inflicted scold, she took herself in hand. With a firm stride, she left the library and its unpleasant odor, and, after a short consultation with Miss Bledsoe, set herself to transcribing from memory the Beethoven piano music she had promised to teach Lissa.

She resumed her task after luncheon, and was still at it well into the afternoon, when, to her surprise, she was summoned to Lord Chamford's bedside.

It was with some trepidation that she entered the cavernous bedchamber.

"Hah!"

The authoritative voice was as she remembered it, but perceptibly stronger. The marquess was sitting up in bed, garbed in a brocaded Turkish dressing gown of almost blinding splendor. His eyes sparkled with pleasure as he beckoned Diana into the room.

"Hah!" he boomed once more. "Didn't think to see me again, didjer? Eh?" He chuckled. "Fooled 'em all! I'll cock up my toes when I'm good and ready, but that won't be for a long spell yet. Demmed if I'd stick my spoon in the wall before the wedding. Sit!" He gestured to a large armchair placed near the bed.

As she settled into its softness, Diana glanced around the room. She perceived that Lady Teague was also visiting the convalescent, and was ensconced in a matching armchair, with an expanse of table linen draped over her lap, and a supply of darning materials at hand. She smiled a welcome.

"Are you not amazed?" she beamed. "I have not stopped marveling at Papa's continued improvement." She did not pause in her neat stitching as she spoke. "Indeed, we are having a task of it keeping him from overexerting. Yesterday he said he would get up, and it was only when the doctor threatened him with a relapse before the wedding could take place that he would allow Fishperk to settle him back among the pillows."

"The doctor is an old woman, and you"—he darted a fiery glance at his valet—"are a prosy old fool. And I'll tell you this—if I don't get something for dinner besides that pap you've been spooning into me for the past two weeks, I won't be responsible for the consequences."

Fishperk, nodding sedately, did not appear to feel himself threatened, but permitted himself a lift of an eyebrow.

"Now, Papa," said Aunt Amabelle with a fond smile, "don't you remember? Dr. Meering promised you could have something solid today, and you'll have a chicken wing, boiled in wine, and some toast. Won't that be nice?"

"Nice!" snorted the marquess. "It might be, if you would add to it a beefsteak smothered in onions and a bottle of port. But"—he sighed heavily, rolling his eyes at Diana—"I suppose I shan't get it. You see how they treat me?"

"How ill-used you are, sir, to be sure." Diana nodded in solemn agreement, the twinkle in her eyes belying her words. "I wonder you don't bring action for cruelty to a starving gentleman."

Turning the subject, she gestured to a well-used ivory chess set resting on a nearby table. "Perhaps, if it will help to keep your mind from your tribulations, my lord, we could have a quiet game?"

"You play, do you?" The marquess rubbed his chin dubiously. "It's been my experience that females have no understanding of the subtleties of the game. However, I suppose we might give it a try. Later, though. Right now, I wish to hear of the wedding. How go things in that direction? What plans have you set in motion? Has anyone sent an announcement to the *Morning Post?*"

Startled, Diana exchanged glances with Aunt Amabelle.

"Why, Papa," quavered her ladyship, "don't you remember? We decided that, since once the news is put about we shall be inundated with visitors, we should wait until you are stronger before issuing any announcements."

"And do you remember that I told you that's all a lot of balderdash? As you pointed out, Amy, I am recovering by leaps and bounds. And I don't see why I need to be concerned about visitors, anyway. God knows I don't want to see the parcel of gabblemongers that'll be parading by. So let 'em come—I'll just send down that I'm not to be disturbed. Hah!" he added, as though deriving no little degree of pleasure in this plan of action.

"Now, about the wedding itself. We must decide where it is to be held. I think the village church, rather than the Court chapel. All our people will want to see what's going—eh, what?" This to the distracted Aunt Amabelle, who was feebly trying to interrupt.

"Papa, I'm sure we must consult—that is, Diana may wish to be married near her own home."

Aunt Amabelle turned an agonized gaze on Diana.

Thus applied to, Diana frantically searched her mind for something to say to stay the marquess in his plans.

"Indeed, sir," she improvised, "I have not been in communication with my mother about this. As you may recall, her health is not precisely stout at the moment, and I hesitate to . . ."

The marquess heaved a sigh of exasperation.

"You mean you have not notified your own mother that you plan to marry? I would have thought Jared had asked her for your hand before he committed himself to you. But you young people do things in such a skimble-skamble manner these days."

Diana felt perspiration breaking out on her forehead.

"Well, you see, my lord," she began carefully, but the old gentleman cut her off with a brusque gesture.

"Never mind," he said roughly. "Forgive my outburst, Diana, but I hope I may be forgiven a certain amount of impatience. Now that Jared has finally brought himself to the mark, I don't want anything to go awry. I want you two bound right and tight as soon as possible."

Diana breathed yet another prayer to Providence as she launched into a speech of placation, and sighed with relief the next moment when Providence, in the form of Fishperk, came through once again. With impeccable propriety, the valet reminded Lady Teague that it was time to dress for dinner.

In the corridor Aunt Amabelle turned to Diana, her soft, brown eyes filled with tears of anger.

"I swear to you, Diana, I could just strangle that boy!"

"If you mean Lord Burnleigh," returned Diana, rigid with indignation, "I will gladly help you do it at your earliest convenience. How like him to concoct this abominable scheme, and then just leave someone else to carry it through! Where is he, anyway?" she asked as an afterthought. "It's been hours since he left for Silverwell with Mr. Brandon."

"Oh, he returned some time ago. Immediately he came into the house, he was intercepted by Simon, and the last I saw of them, they were tramping out toward the Home Wood with their guns in their hands."

"You mean," said Diana with awful calm, "that he returned from an interview, in the company of a magistrate, with two witnesses to a terrifying attack on me, and he did not have the courtesy to inform me if any progress was made in the matter?"

Aunt Amabelle, evidently feeling that nothing she might say in answer would serve to placate the seething young woman before her, wisely made no reply.

"Well!" was Diana's comment.

"Yes, I think so, too," said Aunt Amabelle.

The two ladies spent several more minutes reducing the earl's character to well-gnawed scraps before turning away, marvelously refreshed, each to her own chambers.

14

Three floors below, Jared and Simon entered the house via a side door in the kitchen wing. Both wore top boots, leather breeches, and nankeen shooting jackets, all liberally daubed with mud, and each carried a brace of wood pigeons, which they deposited into the arms of a flustered kitchen maid.

They made their way to the upper floors, comparing the difficulty of the various shots they had made over the course of the afternoon, and congratulating each other on their marksmanship.

"I still say," Jared remarked, "you could have had that hare, if you'd aimed a little to the left. Next time we'll take the hedgerows. I daresay we should be able to pull some grouse out of them, although it's a little early."

"I shouldn't wonder," agreed Simon. "But tell me, speaking of hedge-birds, how did your visit to Silverwell go this morning? Anything of interest to report?"

"No, neither my lord Stedford nor his man saw anything that could possibly be construed as helpful."

"What a chawbacon the fellow is!"

Jared uttered a crack of laughter.

"But, no—how can you speak of a veritable pink of the *ton?* Lord, you should have seen him! He wore a yellow coat with silver buttons the size of coach wheels, a puce corded waistcoat, and striped gaiters. The compleat country gentleman!"

"I hear he's making some rather startling renovations at Silverwell."

Jared snorted.

"You should see what he's done there. The Green Saloon has been gutted. No outdated Queen Anne or Louis Quatorze for my lord. Oh, no! The room now contains the worst clutter of imitation relics of the Ancient World

that you're liable to find this side of an Arabian *souk*.
Etruscan vases on the mantel, settees with crocodile feet,
pier tables covered with Sphinxes, and a wine cooler in
the shape of a Grecian urn.''

"I heard," added Simon, "that he's putting up a Chinese pagoda on the south lawn. Pink of the *ton* or no,
the fellow is making himself a laughing stock. What a
crackbrain!"

"You know, though," mused Jared, "he may be a
court card, but he doesn't strike me as being particularly
stupid. That's why it seems strange that, arriving on the
scene of Diana's attack as soon as he did, neither he nor
his man was able to catch the fellow, or even to see what
he looked like."

"That fellow Churte is pretty stout," replied Simon.
"He probably couldn't catch Aunt Amabelle at a dead
run. And as for our precious Ninian, I'd wager he was
more concerned with keeping his ringlets in place than
with tackling nasty big ruffians in homespuns."

Jared was still following his own line of puzzled
thought.

"Does it strike you that there's something dashed
smoky about that pair?"

In answer to Simon's look of startled inquiry, Jared's
mouth curved in an embarrassed smile.

"To be sure, I may be imagining things, but he was
not at all pleased to find the magistrate on his doorstep
this morning. Oh, he was cordial enough, but he certainly did not give the appearance of one welcoming the
law with open arms. When Brandon asked to speak to
Churte, Stedford at first professed not to know where he
could find the fellow—Churte having decided to go off
on holiday, or some such. However, when Brandon said
he would be glad to return another time, my lord managed to dredge him up quickly enough. And as for
Churte! When he finally did make an appearance, he was
nervous as a cat on hot bricks. You'd have thought he
was in the dock, with the verdict just gone against him."

"Now, wait a minute," interrupted Simon. "Are you
saying the two of them are into something not quite le-
gal? Had you ever met Stedford before he came into the
title?"

"As a matter of fact, yes. One did not, of course, run

into him in the highest of social circles—or even the middle level, for that matter. One was, however, liable to encounter him at the race course, or in the shadier gaming establishments, where the legs lie in wait for greenlings with money—those new to Town and ripe for fleecing. I can't help believing there's something more than a little havey-cavey about him and his man. Stedford is never seen but what Churte is nigh him, as though they were sewn together.''

"I'll agree with you there," said Simon. "What I think is, Stedford's precious henchman has been on the wrong end of a good many official investigations in his time. I mean, just look at the fellow. It's Lombard Street to a China orange he's spent his share of time in Number Nine."

Jared laughed again.

"Newgate? That seems a little harsh, but you may be right. Perhaps Stedford was in the habit of employing him from time to time for a bit of dirty work—card fuzzing, perhaps, or fixing a wager. Our Ninian strikes me as being the type that is not too nice in his dealings."

The two continued on their way through the twisting corridors, where servants were lighting candles against the deepening twilight.

"It's a shame what he's doing to Silverwell, though," reflected Jared. "Stedford gave me a tour of the place after he and Churte talked to Brandon. Do you remember the days we spent there as children, tumbling about the place with Tad and Philip and little Susan? Lord, it's hard to believe they're gone. When I came to the gallery, I couldn't help but remember the foot races we all ran there."

"I suppose he's transformed that into a temple to Isis."

"No, he's left it pretty much as it was, lined with family portraits. There's one missing, though."

"Really, who? Don't tell me he feels one of his ancestors ain't up to snuff in his fashionable new palace."

"I couldn't tell you," replied Jared. "I only realized it was gone because it left an obvious empty space. When I asked Stedford about it, he said one of the servants damaged the frame recently while cleaning it, and it's out for repairs. He had no idea who it was, either. I hope the day never comes when Stonefield is taken over by an outsider who doesn't even know the names of his own ancestors.''

Simon shot him a sidelong glance.

"We know how to prevent that, don't we?"

"I told you," Jared replied coldly, "I am taking steps to—"

"Yes, I know—steps to acquire a bride. But how is it you are still here? Shouldn't you be out beating the bushes, so to speak? Or do you plan to woo your chosen damsel by post?"

Jared stiffened.

"I cannot very well leave until Grandfather is completely out of danger."

"Really? I thought perhaps your unwillingness to depart the family manse had more to do with a certain golden-haired guest."

Jared eyed his brother coldly.

"I hardly think this is the time for dalliance."

Simon lifted his brows.

"I hardly think her the type for dalliance. And I thought you had come to believe that she really is a schoolmistress, and was a victim of some sort of abduction."

Jared shrugged.

"Mmm. Let's just say I'm willing to give her the benefit of the doubt. On the other hand, she is undoubtedly no different from any other female."

"Oh? And how's that?"

"She's very clever at putting her beauty to work for her own ends. I'm sure teaching school is only a temporary measure until she can snare a rich husband or a protector."

Simon gaped at him.

"Good God, Jared! Are you still spouting that bacon-brained nonsense? From what I have seen, she has shown herself to be a lady, in every sense of the word."

Jared made no response beyond a frigid stare. Simon eyed his brother, and at last said slowly, "I think I begin to see. As long as you can convince yourself that she's some sort of slut, you stand in no danger of entertaining any warmer feelings for her. Is that it?"

Jared still made no answer, but his face tightened, and he raised his hand in an unconsciously defensive gesture.

Simon laughed softly.

"I shan't plague you anymore, brother. But I'll warrant you're having the devil's own time maintaining that little fiction. Take care you don't find yourself in the basket over this—one way or another."

With an ironic salute, he turned away and went in the direction of his chambers. Jared said nothing, but stared after him for a long minute before moving off toward his own rooms.

At dinner, Jared pursued the subject of the Viscount Stedford and his doings. He held Aunt Amabelle's complete attention when he spoke of the changes wrought by the new owner of Silverwell.

"A Chinese pagoda!" she exclaimed. "You don't mean it."

" 'Pon my honor, Aunt. And one does not dare sit down in any of his wretched armchairs without expecting some sort of exotic animal to begin gnawing at one's ankles."

"That settles it," interposed Lissa. "We must pay a visit as soon as possible. It sounds marvelous! I only wish that we could have something like it here at the Court. The latest mode of fashion we have is the Italian garden, and that was put in before I was even born."

"Oh, indeed," remarked Simon. "We are sadly behind the times. I'll tell you what, Lissa, you must hasten to Grandfather and demand that we replace the Kent furniture in the library with crocodile feet and Chinese tassels. And be sure you tell me when you are going to do it so that I may come and watch, for it will be a rare show, to be sure."

"Well, of course, I shan't do anything of the kind," said Lissa with great dignity. "But it seems too shabby to live with the same old humdrum set of things forever and ever when right next door the whole place is being done over in what I just know will be all the crack!"

"Not the whole place, Lissa," put in Jared. "So far the blight has only extended to several of the main state rooms. His library sports no tassels as yet, and the gallery is much as it used to be when Simon and I played there as children."

Aunt Amabelle breathed a nostalgic sigh.

"My, we did have some splendid times there. When I was a girl, I used to play frequently with Phyllida; that would be Lord and Lady Stedford's third daughter. We both had the same dancing master, and took our lessons at Silverwell. Lady Stedford would play for us. Such a lovely woman she was, with—" She stopped short, and swung to face Diana. "My goodness—that's it!" she cried in pleased recollection. "She had the most beautiful golden hair, and it was just like yours, Diana. Oh, I am glad to have that cleared up. You know how it is when you are reminded of something, and you just can't place it."

She beamed at the entire group.

"Don't you agree, Lydia? You remember her, don't you?"

Mrs. Sample, after judicious consideration, nodded her head.

"And you, Jared? Do you remember her? There is a beautiful portrait of her in the gallery at Silverwell. Jared?"

But the earl, his hand suspended over a dish of comfits, appeared lost in thought. At last he raised his head.

"Yes, Aunt—yes, I think I do. In the painting, her hair is piled in great swirls on top of her head, and she's wearing"—he paused for a moment, his expression intent, before continuing—"some sort of filmy fichu around her shoulders. Is that right, Aunt?"

Simon shot his brother a curious glance, and Aunt Amabelle laughed delightedly.

"Yes! Exactly right! Lord Stedford insisted she be painted *sans poudre* because he wanted that beautiful crown of hair to show to advantage."

She gazed at Diana once more.

"How remarkable to see that same unique shade on another lovely young girl."

At this, Mrs. Sample felt compelled to add her mite.

"Not at all," she rumbled, her superfluity of chins quivering earnestly. "There was Coretta Tanner, don't you know, the parson's wife in Little Bobbingdon. My old home," she explained to those who might be ignorant of this fact. "She had a birthmark on her cheek in the shape of a swan! Yes, it's true."

She swung around, her massive bosom heaving, ready

to defend her statement to any that might accuse her of delivering a falsehood.

"People used to come to church on Sunday not to hear the parson's sermon, but to glimpse that peculiar mark. Coretta was quite proud of it, and she was sure there must not be another like it anywhere, but what do you think?"

She paused for dramatic effect.

"One day a peddler appeared in the village, and he bore an identical mark, and on the very selfsame spot. Yes! It quite took the wind out of Coretta's sails, I can tell you, for what good is a birthmark of distinction when one may see it reproduced in someone of such low order?"

"Yes, but Lydia," gasped Aunt Amabelle, "it's not the same thing at all. That is, Amanda's hair hasn't been reproduced in a person of . . . I meant, that is to say . . ."

Aunt Amabelle's bracelets, those barometers of her mood, vibrated in agitation.

Jared, unable to contain his amusement any longer, laughed aloud and glanced at Diana, whose eyes sparkled responsively.

Later that night, Diana again found herself frowning sleeplessly at the ceiling over her bed, and again her thoughts were of the arrogant earl. It disturbed her to discover that it was becoming more and more difficult to think of him in those terms. She tried to reconcile her feelings for the man whose eyes laughed into hers with her anger at the wretch who had contemptuously dismissed her as a strumpet, and who still seemed to think of her as a cold, grasping harpy.

There was no doubt that she truly detested him, but why did she find such enjoyment in his company? She was forced to admit to herself that she even relished the confrontations between them, that she had never felt so alive as when matching wits with him.

This was dangerous. A physical attraction was one thing. She could deal with that. But to feel so comfortable when she was with him, to be drawn to the man who lay behind the cynical facade of the Corinthian—that was madness.

Her eyes grew heavy, but as she turned once more into her pillow, she resolved to keep foremost in her mind the fact that the earl's charm could be turned on at will, and could be turned off just as quickly. Should she flout his plans, she would no doubt be faced again with the arrogant, cold-eyed peer who had insulted her in the library on that first day.

"And see that you don't forget it," murmured the Schoolmistress sleepily, before she, too lapsed into silence.

15

"My Lord Chamford!" exclaimed Diana in mock severity. "I can scarcely credit it of a peer of the realm, but I believe you are laying a trap for me!"

She raised her eyes from the chessboard to observe the delight written on the marquess's face. He narrowed his eyes and laid a bony finger alongside his nose.

"Hah! Thought to outflank me, didjer? You must know, m'dear, that you are dealing with a hardened campaigner, and I shall show no mercy. But where did you learn the game? You have an excellent grasp of the finer points—for a female, that is."

Diana twinkled back at him, thinking that the improvement he had made over the last few days was nothing short of miraculous. The day being fine, he had been settled into a bolstered armchair and carried downstairs by four stalwart footmen into the rose garden. Here he basked in the sun, gaining strength and health seemingly by the minute.

Diana had been pleased when he remembered her offer to play him at chess. She enjoyed the old gentleman's company, and grasped at the opportunity to lift her mind from her most pressing problems.

It had been three days since the marquess had begun his remarkable recovery, three days since Diana had suffered the kidnapping attempt in the churchyard. During that time she had seen little of Lord Burnleigh. Was he purposely keeping out of her way, she wondered, in order to forestall any pointed questions from her on his progress in what she was coming to think of privately as the Great Marriage Mart Sweeps?

Perhaps he was even now combing the castles and manors of England for his perfect peeress. How unfor-

tunate, she thought bitterly, that he had not thought to
tuck a glass slipper in his greatcoat pocket.

Not that any of it mattered to her. By the time wedding
bells rang out over fashionable St. George's in Hanover
Square for the earl and his new countess, Mademoiselle
St. Aubin would have returned to her snug little nest in
Madame Justine Du Vrai's select establishment for young
ladies. Somehow this idea, which had up until a few days
ago seemed the most important goal in her life, aside
from whatever predicament Marcus had got himself into,
had unaccountably lost a great deal of its appeal. She did
not understand why this should be so, because until her
abduction and the encounter with Lord Burnleigh she had
been content with her life. She had a rewarding position
as a teacher of young girls; she had friends and, yes, even
a few suitors.

She pictured a certain young solicitor, who of late had
spent many evenings in Justy's parlor, reading to her from
slender volumes of wistful verse. He was handsome, and
she had taken pleasure in his gentle charm. She had even
considered accepting the blushful proposal that she was
sure would come before many more evenings in front of
the fire. But now . . .

Now she could hardly remember what the young man
looked like, and the prospect of spending endless evenings listening to his bland voice spouting poetry seemed
rather dreary.

Her mind was unexpectedly filled with the earl's harsh-
featured face. So clearly was his image etched in her
brain that she could almost feel her fingertips tracing his
strong jawline. And that recent evening when she had
stood so close to him in the silent music room. Her heart
quickened at the remembered touch of his hand. And the
firelight in his eyes.

She realized with a start that Lord Chamford was
harumphing in an alarming manner.

"Oh, I do beg your pardon, my lord. I was woolgath-
ering. Is it my turn?"

Distractedly, she moved her queen to forestall an attack by the marquess's rook. This earned a quick frown
from her opponent.

"Good God, girl, where are your wits? You've left

yourself vulnerable, and now''—he reached for a knight that had escaped Diana's attention—"checkmate!''

Even as Diana expressed chagrin at her defeat, and admiration for Lord Chamford's strategy, she found herself drifting back to her daydream. The fire shine had not been the only light deep in the black velvet depths of those eyes, and she shivered at the memory of the response drawn from her by that primal flicker. She was brought up short as the Schoolmistress made herself heard.

"Are you going to let a handsome face and a well-filled morning coat blind you to the fact that this man is your enemy? He thinks you a grasping harpy, and you can well imagine what ideas lurk behind that compelling gleam.''

Diana sighed and turned to the marquess, who was again speaking to her.

"I wish to talk about the wedding.''

Diana's heart dropped to the tips of her jean half boots.

"I think,'' continued the marquess, "that it would be best to hold it here at Stonefield. Not in our chapel, of course, but in the village church. Have you any objection to that? Will your mother be up to making the journey here soon? And have you and Jared settled on a date? We don't want to be precipitate, I know these things take time, but perhaps in late summer. Shortly after harvest would be . . .''

The marquess stopped and directed a suspicious frown at her.

"You have written to your mother, have you not?''

When he received no answer beyond an apprehensive glance, he sat bolt upright in his chair and fixed Diana with an awful stare.

"Why have you not attended to this? Jared, too, should have written to her to ask properly for your hand, and I suppose he has not done that, either?''

There was only silence from the hapless young woman seated before him, casting wildly in her mind for a response.

"What the devil is the matter with you two?'' roared his lordship, now in full spate. "In my day, when an engagement took place, a wedding was expected to follow within a reasonable time. Yet nothing has been set in motion. Nothing is happening. How will there ever be a wedding if the pair of you sit around on your thumbs and do nothing? This is—"

"Grandfather, you will bellow yourself into a relapse."

Diana whirled at the sound of the cheerful voice, and nearly cried out with relief at the sight of Simon making his way toward them from the house.

Perceiving the appeal in her eyes, Simon hurried to grasp the old man's hand.

"I have come to say good-bye, Grandfather."

These words effectively quelled Lord Chamford's diatribe, and he lifted his eyes to Simon's.

"So soon, my boy? It seems you just arrived!"

Diana rose and moved away.

"I shall leave you alone."

"I'll only be a moment," said Simon. "Will you wait at the end of the garden? I should like to speak with you before I leave."

She hesitated, then nodded and walked away. A few minutes later Simon joined her.

"Since you will be leaving Stonefield soon"—there was a smile deep in the eyes that were so like his brother's—"we shall not likely meet again."

Diana started, but her gaze was calm.

"So Lord Burnleigh did tell you about me."

Simon made no response, but continued to watch her. She drew a deep breath.

"I live in France. Did he also tell you that?"

"Yes, but he said that you told him you are English by birth. You live in Paris, and were abducted by persons you do not know, for reasons you do not understand."

Diana's lips twisted into a faint smile.

"That about sums it up. Put like that, my story sounds like a piece of Gothic fiction."

To her surprise, Simon returned the smile.

"Jared's very words." He chuckled.

"And you, Simon," she asked gravely, "do you believe I'm a cunning adventuress?"

Simon's eyes were calm as he looked into hers.

"No," he replied simply.

Tears stung Diana's eyes. Why it meant so much to be accepted by this open-faced young man she could not tell, but she felt a rush of happiness. Impulsively she bussed his cheek, and dashed the tears from her eyes.

"If I say something else nice, will you kiss me again?"

Simon's grin was contagious, and suddenly she felt very much at ease.

"You take liberties, my good man," she said with mock severity, but then sighed. "I wish your brother were not so difficult to convince."

"Jared is a slightly different kettle of fish. He is—a little harder than most."

Diana made a noise that sounded suspiciously like a snort.

"All right, he's downright cynical and bitter. But he has more reason than most to be that way. No, no, it is not for me to discus Jared's quirks," he said in answer to Diana's lifted eyebrows. "I just wish . . ."

Diana cocked her head.

"You wish what, Captain Talent?"

But Simon had apparently decided not to disclose what was on his mind. He laughed instead, and bestowed a hearty kiss on her forehead.

"I wish you well in your efforts to confound your enemies, whoever and wherever they may be."

Diana blinked.

"My, that sounds quite pontifical."

"Yes. Well, we Army men tend to take the long view. All right, Aunt," he called to her ladyship, who was beckoning from the terrace window, "I'm coming."

He started up the broad stairs leading to the terrace, but then turned back.

"One more thing. Jared is not your enemy. Do not fear to trust him. I have a feeling he will take great care to see that no further harm comes to you."

He touched her cheek gently, then turned and ran up the stairs and into the house.

Diana followed more slowly, turning his words over in her mind. When she reached the hall, she found the other members of the family gathered to bid Simon farewell. The good-byes were brief and as cheerful as possible as the party accompanied Simon through the great doors. Aunt Amabelle almost managed to conceal the quaver in her voice, and Lissa turned away only momentarily to brush off a few betraying tears. Jared contented himself with a quick, fierce handclasp.

"Take care, halfling!" he called brusquely as Simon mounted the carriage that would take him to Portsmouth.

The captain waved a last farewell to his loved ones, and touched his hat to Diana. Then, with a clatter of harness and hooves, he was gone.

The afternoon seemed grayer as the little group turned to reenter the house. Aunt Amabelle surreptitiously put her handkerchief to her face, and Diana moved to her.

"My lady," she said diffidently, "we left Lord Chamford unattended in the rose garden. Fishperk is nearby, of course, but I thought perhaps . . ."

"Thank you, my dear. You are quite right. I shall go to him at once."

She walked swiftly to Jared and spoke a few words to him. He nodded, and the two left the hall together.

Less than an hour later Diana, descending the stairs after repairing the effects of sun and breeze on her hair, turned toward the sound of voices emanating from the south terrace. To her surprise, she found Lissa in animated conversation with the Viscount Stedford. Glancing about, Diana saw that no other member of the family was on the scene, and she experienced a twinge of concern. Lissa surely knew better than to entertain a gentleman alone in such an informal manner. Even if she did not, the gentleman, several years her senior, and knowledgeable in the ways of the *haut monde,* must be aware of the solecism they were committing.

She observed Mallow making his stately way toward her from the other end of the hall, and she quietly requested that he summon Lady Teague. The perspicacious butler, after one glance at the scene on the terrace, allowed a glimmer of comprehension to flicker in his eyes. With an almost imperceptible bow, he reversed course and sailed out of sight down the corridor from which he had just come.

Diana, a bright smile on her lips, hurried onto the terrace. The viscount had seated himself on a stone bench, close to a blushing Lissa, and was delivering himself of a fulsome compliment. Diana watched as he brought Lissa's fingertips to his lips in a caressing gesture.

Diana coughed peremptorily, and the pair swung toward her. Lord Stedford sprang to his feet, smoothing his hair with one hand. Lissa burst into a nervous giggle as she greeted the older girl.

"Oh, Diana! Look who has come to pay us a visit. Isn't it famous?"

Diana smiled faintly.

"Indeed. But when did you arrive, my lord? I did not hear the bell."

Ninian flushed a little, and Lissa rushed to answer for him.

"Oh, it was so droll, Diana. I had come out to the terrace to take the air—after Simon left, you know. I was looking out over the park, and who should I see riding through the copse—yes, that one over there—but Lord Stedford and his man. It put me in quite a fright at first, because I could not see who it was. I watched them for ever so long, picking their way back and forth along the edge of the wood, just behind the trees."

Ninian chimed in to take up the thread.

"It was the merest chance. Churte and I rode out— taking the air ourselves, don't you know? Churte noticed an old, overgrown path, and we decided to follow it to see where it might lead us." He smiled disarmingly. "You know, I am still exploring my land, and have not yet covered the half of it, I daresay. At any rate, we wound through fields and woods, and just when we were thinking ourselves hopelessly lost, I looked up and there was Stonefield Court! We had found an old shortcut between our two estates. You can imagine how pleased I was to see Lady Lissa strolling in the sunshine, looking like a Botticelli nymph."

Lissa attempted an expression of coquetry, but succeeded only in looking deliciously confused. Diana stared in consternation at the blatant adoration on the girl's face.

"I waved immediately," continued Ninian, "and when the fair nymph called an invitation to join her, I accepted with alacrity."

For a fleeting instant Diana wondered why, once he had spied the Court, the viscount had stayed so long hidden in the copse before making himself known to Lissa. The main portion of her attention, however, was centered on his attire.

Today, my lord was a vision in lavender. His coat, a subdued shade of that color, was adorned with large silver buttons, carelessly done up to allow the merest glimpse of a wine silk waistcoat, from which dangled several fobs. Pantaloons of a delicate lilac tapered to mirror-polished Hessians, trimmed with long silver tassels. A lace-edged handkerchief of finest lawn trailed from the fingertips of one hand, while the other caressed his long-stemmed quizzing glass. An amethyst pin, nestling in the snowy folds of his neckcloth, completed the ensemble.

Good heavens, thought Diana, Jared was right. The Viscount Stedford was precisely the stuff of a schoolgirl's dream. And it was all too obvious that Lissa, though just emerging from that state, was painfully susceptible to his spurious air of elegance.

At this moment Aunt Amabelle, followed by Mrs. Sample, swept onto the terrace, very much in the manner of an angry partridge hen, feathers astir. She smiled courteously, but no one, observing the disapproving fire in her eye, could mistake her mood for one of affability. For once there was no hesitation in her manner, no clatter of beads and pins as she extended a hand to the viscount.

"Lord Stedford! What a pleasant surprise."

In a smooth flow of motion, she led Ninian to another stone bench, where she seated herself and drew him down beside her, thus effectively removing him from Lissa's vicinity.

"You have no doubt come," she continued, "to inquire about Papa's health. How very thoughtful of you!"

Diana watched in appreciation, while Lissa's underlip showed itself in a thwarted pout.

Ninian, his suave demeanor temporarily deserting him, managed only a flustered, "Why—why, yes, indeed. Um, how is Lord Chamford? Well on the road to recovery, I trust?"

Aunt Amabelle murmured a phrase of frigid politeness. In an effort to smooth over an awkward situation, Diana turned the conversation to the projects underway at Silverwell. The topic proved fruitful, as Lord Stedford launched into an enthusiastic monologue, describing in detail the changes he had already brought about and his plans for future renovations.

Where do you contemplate your next effort, my lord?" queried Aunt Amabelle.

"Ah, that's an excellent question, dear lady. My designer—yes, I did hire one to assist me; not that my own taste needs arbitrating, but he has been helpful in locating the items I desired—believes that we should move in an orderly plan, completing one floor at a time, but I"— here he paused, lifting a white hand to his brow as though courting his muse—"I, who am in tune with the spirit of the house, feel that we should let our plans flow in a natural progression. Thus—"

"Spirit of the house!" interrupted Lissa, her voice a high squeak of excitement. "You are never saying Silverwell is haunted! But how famous!"

A hint of irritation crept into his lordship's voice.

"No, no, my dear. I meant the soul of the place, the essence, as it were. At any rate," he finished in rather a rush, "I believe I shall start next on the upper floor."

Aunt Amabelle spoke, a distinct edge in her tone. It was apparent that if asked, she would no longer have categorized the graceful tulip before her as unexceptionable.

"And how, my lord, did you acquire such an intimate knowledge of the, er, essence of Silverwell? To my knowledge you never set foot there until old Lord Stedford's death, and I don't believe you were acquainted with the family."

For an instant, Diana caught in the viscount's wide sapphire gaze a look of pure hostility, but it was replaced so quickly by one of limpid warmth that she thought she must have imagined it.

"You are right, of course, Lady Teague," he said smoothly. "My time in residence is short, but I am the end product of the generations who have lived there before me. My ancestors speak to me in a way others cannot possibly fathom."

The viscount lifted his eyes, as though lost in dreamy communion with the ghosts of his progenitors.

Lissa sighed.

"Oh, Lord Stedford, that is simply poetic!"

Aunt Amabelle looked as though she were about to be

ill, and Mrs. Sample rumbled inarticulately. With an effort, Diana controlled her own distaste, and it was with a sense of relief that she observed Jared's tall figure stroll through the French doors that gave onto the terrace.

"I wondered where you had all got to," he remarked mildly. "Are we having an alfresco gathering?"

Lissa again explained Lord Stedford's unexpected appearance at the verge of the Court's south lawn, and the earl nodded in bored but courteous attention. He then turned to his aunt and drew her aside.

"I just left Grandfather. He has returned to his bedchamber, and asked that I send Simmons up to him. He refused to tell me what he wants with our bailiff, but he was most insistent. Simmons is on his way up now."

He glanced toward the viscount, who had again drawn near to Lissa and was deep in conversation with her.

"What the devil," he asked in irritation, "is that man milliner doing here? Is creeping about our back lawn his idea of paying an afternoon call?"

Diana, observing this conversation, was struck by the difference between the casually elegant appearance presented by the earl and the foppish dandyism affected by the viscount. Her mind continued to embroider on this theme, with more and more emphasis settling on Jared's muscular form, his almost palpable virility, the way that unruly lock of hair persisted on falling down over his forehead, the strength of his . . .

She came to herself with a start and turned toward Lissa. That damsel had by now drawn very close to the viscount and was giggling in appreciation of his witticisms.

"But, Lady Lissa," his lordship was saying, his eyes twinkling roguishly, "you did not tell me that you are an expert in London ways. Do you visit the city often?"

"You mean, take a bolt to the village?" She laughed, her efforts at playing the sophisticate only betraying her innocence. "No, we are bound here in stuffy old Kent. I never get to go anyplace."

"Why, Lissa," interposed Aunt Amabelle, scurrying to insert her plump self between the two, "you just returned from Tunbridge Wells!"

"And don't forget," intoned Mrs. Sample, "we were in London only three months ago. Don't you remember how cold it was? We shivered the whole time we were there.''

"Oh, yes!" Lissa gurgled in delight, and turned to Ninian. "We went to town to shop. We must have visited every modiste and linen draper there. You know," she added for the viscount's edification, "I am to make my come-out this year."

"No! But how exciting!" The viscount clapped his hands in pretty enthusiasm. "You will be the Toast of the *Ton*, Lady Lissa. It behooves me to extract a promise from you right now to save a dance for me at Almack's. Your arrival will cause *such* a stir. There is no doubt your card will be filled immediately and I shan't be able to come near you for the crush of beaux!"

Lissa giggled and blushed adorably.

The viscount's face assumed a fatuous expression of satisfaction until, looking up, he caught Lord Burnleigh gazing at him in a manner that could hardly be called promising. Rising hastily, he announced his intention of taking himself off before he wore out his welcome. With genial good-byes to the assemblage, he moved in the direction of the tree-fringed verge, where Churte could be seen minding the tethered horses. Ninian encountered Diana standing a little apart from the rest, and drew her aside.

"I had hoped I might have an opportunity for some private conversation with you while I was here," he murmured, his voice suggestive.

"That is quite all right, my lord," she replied coolly. "I could see that you were otherwise occupied."

The viscount, apparently taking this as a display of jealousy, laughed delightedly.

"Now I must make *sure* that we have some time together. Will you come riding with me tomorrow?"

With some dismay, Diana cast about in her mind for words to frame a refusal that would not reveal her extreme reluctance to endure two or three uninterrupted hours in the company of this tiresome coxcomb.

"I'm afraid, Stedford," Jared's quiet voice broke in, "that Miss Bavister will be otherwise occupied tomorrow. She has promised to go riding with me. I have so far not had the opportunity to show her our lands, and we will be going out early so that we may cover at least the main portion of the estate.''

Ninian's blue eyes narrowed to slits, reminding Diana of a cat deprived of its saucer of cream, but he recovered himself quickly, and the dazzling smile appeared once more.

"I quite understand." He laughed softly, glancing from Jared to Diana. "A case of striking while the iron resides within your own walls, if you don't mind a mixed metaphor."

With a careless wave, he set off across the sweep of lawn that led to the copse.

The earl turned to Diana and smiled.

"I trust, Miss St. Aubin, you are not disappointed at the prospect of a day without Lord Stedford's company."

"Since you ask," replied Diana with asperity, "I must say that I very much resent your interference, my lord."

Observing the sardonic expression in Jared's eyes, she confessed ruefully, "At least, I would if I were not so grateful."

She burst into laughter, in which the earl joined with frank enjoyment.

"Really," she gasped, "he is the most absurd fribble."

The two walked in companionable conversation through the wide doors into the house.

"I wish my tiresome little sister shared your opinion of Lord Stedford," the earl said with a sigh.

"She is very young," replied Diana, "but she has a good head on her shoulders. I'll wager that a little time spent in his company will create a strong reversal of her views."

"I trust you are correct. By the by, what time can you be ready tomorrow for our tour of inspection?"

She glanced at him in surprise.

"Our tour? You mean you really intend to take me riding?" She laughed uncertainly.

"But of course. Did you think my invitation was merely a ploy to rescue you from the attentions of the viscount?"

Since this was precisely what she had assumed, she felt herself at a loss for a response. Instead, she looked at the floor, her heart beating uncomfortably.

Jared continued in a caressing tone that did nothing to steady her pulse.

"I would very much like to show you the estate, now that it is dressing itself in all its spring glory. Will you come?"

Diana lifted her eyes to Jared's, and suppressed the trembling that had begun deep within her.

She smiled, and responded demurely, "That would be very nice, my lord."

16

When Diana descended to the breakfast parlor the next morning, she found Jared already there, dining in solitary state with his copy of *The Gentleman's Magazine* propped before him. She paused for an instant in the doorway, and, having ascertained that neither footmen nor parlor maids hovered in the vicinity, walked directly to him. Diffidently, she placed a packet beside his plate before turning to the sideboard.

"But what is this?" he queried.

"It is the money you gave me. It is all there—I have spent none of it."

"I don't understand."

"There is nothing to understand. I am returning your money."

Jared sat, stunned and at a loss for words. Never, in his wide experience of the female sex, had one of them returned money. Ever. He raised his quizzing glass to inspect the packet, then transferred his gaze to Diana.

"Returning it?" he asked stupidly.

"Yes. I can no longer keep it, of course. Everything changed when your grandfather began his recovery. Before that, I had been more or less coerced into pretending to be your fiancée."

Jared had the grace to blush.

"But," she continued, "when it became apparent that he is not going to—that is, when I realized that his continued improvement relies on my presence here, it was my own decision to remain. So, you see, our bargain has been canceled, and I am returning your money."

It was several seconds before Jared fully absorbed her declaration. He rose hastily and crossed to the sideboard, where Diana had begun to fill her plate.

"But—but . . ." he sputtered, "this is ridiculous! Of

course you will not return it. That is"—he paused, observing the set expression on her face—"you need money. You cannot argue with that. And the carriage and the abigail, and all."

Diana nodded stiffly.

"When we locate Marcus, he will make all the necessary provisions for me."

"Yes, but in the meantime you cannot live like a pauper."

For some reason this conversation was making Jared feel guilty in the extreme, and he paced beside Diana in agitation.

"Look here, why don't you keep the money—for the time being, that is," he added hastily, "and we'll call it a loan. When you leave Stonefield . . ." He experienced an odd pang as he said those words. "When you leave Stonefield," he repeated firmly, "you may return it all at that time. Would that be satisfactory?"

Why, he wondered, was he pleading with her to accept money that she had wrung from him in such an unprincipled manner only a few days ago? And why was he finding it so difficult to maintain with her the cool detachment that he had perfected in his relationships with women?

Taking a seat at the table, Diana sighed and turned to him with a confiding smile. "To tell the truth, I was hoping you'd say that. I rather hate being penniless, but of course I had to return the money. It's a matter of honor, after all."

"I quite understand."

He did not understand at all. In fact, his world had been jarred considerably. He had insulted this woman in every possible way, yet she thrust money at him and spoke of honor! He had never before known a female whose vocabulary included the word.

Beckoning a footman from the corridor, he ordered the little packet returned to Miss Bavister's chambers. He poured Diana a cup of coffee, and seated himself beside her.

"Speaking of Marcus," he began after a moment's hesitation, "I'm afraid I have bad news. No, no," he added hastily, as Diana whitened. "It's just that Roberts, the man I had sent north to find him, returned early this morning, and reports that he can find no trace of Marcus in Scarborough. Roberts discovered that the acrobatic troupe is now in Newcastle, and he traveled there, only to be told that Marcus quit the troupe some three weeks ago, saying that he had important business here in Kent.''

"Then he must still be in the area," cried Diana, her forehead wrinkled in concern. "Why hasn't he contacted me? Dear God, do you suppose. . . ?"

"What I suppose is that he has found an adventure more to his liking than tumbling about in a circus tent for an audience of rustics. He said he would return to Aylesford, and I'm sure when he's had his fill of whatever lark he's up to, he will do just that. In the meantime, I'll continue my inquiries.''

As though to change the direction of her thoughts, he raised his quizzing glass to inspect her attire.

"I thought you agreed to my invitation to go riding this morning.''

Diana realized that the earl was trying to alleviate her concern, and, indeed, his words, spoken so matter-of-factly, served to ease the worry she felt. She looked down at her morning gown of pomona-green muslin, wishing her borrowed wardrobe had contained a fashionable carriage dress.

"I'm sorry I'm not quite properly attired," she apologized, "but it is the closest thing I have at present." She laughed. "Perhaps I shall take some of that vast quantity of pound notes and purchase something dashing.''

The earl was garbed in buckskin britches, top boots, and a superbly fitted jacket of kerseymere. He looked, Diana thought, absolutely magnificent. Her hand twitched with the impulse to smooth back that unruly lock of hair. As she had so many times in the last few days, she flushed at her own wayward thoughts.

Misconstruing the delicate color that flooded her cheeks, Jared hastily added, "How stupid of me. Of course you do not have a riding habit—the talent of my aunt's needlewoman extends only so far. But I don't think that poses a problem; since we shall be staying within the estate boundary, we will meet no one but our own people.''

Jared smiled winningly, but Diana fastened to one phrase.

"Riding habit?" she asked with misgiving. "I thought when you said 'riding' you meant in a vehicle."

"No, no. I wish to show you Stonefield. The orchards are beginning to blossom, and the fields are choked with wild flowers. You must be on horseback to appreciate it all."

"But," Diana said firmly, "I do not ride."

"Do not ride?" echoed Jared in a blank voice. "Do not ride."

"But that's nonsense. That is—everyone rides."

"That is not quite true, my lord, for I . . . do . . . not . . . ride. I have never," she added in case there might still remain in his lordship's mind the slightest misunderstanding of her words, "been on a horse in my adult life. When I was small, my father took me for pony rides in the park, but other than that—"

"But that's impossible. Everyone rides," he repeated.

"My lord," Diana continued patiently, "I live in Paris, and I exist on a modest income. I, like thousands of others of my station, do not own a horse. When I wish to travel about, I walk. Or hire a chair, or a cab. Or go by post, or *diligence*. Or—"

Jared held up a hand.

"Thank you, ma'm'selle, I apprehend your meaning." He smiled broadly. "Well, then, now it is my turn to instruct the schoolmistress. Today we shall begin your first lesson in the equestrian arts."

Diana bestowed upon him a look bordering on hostility.

"I don't think so, my lord. I have no desire to hoist myself on the back of some unfortunate beast merely to transport myself from Point A to Point B."

"And yet you have no objection to harnessing one or two unfortunate beasts to a vehicle to accomplish the same end," retorted Jared, amused.

Diana stared at him for a moment, nonplussed.

"That's different," she replied haughtily.

Jared smiled with a heart-stopping grin that smoothed his harsh features and warmed those eyes of black granite. He moved to Diana and, grasping both wrists lightly, pulled her to her feet. Sensing her hesitation, he peered into her face, and made a discovery.

"Why, I believe you're frightened! If you have a fear of horses . . ."

"I am not afraid," she responded with great precision. "That is, not exactly."

Jared raised his brows questioningly.

"I—I know there is nothing to be afraid of. I know they mean me no harm. It's just that when I am standing next to one, I am not sure it quite knows what it's doing with all those feet," she finished in a dignified tone.

"To be sure," Jared responded gravely, the smile still lurking in his eyes. "Being stepped on by a horse is not a pleasant thing. And it can happen, if the animal becomes frightened or confused. But that is a rare occurrence, and I promise I will provide you with the most unflappable steed in our stable."

Thus, in less than an hour, Diana found herself seated atop a gentle mare of rather advanced years.

"Her name is Sukey," Jared informed her, "and she was Lissa's first mare. She has the temperament of a sofa cushion, and approximately the same gait."

Diana found this to be true, and as she progressed in stately fashion, she relaxed and began to enjoy the beauty of the spring day and the company of the man beside her.

Jared rode his hacking mount, a mettlesome, well-ribbed-up gray named Thor, which the earl controlled with an easy grace.

They moved slowly through the extensive park land surrounding the Court. Peacocks made their way in iridescent majesty over lush, exquisitely trimmed lawns, and in the distance, a small herd of deer flowed gracefully past a stand of birches.

"It's like a landscape from a fairy tale," Diana exclaimed in delight.

"Much of it is my mother's doing," replied Jared, smiling. "The park, of course, has been here for hundreds of years, but it was she who had the notion of adding 'ornamental animals.' We had guinea fowl for a while, but they made such an incessant racket that they were soon consigned to the cookpot."

"And where is the famous Italian Garden?"

"That is laid near the west wing—on the other side of

the Court. We can save it, and the orangerie, for another day, when we are on foot."

Their meanderings eventually led them from the immediate environs of the Court, where park land gave way to rolling fields and neat hedgerows.

"The Home Farm," Jared indicated with a sweep of his arm. "Our chief crop is oats, but we have a sizable acreage in hops. As a Frenchwoman, you no doubt have a nose for fine wine, but we English are proud of our beer. Our estate is famous for the excellence of our hops, which are the prime ingredient of some of the finest brews in the land."

"And over in the distance, are those blossoming orchards yours?"

"Indeed. Those are cherry trees, but we also have extensive apple and plum orchards. Perhaps later in the day we will stop at one of the cottages. The farm wives hereabouts pride themselves on their plum wine."

"Another treat for my fine French nose." Diana chuckled. "Goodness, what with home-brewed in kegs and plum wine in bottles, I should imagine the harvest festivals in this area are something to experience."

"Ah," replied Jared solemnly, "you have hit on the secret of our productivity. Our local damsels become extraordinarily accommodating during these events, doubling our birthrate, and thus ensuring a constant labor supply."

At this, Diana gasped a little and blushed. Jared stopped and reined in.

"Allow me to apologize. I—we have been conversing in such an informal manner, that I fear I forgot . . ."

Diana shook her head vehemently.

"No apology is necessary, my lord. I did not mean to be missish. I enjoy good conversation, and I would not wish you to guard your tongue simply because I am a female."

Jared stared at her. He really had forgotten for a moment that he was speaking to a member of that sex with whom one had constantly to be on guard lest they be scandalized and offended. In fact, he could not recall ever conversing so amiably and enjoyably with a woman. He had not once complimented her on her eyes, or sung any of the other flowery praises necessary to conversation with the London belles of his acquaintance, nor had he found it necessary to rack his brain for such insipid topics as might appeal to the shallow minds of those ladies.

How strange, he reflected. His talk had been almost entirely of the lands of Stonefield, of the experimental farming methods he persuaded Grandfather to try, and of his success in converting worthless marshlands to profitable acreage. He might have expected her to be bored, but she surprised him. Not only did she listen with interest, but responded with intelligent and thoughtful comments of her own.

Diana, too, had been provided with much food for thought. How Jared loved this land! He was completely transformed from the hard-eyed Corinthian she had despised at their first meeting. Her guard, which had been raised so firmly against that arrogant rake, was giving way under the charm and warmth of the man who spoke so enthusiastically of his home and family.

At last they came into a small, fragrant meadow, fringed with ancient oaks. Beside a chattering brook, Jared stopped and dismounted. He assisted Diana from her saddle, and together they spread the picnic lunch packed in the roomy hamper that had been strapped to Jared's saddle.

He heaped her plate with cold chicken, ham, fruit, and yeasty rolls lavishly spread with fresh country butter. He poured the wine with a flourish.

"An excellent claret," he pointed out, "safely tucked away in our cellars before the outbreak of hostilities between our two countries. And," he said, through a comfortable mouthful of ham, "speaking of our two countries, you have not yet explained how you, a charming English rose, happened to blossom in Paris."

"But I told you, sir. My parents sailed to France almost immediately after they were married. Something—something very bad—happened to my father. So awful that Marc and I were never told about it. As we grew older, we began to think he perhaps had done something unlawful and was forced to flee the country."

"Had you any reason to believe that might be so?"

Diana's mouth twisted.

"No. Neither my mother nor father was forthcoming,

except to say that Father had been treated very badly by his family over the incident. They would not speak of it further. I do not even know from which part of England they came.''

"Are you not curious?''

"Indeed I am—and Marcus even more so. One of his reasons for coming to England was to try to discover our roots. He took all our family papers with him before he left, much against my wishes. Knowing him, he will have lost them all by now. And before I return to Paris, I would like to make my own inquiries. As soon as I hear from Marc, that is. But,'' she continued helplessly, "I don't even know where to begin.''

"Well, the name 'St. Aubin' is not all that common in this country. Perhaps if you—''

"Oh, no!'' interrupted Diana. " 'St. Aubin' was not my father's name.''

She stopped at Jared's look of confusion.

"Perhaps I'd better start at the beginning. You see, my father died when my brother and I were still very small. I was only five, and Marc, three. Father had been ill for a long time. He was a scholar, and wrote several well-received treatises on classical subjects. Mother told us that he was only truly alive when, through his books, he wandered the streets of ancient Greece and Rome. He even gave his children popular names of the era.

"His best friend in Paris was Jacques St. Aubin, a local merchant. It happened that Monsieur St. Aubin's wife passed away several months after Father died. An attachment grew between two lonely people, and within a year, he and my mother married. Because of the war between England and France, Papa Jacques, as we called him, feared for our safety. He formally adopted Marc and me so that we could be granted French citizenship, thus protecting us from any difficulties that we might otherwise have experienced.''

"But you no longer live with them, and Marcus has gone to make his own way.''

Diana sighed. "It was so very sad. Mama's second marriage did not last even as long as her first. Papa Jacques lost his life as an innocent bystander in one of the last street riots of the Terror. His business had suffered during the upheaval, and Mama was left nearly

penniless. She made the acquaintance of Justine du Vrai
soon after, and she took the position of English Mistress
at Justy's *pensionnat*. We lived there until Mama's death
six years ago. By that time I had demonstrated my teaching ability by helping out with some of the younger pu-
pils, and madame gave me Mama's old position almost
immediately.''

"And you scarcely out of the schoolroom yourself!''
exclaimed Jared, his sympathy touched despite himself.

"And greatly relieved to have work with which to support myself,'' Diana retorted tartly. "Justy is an excellent employer and a good friend. She pays me an
exorbitant salary. But then''—Diana lowered her lashes—
"I am very good at what I do.''

"So I have observed." Jared chuckled. "You have already worked wonders with my tiresome little sister. But
what was your father's name—your real name?''

"It's Crowne. My father's name was William
Crowne.''

Diana, gathering together the remains of their lunch,
did not observe Jared's sudden stillness or the arrested
expression in his eyes.

He moved to help her tuck the plates and silver back
into the hamper.

"By the by, I see you do not wear your necklet today.
I thought you wore it always.''

Diana flushed slightly, remembering the last time a
discussion of her little pendant had risen between them.
With a studied air of nonchalance, she ran her fingers
beneath the neckline of her gown and produced the little
pendant.

"Unfortunately,'' she said, "the color of carnelian
cannot be said to agree with many others. I usually keep
it tucked away.''

She prepared to return it to its hiding place, but he
forestalled her by taking the pendant in his fingers, as he
had those few nights ago. He bent his gaze to the little
jewel and examined it.

At his nearness, Diana felt her heart begin to beat in
a panicky thud.

"Good heavens,'' scolded the Schoolmistress. "Can
you not come within two feet of the man without going

into a semi-swoon like the heroine of one of those wretched novels you persist in reading?''

But steel herself as she would, Diana once more became aware of the earl's solid maleness. The scent of him filled her senses, and she lifted her hand as though to fend off her own wayward feelings.

"You say it was a gift from your mother?" Jared continued. "How did she come by it?"

With an effort, Diana marshaled her thoughts.

"She—she received it from her mother. No, no, that's not right. She had it from Father."

Now Jared, too, seemed to have lost interest in the history of the pendant. He lifted his eyes to Diana's, gazing into their smoky depths. He brushed a golden, breeze-swept curl from her temple, and she could not quite control an involuntary trembling at his touch. Feeling suddenly shy, she lowered her gaze, allowing long, silky lashes to shadow her cheek.

Cupping her chin, Jared gently raised her face, as though he were turning a flower to the sun. His dark gaze held an intensity that both frightened and delighted her. There was something else lurking in those black depths, something flamelike and dangerous. Diana shivered. She felt mesmerized by the light that glowed there, and by the touch of his hand.

Jared bent his head, and Diana felt his breath stir the tendrils of hair that lay against her temples. His lips brushed her cheek with butterfly softness, and from the deepest part of her an unexpected response surged forth to engulf her.

With the last of her willpower, she turned her head away.

"No!" she whispered, "Please, no."

"But we are betrothed." He laughed softly, his breath warm against her face.

With a dizzy sigh, the Schoolmistress vanished without a trace. When Jared's mouth continued its trail of wondrous torment, Diana moved her own to intercept it. His lips met hers in a kiss that was tender, yet firm and demanding. Diana was possessed by a longing and passion that she had not known was possible. Without volition, her arms crept around his neck. Her lips opened under his, warm and welcoming.

Jared tightened his arms around her, his breath uneven, and Diana melted against him, reveling in the feel of him against the length of her body. His hands moved sensuously along the curve of her back. He pressed warm, tantalizing kisses along the curve of her chin, marking a path down to the base of her throat, where he covered the pulse that beat there.

It was not until his fingers gently began working at the ribbons fastening her bodice that she was brought to a sudden awareness. She thrust herself away from him, gasping. She was astonished and frightened at the intensity of her response. Never had such emotions taken possession of her! She pressed her fingers to her lips and stepped back, staring at Jared.

His returning gaze was filled with a confusion she had never seen there, and as he turned abruptly to gather up the remainder of the picnic lunch, he seemed almost angry. However, when he spoke a few minutes later, his voice was controlled, his tone, amused.

"What a charming interlude, to be sure," he drawled, "but must I attend to these domestic details by myself?"

For an instant Diana searched his face, but the warmth had fled from his eyes. It was as though she had only imagined the compelling fire that had blazed there moments before. Still shaking, she hurried to assist him with the last remnants of the lunch. She could not look at him as she hurriedly replaced the silverware and empty containers in the hamper.

The kiss had meant nothing to him! It was merely a way to pass a spring afternoon. Well, she had been warned that he was a rake. She had seen the evidence herself in those utterly tasteless billets-doux, which had made four more appearances on the silver post salver. Not that she was counting! He had made it more than plain at the outset that he thought her a demi rep. He had apparently realized he was wrong, but it was evident that he considered a lowly schoolmistress, unused to the attractions of a polished libertine, to be ripe for a moment's dalliance. How could she have so willingly proven him right?

Diana did her best to converse casually with Jared as they remounted and started back to the Court, but she could hardly speak for the tears that thickened in her throat. There was none of the comfortable informality they had enjoyed earlier, and Diana was relieved when they reached the stables. On being lifted from her placid mount, she murmured a disjointed thanks to Jared for a most enjoyable afternoon and, of course, such a lovely picnic. Then she turned and fled into the house.

Her path led directly to the music room, where she could loose her inner turmoil at the piano. As she entered the room, she brushed unseeing past a youthful footman, and murmured a distracted apology. She had reached the piano when a voice behind her exclaimed, "Danny!"

Diana whirled. Only one person had ever called her that. She stood rigid for a moment, then gasped and raced into the waiting arms of the young footman. With a glad cry, she called out one word.

"Marcus!"

17

Upon emerging from her brother's suffocating bear hug, Diana promptly began pelting him with questions.

"Marc, where have you been? How on earth did you get here—and what are you doing in footman's livery?"

"What d'you mean, what am I doing here?" the young man before her replied indignantly. "I've been looking for you! You might have told a fellow you were living in the lap of luxury. Good God, if you knew what I've been through!"

"How did you know where to find me? Did you get the message I left for you at the Swan?"

"Of course I did. Why else would I be here? What I don't understand is what you're doing here. Why didn't you come to the Swan as I asked? You've put me in the deuce of a pelter, y'know."

"Oh, Marcus!" exclaimed Diana, "I've had the most wretched time. I was on my way to the Swan, but I was abducted, and then—"

"Abducted! My God, are you all right?"

"Yes, but you cannot imagine how dreadful it was, and then the earl—"

"Yes," interposed Marcus, "I must hear all about it, but not now. I'm one of the hired help in this overgrown puzzle box, and I can't be seen standing around chatting with the nobs."

"I must tell Lord Burnleigh of your arrival. He has already—"

Marcus gripped her arm.

"No! Don't tell him anything—or anyone else, for that matter—until I have had a chance to talk to you, to explain . . ."

"Explain what?"

"Ssh," he hissed in a stage whisper. "Later. We'll

have to meet after everyone's bedded down for the night.''

"I suppose that is the best plan," replied Diana, herself whispering, although they were alone in the room. "Meet me right here, a little after midnight."

Marcus nodded, and tiptoed out of the room, darting a conspiratorial wink toward his sister. Diana fairly danced around the room in relief and joy; then, seating herself at the piano, she gave vent to her feelings in an exuberant tarantella.

Jared, passing the room a few moments later, marveled at the change in her mood from the one of cool distance in which she had left him at the stables. Suffering from an uncharacteristic feeling of awkwardness, he refrained from entering the chamber, but stood in the corridor for some time, enveloped in a brilliant shower of notes.

His mind was on the events of the morning. What in God's name was the matter with him? he reflected dazedly. Why was he unable to stay at arm's length from her? When he was alone, he had no difficulty in vowing to treat her with cold propriety and nothing more. But once he was with her, all his intentions were swept away in the sparkling enjoyment of her company.

All he had meant to do when he lifted the little pendant from her collar was to examine it—and then he had been overcome by her nearness. It had seemed as though all the laughing silver brilliance of the stream beside them had gathered into the huge eyes lifted to his.

When he had bent his head to hers, he had only a moment's dalliance in mind, but her lips had melted against his with such an aching sweetness and innocence that he had been moved as he had never been before by the touch of a woman.

Yes, she was an innocent, he admitted to himself. His instinct had told him that after five minutes in her company, if only he could have brought himself to listen. She had shown herself to be a woman—a person—of wit and strength and sincerity. She had offered him the warmth of her kiss freely and without artifice, and he, the most experienced Corinthian in London, had behaved like a love-struck schoolboy. And, he wondered desperately, what was to keep him from doing it again? It seemed that every time he was near her, all he wanted to do was take her in his arms and hold her, and never let go.

With an effort, he turned his thoughts to the other results of his outing with the enchanting Miss Crowne/St. Aubin. He was at once pleased, astonished, and truth to tell, a little apprehensive at the discovery he had made. Just what he was going to do with the information he had uncovered was the next puzzle to be solved.

Whistling a soft accompaniment to the gay Mediterranean dance, he continued thoughtfully on his way down the corridor.

For Diana the next few hours took several centuries to pass, but somehow she managed to conduct herself in a reasonably natural manner. She felt that the questions churning in her mind must be buzzing audibly, and such was her preoccupation, that in chatting innocuously with Jared over dinner, their contretemps earlier in the day was, if not entirely forgotten, successfully pushed to a far corner of her mind for later examination.

At last good nights were said, and the family members drifted away to their respective bedchambers. Diana did not disrobe, but curled up on her bed with another of Lady Teague's religious tracts, and tried without success to immerse herself in its dismal contents. In another hour the house became quiet; the hands on the little clock near her bed crept to half-past twelve.

Grasping her candle, she stole noiselessly to the door and let herself into the corridor. Satisfied that no one stirred in the vast pile, she made her way through the dark, silent passages.

In the music room she found her brother awaiting her. He had discarded the formal portions of his uniform as well as the powdered wig that the marquess considered *de rigueur* for liveried servants. He was dressed only in shirt and breeches, and his pale blond hair gleamed in the light of the candle he had placed on a sofa table.

He was a tall young man, straight and slender and well-proportioned. He bore himself with an athletic grace that gave him a maturity beyond his twenty-two years. Oddly, his face was all schoolboy, with strong, square features dominated by a pair of mischievous hazel eyes. He was pacing the floor, and had just made a turn at the far end of the room, near the fireplace. At Diana's entrance he hurried to her, and once more Diana found herself enveloped in a rib-cracking hug.

"Oh, Marc!" she exclaimed, emerging disheveled and breathless. "You dreadful boy! I have been in an agony of worry over you."

"*You've* been worried! When you didn't show up at the Swan, I was imagining all manner of horrors. You say you were abducted? Good God, Danny, tell me what happened."

"First," replied his sister with some asperity, "I want to know why you left the troupe at Scarborough, and where you have been ever since. And, for Heaven's sake, why are you posing as a footman?"

She drew him to a nearby confidante, where they huddled together in the little pool of light created by their candles.

Marcus drew a deep breath.

"It all started shortly after I arrived in England. Now, don't say, 'I told you so,' but I had the deuce of a time with that packet of family papers I took with me. It's bulky, and every time I traveled from one place to another, I had to jam it any old which way into my luggage."

"Yes," interposed Diana impatiently, "but what has that to do with anything?"

"If you will let me speak," replied Marcus in an injured tone of voice, "I'm trying to tell you. As you may imagine, the journey was hard on the packet. It is leather, you know, with a silk lining, and it was not long before the silk began to fray. When we finally arrived in Scarborough and settled into an inn there, I tossed it into a cupboard, and one whole side split open."

Marcus's eyes lit, and he grasped his sister's hand.

"Danny, there was a letter inside. From Mama!"

"From Mama?" echoed Diana in bewilderment. "To whom?"

"Why, to us, of course."

"But why would she write to us? Up until the time of her death, we had never been separated from her, and we were both with her when she—at the end, that is."

Marcus twisted uncomfortably.

"I must first ask you—I don't know yet how you came

to be in this house, Danny, but—how well are you acquainted with Lord Burnleigh? More to the point, do you trust him?''

Diana was startled by the question, and it was several moments before she answered.

"My association with him so far has not been what one could call cordial. In fact, when you hear what I have been through because of him . . . But, yes,'' she concluded almost in surprise, "yes, I do trust him.''

"And his neighbor, the Viscount Stedford?''

"What a charming spot for a midnight rendezvous, Miss St. Aubin.''

Even though the speaker was concealed in the darkness near the doorway, Diana had no difficulty in recognizing his voice. She rose precipitously, thrusting past Marcus, who had also risen to place himself in front of her.

Jared, shocked at the flame of jealousy that shot through him at the sight of Diana seated with her head close to that of another man—one of his own footmen, if he were not mistaking the matter—strode into the room. He promptly barked his shin on a carelessly placed footstool.

In the few moments it took to recover his equilibrium, reason returned to the earl, and he continued in a milder tone, "Might one inquire as to what the devil is going on?''

Incensed at the interpretation Jared had placed on the scene, Diana replied stiffly, "My lord, may I present to you my brother, Marcus St. Aubin.''

Lord Burnleigh, that noted ornament of society, not to put too fine a point on it, gabbled.

"But—but . . .'' He drew a deep breath and forced himself to calm, while Marcus, always nice in the finer points of etiquette, moved forward with his hand outstretched.

"Happy to make your acquaintance, sir. I can understand where you might think this a dashed awkward situation, but I assure you . . .''

Jared straightened abruptly and gazed intently into the face of the young man standing before him. His mouth curved into a smile as he shook the hand extended to him.

"Ah, yes, I see—Marco the Magnificent.'' He waved

the two back to their confidante, and sank into a nearby armchair.

Diana smiled stiffly.

"Marc was just explaining to me what he is doing here in livery." She turned a questioning expression on her brother.

Marcus hesitated, and his first words were addressed to the earl.

"I had thought to be alone with my sister while I shared certain information. No, no," he added hastily as Jared rose with a murmured apology. "Please stay. I believe at this point we could use some outside counsel—and, perhaps, an ally."

He paused for a moment.

"May I ask you, sir—how you stand with your neighbor, the Viscount Stedford? Are you good friends?"

For an instant Jared stared at him, unwinking.

"Hardly what one might call good friends," he replied drily.

Marcus gazed searchingly at the earl. As though satisfied, he gave a slight nod.

"But Marc," asked Diana in a bewildered tone, "what has the viscount to do with your turning up here in footman's garb? And you still have not told me what you are doing in Kent, when you should be in Scarborough—or Newcastle, by now. Why in the world did you want me to meet you in Aylesford? What in the world could there be in that place to interest you?"

Looking very much harassed, Marcus continued hastily.

"Nothing. Aylesford has nothing to do with anything, but I had to go there to find the direction of—"

"Silverwell!"

Two voices uttered the word, and both Marcus and Diana swung in astonishment toward Jared, who had chimed in as Marcus finished his sentence.

Marcus simply stood, gaping at the earl, while Diana's glare flew from one man to the other.

"Lord Stedford! And now Silverwell! Marc, if you do not explain this instant . . ."

In answer, the young man strode to the fireplace and plucked a piece of paper from the mantelpiece. Returning to Diana, he placed it in her hands. His eyes were somber.

"This is Mama's letter, Danny. It will answer most of your questions and, I think, present you with new ones."

Curiously, Diana turned the paper in her hands. She noted the neat, faded handwriting and felt a tug at her heart. She raised her eyes once more to those of her brother, then took the letter and began to read.

My Dear Ones,

I have thought long and hard over the writing of this letter. I am not sure I can bring myself to put it in your hands, but I feel that certain facts regarding your background should be recorded.

I know you have been curious on the subject, which is entirely natural. Perhaps, in the telling, you will come to understand why such details were kept from you. It is a painful subject for me, and I will be as brief as possible.

Your father, William Crowne, was the son of Charles Crowne, the Viscount Stedford. He was raised on the family estate, Silverwell, some fifteen miles north of the town of Aylesford, and directly beyond the village of Stonebury, where I was raised. I was the apothecary's daughter.

With a gasp, Diana faced Jared.

"Silverwell! And you knew? You knew all this time and you didn't tell me?"

Jared moved to her side, his hand raised in placation.

"No, I did not know. Over the last day or so I had come to guess the truth, but I was not sure. I had planned to investigate, and I would have told you as soon as the facts came out."

Diana shook her head dazedly, and returned to the letter.

We fell in love and planned to marry, but when Lord Stedford learned of our betrothal, he made his implacable opposition known in a series of cruel and hurtful outbursts. He informed William that if he were to marry "that importunate nobody" (one of his kinder terms for me), William would be dis-

inherited, banished from Silverwell, and cut off from his family forever.

My own family was equally opposed to the liaison. My father was a staunch believer in the separation of the classes, and he feared the viscount's wrath.

William acquired a special marriage license, and one day, after a particularly acrimonious argument with his father, he left Silverwell forever. He paused only to bid farewell to his mother. This gentle lady, though opposed to our marriage, had been kind and sympathetic to me. In order to foil any effort by his father to pursue us, William told Lady Stedford that he and I were setting off for America. She was devastated at this final rift, and gave to William as a parting token a small pendant which had been given to her as a child by her parents. Your father gave it to me as a wedding gift—it was all he had—and I gave it to you, Diana, on your twelfth birthday.

I abandoned my own family to go with your father to France, where he had friends with whom we could stay. We were married just before dawn in a tiny church in Bythorne, one of the villages through which we traveled en route to the sea.

Such was our pain and outrage at the treatment William and I had received at the hands of our families that we determined never to have any contact with them again. Nor did we wish our children to have any knowledge of them.

This, then, is why we concealed your background from you. Now, perhaps, it is time for the bitterness to end. At least now you know what happened. Use the facts as you see fit, and remember that your father and I loved you very much.

                                        Mama

Numbly, Diana let the pages fall into her lap. She dipped her fingers inside her collar and brought forth the pendant. She lifted it toward Jared, her eyes questioning.

"Yes." He smiled. "Her name was Amanda Lacey. 'A.L.' She wore it when she was painted as a young bride. I must have seen her portrait a hundred times in

the days when I played so often at Silverwell. That was
why I recognized the pendant, though I couldn't recall
why. Diana, you inherited not only Amanda's beautiful
golden hair, but her necklet as well.''

Diana, her emotions overwhelmed by all that had been
revealed, felt her eyes brim with tears. She turned to
Marcus.

''I—it's all so incredible!''

Her brother nodded and, reaching into his shirt, produced three folded sheets of thin parchment.

''Their marriage certificate, and Mother's and Father's
birth certificates. They were in the lining with Mama's
letter. Do you remember, Danny? When we were going
through her papers, we wondered why her marriage lines
were not among the other important documents she had
saved—our birth certificates and such. I don't know why
she hid them. Perhaps, at the last, she changed her mind
about telling us the story she had kept to herself for so
long.''

''All those years,'' Diana whispered, ''Papa, the son
of a nobleman. Why, he grew up not five miles from
here. And Mama, as well. I cannot take it all in!''

She rose and stared at Marcus and Jared, her brow
furrowed in concentration.

''But if all this is true, if Silverwell was my father's
home . . .'' Her eyes widened. ''My father was the old
viscount's—Charles's—third son. The one Lady Teague
told me of.''

She paced the floor, her words almost tumbling over
each other.

''And if that is so, with the other sons and grandsons
gone . . . Oh, Marcus,'' she said incredulously, ''you
are the Viscount Stedford!''

''Yes, I rather think I am,'' the young man before her
replied in a diffident voice.

18

For a moment there was a silence among the three gathered in the shadowy room. Diana felt that her world had been turned on end, and she stood, staring at her brother as though he were a changeling.

"I cannot believe this."

Jared went to her swiftly, without thinking, and settled his arm about her shoulders. Diana was aware of the sense of comfort and security his touch brought, but her mind was still occupied in rapid thought. Finally she straightened, and spoke again to Marcus.

"But what are you doing here? And in this absurd disguise?"

"When I arrived in Stonebury, I began scouting out the territory, and that was when I discovered that there was already a claimant to the title. After Charles's death, an effort was made to discover if William Crowne had really died, but no trace could be found of him. So all concerned were satisfied that Ninian Crowne was Charles's closest remaining relative. I, of course, am living proof to the contrary, but I could not just go marching up to the front door at Silverwell and inform the present incumbent that he must vacate the place because I, the true viscount, have come to collect my inheritance."

"Why not?" asked Diana in bewilderment.

Marcus stared at her blankly for a moment.

"Well," he said after a moment, "because that's not how things are done. I mean, I figured I should first go to a solicitor, or something, and show somebody the papers proving my claim. Besides," he continued in a more assured tone, "by that time I was beginning to worry about you. When you didn't show up as scheduled at the Swan, all sorts of unpleasant explanations began thrashing around in my mind, particularly when I received a secondhand message that you were ensconced in the home of Stedford's nearest neighbor.

"So I figured the best thing to do at that point was to come here incognito, so to speak."

Diana sighed.

"I might have known. You couldn't just manage things in a straightforward manner; you had to make a bad play out of it all. Go on," she added, as Marcus cast her a reproachful look.

"Anyway," he continued with great dignity, "I came to Stonefield to find you, and because I felt it would be a good observation post—to spy out the lay of the land at Silverwell, you know. I discovered there was a need for a footman. They're a bit shorthanded, owing to three of the lads having recently taken the king's shilling—hoping they might get sent to the Continent in shiny red tunics, as I understand it. I was hired on the spot. Not a bad job, either," he added reflectively, "though not the sort of thing I'd like to make a career of."

"Oh, you ridiculous boy," gasped Diana between bursts of laughter. "I might have known you would pitch yourself into some absurd situation."

"That's all very well," Marcus said in some indignation, "but it is nothing to the absurd situation I discovered here. Before I'd had a chance to ask about you, I was called upon to serve at luncheon, where the featured guest was a Miss Diana Bavister from Wales. When I saw precisely who this Miss Bavister was, I nearly dropped a soup tureen in Lady Teague's lap."

"You were there!" exclaimed Diana, round-eyed. "Oh, Marcus, I never dreamed—that is, it's a dreadful thing, but one so rarely really looks at the servants. But why didn't you say something?"

"Oh, certainly—a precious cake I would have made of myself! 'Um, pardon me, Miss Bavister, or Miss St. Aubin, or whatever you're calling yourself today. If you would care to step over here and glance under this large and extremely uncomfortable wig, you would find a delightful surprise.' If that wouldn't have flung the cat among the pigeons! This afternoon was the first moment I've had a chance to find you alone."

He fixed his sister with a minatory stare and demanded, "Just what smoky game are you up to, Diana?"

Diana uttered an affronted gasp.

"Do go on, Miss St. Aubin," encouraged Jared, his eyes alight. "I'm sure your brother will find your adventures, er, stimulating, to say the least."

"And you were always the sober, serious one," commented Marcus. His eyes narrowed in sudden suspicion. "You ain't running a rig on his lordship here, are you? If what I've heard since I've been here is correct, that won't fadge, Danny."

Jared burst into a peal of laughter as Diana stiffened with outrage.

"If you call being abducted, and forced to participate in a perfectly appalling deception, running a rig. . . ."

She recounted the whole of her ordeal since she had been taken from the Green Men so many days ago. In her tale, the earl figured as the most dastardly of villains—an abductor of innocent females, and keeper of same in durance vile. When she had finished, Marcus shook his head.

"Well, I daresay it's all a hum, at least that last part. You're living in a ruddy castle, with servants running at your beck, and dressed in a finer gown than any I ever saw you wear. I'd hardly call that durance vile. As for this bethrothal charade—well, all I can say is, I never want to hear a word out of you, missy, about *my* crack-brained schemes."

At this Jared, discerning flashes of lightning rising in Diana's storm-cloud eyes, made an effort to suppress the laughter that still shook him.

"I suggest that you two call a truce," he said. "We have not yet discussed the crux of your problem."

Marcus and Diana looked at him with identical expressions of puzzlement.

"What is to be the next step, now that we know the identity of Diana's kidnapper?"

It took only a few seconds for puzzlement to change to comprehension.

"Ninian!" gasped Diana.

Jared nodded. "I think we can agree that the estimable Churte hired the sharper who carried out the actual deed."

"Yes!" cried Diana. "It must have been. Even though I never saw the face of the second man, the one who waited in the carriage outside the Green Man, my impression was of a man—squat and broad—who could have been Churte. Oh!" she added in indignation, "and there he was, the very next day, tipping his hat to me from Ninian's curricle. No wonder he looked so peculiar."

"And," continued the earl thoughtfully, "I think we can also assume that it was Churte who carried out the attack, no doubt engineered by his lordship, at the vicarage. When Lissa and Patience arrived in such a timely fashion, Ninian was forced to reverse his role from abductor to rescuer. The cloak used to muffle your screams looked as though it was tailored to fit someone of Churte's rather unique build."

"Yes! It must have been, for now that I think of it, I only heard one set of footsteps running away when Ninian came to my supposed rescue."

Diana paused, struck by another circumstance.

"Why, I saw Churte earlier at the Court. But that was before Lissa decided on her visit to the Smalleys."

"It's possible," replied Jared after some thought, "that he had already bribed one of our servants to keep him posted on your activities."

Marcus had been thinking, and now he chimed in excitedly.

"When this Ninian person was made Lord Stedford, he must have taken steps to ensure that his grip on the title was secure. His agents must have been more persistent than those hired by the estate attorneys, and he discovered that William had gone to France, not America, and that he did not die before producing an heir. Naturally, Ninian made it his first order of business to ensure that the heir would never surface. As long as Diana and I remained in France, living our lowly little lives, unaware of our exalted station in life, we were no threat to him, but once I set out for England, he must have been concerned. When you trundled over here after me, he found it necessary to take steps."

Diana choked.

"Do you mean that Ninian intended to. . . ?"

"To kill Marcus?" Jared interposed. "No, I think not. I'm not at all sure murder is beyond him—I assuredly believe it is not beyond the capabilities of the vile Churte—but Ninian need not carry matters that far. All he must do is destroy the documents that prove your identity. He would have assumed that as head of the family, so to speak, Marcus would have the papers in his possession.''

"But," Diana concluded, "he couldn't find any trace of Marcus, since he was so cleverly posing by now as Signor D'Angelini.''

Marcus nodded in ready admiration of his own genius.

"So Churte was forced to nabble you in the hope that you would lead him to me and the documents. Well, the scoundrel will have a precious time ferreting out the papers now. I keep them tucked away, safe and secure under my mattress, three floors straight up.''

"Will you summon the authorities, my lord," asked Diana, "so that we may put them in possession of the facts?''

To her surprise, the earl did not answer immediately, but said, after a few moments of thought, "I am not at all sure that is the course of action we should take.''

Marcus faced him.

"But I don't understand, Lord Burnleigh. How else am I to claim my inheritance?''

Diana, too, swung to the earl, her eyes flashing.

"Indeed, my lord, what is your suggestion as to the direction we should pursue? Or do you believe still that I am an adventuress? That I have brought in an accomplice to further dupe you with yet another tissue of lies?''

Jared stiffened. He opened his mouth to utter a suitably cutting rejoinder, but observing the hint of tears in her eyes, and the break in his voice, he refrained. He had hurt this woman, and he had never so much as offered a regret for his inexcusable behavior. She had every right to flare up at him. A light hand, he told himself, was what was needed at the moment.

He allowed his face to relax in the disarming grin that had rarely failed to soothe, no matter how wrathful its recipient.

"That still rankles, does it? I will take this occasion to offer my most profound apologies for my disgraceful conduct, Miss St. Aubin, or rather, the Honorable Miss

Crowne. Perhaps you will grant me the opportunity later to atone for my behavior.''

Jared searched Diana's face for signs of a thaw, but was not encouraged by the thin smile that was her response.

"Good," he continued heartily. "Let us cry friends, then. Now, there can be no question of the truth of Marcus's claim to the Stedford estate. Aside from the impeccable array of documents in his possession, there are other facts which stand in your favor. You see," he said in response to another questioning stare from two pairs of eyes, "aside from Diana's possession of the little carnelian pendant, there is that glorious head of golden hair, which she inherited from Amanda, as well. There is also," he said, turning to Marcus, "a portrait of Charles hanging in the gallery, painted when he was twenty-one or so. If he were not dressed in the satins and peruke of the last century, one would assume the young man portrayed to be you. And if that were not enough, there appears in that same gallery, in portraits of your ancestors dating back hundreds of years, a certain ring."

Jared allowed his gaze to rest pointedly on the hand resting at Marcus's right side. Puzzled, the young man lifted it into view.

The three gazed with fascination at the oddly designed silver ring that could be seen adorning his little finger.

"It was Mama's wedding ring," said Marcus, his voice breaking. "She gave it to me not an hour before she died, and told me to keep it always."

"It is a talisman ring," added Diana softly. "I asked her once why Papa had chosen such an unconventional wedding ring for her, but she just laughed, and said it was a very special ring, and meant the world to her."

"I don't understand its significance," Jared pondered aloud, "but it evidently has been in your family for a very long time. Yes," he continued, smiling, "your claim is undoubtedly valid, and you could probably be installed at Silverwell by week's end, should you choose. But"— and now he turned back to Diana—"have you considered? We have no proof that Ninian was behind your abduction. When Marco the Magnificent is transformed into the Viscount Stedford, Ninian will be out of Silverwell, but he will still be at large. Having come this far, will he simply bow apologetically out of the picture? Given what I feel is the accurate picture we have drawn of his character, I think it likely that he will at last bring himself to arrange the one circumstance that will assure him of the title.''

Diana's hand flew to her mouth.

"I did not think of that," she murmured, her face white.

"Nor I!" exclaimed Marcus wrathfully. "I'd like to see his head stuck on a pole at the crossroads."

Diana stared fixedly at the earl. "How, then, shall we proceed, my lord?"

"There are several routes I think we might take," mused Jared. "However, some further planning is necessary. In the meantime, I believe it would be unwise to leave either of you unguarded against Ninian's wiles. He is certain to continue his efforts to secure the documents that can prove his undoing."

He turned to Marcus.

"It is essential that he not discover your presence in the neighborhood. You will be safe here, as will your sister. I think it will be best for you to continue in your role as footman, for the time being. If your own sister did not spot you under that wig, I doubt if your enemies will."

Marcus reluctantly agreed to this plan.

"In the meantime," continued Jared, "we will consider how best to bring the iniquitous pseudo-Stedford to justice. Tomorrow we three shall meet again, like Shakespeare's witches on the heath, and see what plots we must hatch. As for now, the night is far advanced, and daylight will come before any of us is ready for it. So up to your garret, young Marco, and if my can of hot water is late tomorrow morning, I shall tell my man to berate that loutish new footman we just hired."

After bidding good night to Jared and her brother, Diana did not immediately seek her bed. For some time she sat in the little chair by the fireplace in her chamber, staring into the embers and trying to absorb the meaning of Marcus's revelations.

To think that her father, that gentle, shabby scholar,

was the son of an English nobleman! He had whistled away a title and a fortune, all for love. Well, yes, at the time he was merely a younger son, one of that vast, unfortunate breed who, though of noble birth, generally had little money of their own. Their fathers were men of wealth and privilege, but that wealth was largely entailed, and went for the upkeep of their vast estates, which were also entailed and must be passed on to the heir. Such was the sanctity of this system that, even though Charles in his rage had cut off his youngest son from the family, he could not keep him out of the line of succession.

What a strange and tragic sequence of events, she thought, had led to her brother's accession to the title. And what an upheaval it would bring in both their lives. Marco d'Angelini would cease to exist, as would Mademoiselle St. Aubin, instructor in English to genteel French damsels.

She drifted into a fantasy in which she floated bejeweled and gowned in silks. Even as she laughed at her own nonsense, she pictured herself courted by all the dashing young blades of the *ton,* positively awash in bouquets and gifts and odes to her fine eyes. Her dream was interrupted by the vision of a tall, dark figure with cold eyes and harsh features, who strode onto the scene.

"Yes!" she thought triumphantly. "When we meet at the Duchess's ball, or the Regent's dinner party, I think, my lord, we will have no more 'see here, my girl' from you. Or 'you *will* do as I say!' "

And no more kisses stolen in sunlit meadows.

She tried to smother that thought before it could go farther, but the damage was done.

The reflection that everything now would be different between her and the arrogant earl did not cheer her. Somehow, it gave her no pleasure to imagine Jared mouthing polite nothings to her at the endless series of staid social functions that comprised life in the polite world.

She rose abruptly from her chair, undressed hurriedly, and plunged into bed, burying her head in her pillow. Resolutely, she attempted to thrust all thoughts of crisply curling black hair and deep-set eyes from her mind.

Still, sleep did not come until her chamber window began to fill with dawn. Her rest was brief, and the sounds of the household coming to life aroused her some two hours later.

19

Arrayed in a morning dress of worked French muslin, Diana entered the breakfast parlor to find that Aunt Amabelle had already put in an uncharacteristically early appearance.

"Why, good morning, Diana." Her ladyship gestured with a piece of toasted bread, entangling several bracelets in the fringe of her shawl as she did so.

Diana returned a smiling greeting, and then, noting that Aunt Amabelle was garbed in a carriage dress, added, "Are you going out, ma'am?"

"Yes, such a bother. Cook's mother is down with a sprained ankle, and I have promised to go to her with some of my 'mixture.' It is one of my hobbies," she explained, "making decoctions and infusions from herbs and roots that I grow myself." She nodded modestly. "If I do say so, my cures are much in demand throughout the neighborhood. Even Dr. Meering says that they are extremely efficacious, and he has asked for my recipes."

Diana gazed at the plump little lady with new respect. Impulsively, she placed her arm over the older woman's shoulders and drew her into a warm embrace.

"What a wonder you are, my lady! Chatelaine, nurse, and good friend to your family. I have never properly thanked you for your kindness to me. I know how difficult it has been for you—forced to house an unknown female in such outrageous circumstances. You were told I was a—a woman of the streets, but you have treated me with compassion and every courtesy."

Aunt Amabelle jerked upright, fairly bouncing in her seat, her eyes snapping.

"Well, that's just—just nonsense, my dear. Woman of the streets, indeed! I should think I know a lady when I see one, and any idiot can see that's what you are. As for courtesy, all I've done is provide you with a few bits of clothing, all in aid of that wretched boy's plots and schemes. The thing is, Diana, you have more than repaid all of us for any consideration we might—that is, Papa has shown such marked improvement, and I'm sure much of it is due to the time you have spent with him. And the change in Lissa is incredible. She actually sought out Miss Bledsoe yesterday and asked for more French vocabulary words to study, so that she may deal better with Odile! You have quite become a part of our family, my dear, so let us have no more talk of—ah, here is Mallow with the morning post.''

She received the correspondence from the butler, and Diana, despite herself, craned to see if the color pink was in evidence among the assorted missives. Yes, there it was—she had caught its scent even before it leapt out at her from behind the notice of a horse auction in Canterbury. She ignored it.

Lady Teague, after perusing the letters on the silver tray, turned to the *Morning Post*. Opening the newspaper, she regaled Diana with the society pages of that periodical. The fact that Diana was unlikely to be acquainted with any of the personages named seemed immaterial to her ladyship.

"Oh, look, Janie Rutherford has finally been delivered of her child—a boy! That's their third, you know, but the first were two girls. She must be so pleased to have presented her husband with an heir. And mercy, the Fishburtons are visiting at Oatlands again. I wonder they can stand the pace. Last time they were there, Lady Fish was bitten at least three times by the duchess's wretched dogs.''

She scanned the page with relish, apparently deriving great pleasure from the doings of persons she saw rarely, and cared for even less. At last, as she was about to put down the newspaper, a small, discreetly placed article caught her attention. She began a casual perusal of the item, and her eyes suddenly widened. Her grip tightened on the paper, and as she continued reading, her breathing erupted into horror-stricken gasps.

"What is it, my lady?" asked Diana, alarmed.

"Mmpshfmump!'' was the only response, spoken through a mouthful of toast, which Lady Teague had inadvisedly placed between her teeth a few moments before. She semaphored wildly with the *Post*.

"Rarsterf—woobfum!" she cried in appalled accents.

With one final agonized gulp of air, her ladyship inhaled the remainder of the toast crumbs, and lapsed into a paroxysm of strangled coughs. Unable to speak, she thrust the newspaper at Diana, jabbing with a shaking finger at the offending item. She irritatedly waved away Diana's attempts at assistance, commanding her instead, with anguished gestures, to look at the passage indicated.

To an accompaniment of gradually subsiding hiccups and wheezes, Diana began to read. To her unbelieving eyes was thus delivered the intelligence that the engagement was announced between the Earl of Burnleigh and Miss Diana Bavister of Wales.

Her eyes widened in horror no less expressive than that displayed by Aunt Amabelle, and for a few moments the only sound in the room was an inarticulate sputtering emerging from two throats.

"But this is abominable!" cried Diana.

"Yes, abominable," moaned Aunt Amabelle, recovering her voice at last.

"It's absolutely outrageous!"

"Outrageous," intoned the antistroph.

"Who in the world could be responsible for this?"

"I can't imagine," breathed Aunt Amabelle, her bracelets, rings, and necklaces fairly vibrating. "The only persons who knew of the pretended betrothal were you and me, and Jared—and Simon. I cannot imagine that Jared would—"

"Certainly not," snapped Diana, annoyed to find herself flushing. "Such a wicked joke is not beyond him, of course, but he would certainly not jeopardize his genuine betrothal plans with a—a stupid prank."

"And I'm sure it was not Simon," continued Aunt Amabelle. "He was forever playing tricks on his older brother, but he would never do Jared any real mischief."

Diana, her forehead wrinkled, nodded in agreement. Suddenly, she sat upright.

"Lord Chamford!" she exclaimed. "He has become increasingly vexed that the wedding plans have not been going forward. He specifically mentioned inserting an announcement in the *Post*. Do you suppose. . . ?"

Lady Amabelle moaned faintly.

"Papa! Yes, it must have been Papa. *That's* what he wanted with our bailiff the other day. Not an hour after leaving Papa's chambers, he was on his way to London. Oh, dear. Oh-h-h, dear!" she repeated dismally, as the implications of the news item unfolded in her mind. "The whole world will believe Jared to be betrothed—and the scandal when the fraud comes out. Good heavens!" She started, as a fresh horror raised its head. "What else do you suppose Papa has been up to? Oh, Diana, what if he's written to your mother? That is, Lady Bavister, in Wales?"

She rose and, grasping Diana's wrist, towed her from the room.

"We must go to Papa at once!"

"But should we not see Lord Burnleigh first?" interposed Diana.

"Jared is not here—of course!" responded her ladyship bitterly. "He left the house early this morning, saying he did not know when he would return."

The two ladies left the breakfast parlor in despairing silence.

When they reached the marquess's bedchamber, they found him occupied with his own copy of the *Morning Post*. He sat in a huge armchair by the fire, chuckling as he read aloud to Fishperk.

" 'An autumn wedding.' Good touch, that, don'tcher think? Finest time of the year, to my mind, and—hah! Good morning, Amy. And Diana, too. Have you seen this?"

Lady Teague nodded.

"If you were referring to the announcement of Jared's betrothal, Papa, yes, indeed I have, and was never so mortified."

"Mortified!" came the answering roar. "Nonsense! The chaps at the paper printed it up exactly as I composed it. Close your mouths and sit down, both of you. You look like landed flounders."

As they obeyed he continued, addressing himself to Diana.

"For some absurd reason, you and Jared have been shilly-shallying about your wedding plans. You needed a

fire built under you; I have merely supplied the tinder.''
He laughed aloud in pleased appreciation of his own wit.

Diana raised a limp hand in protest, but was forestalled by the bustling entrance of Lissa, who was fairly
shooting sparks of excitement.

"Oh, good!" she cried, "everyone is here. Is it true?
Diana, are you and Jared really engaged to be married?"

Diana closed her eyes. She felt as though she were in
a dream, from which she could surely wake at any moment. None of this could possibly be real.

It was Aunt Amabelle who finally responded.

"How—where did you hear such a thing, my dear?"

"Why, Odile told me. Trust the servants! She told me
it's all over the stewards' hall."

She ran to Diana and hugged her ruthlessly.

"What a sly boots you are. I knew there was something going on. I can't imagine why you denied it in the
first place, but I am so very glad you are going to be my
sister. I am going to go right over to the vicarage to tell
Patience! Then we will ride to the Marstons, and—"

"No!" exclaimed Diana and Lady Amabelle as one.

"That is—um," continued her ladyship feebly. "Perhaps you should remain here, Lissa. We are sure to have
visitors. Papa, of course, will not want to receive, so the
rest of us must be on hand to—"

"Nonsense!" Lord Chamford smiled sunnily. "I have
almost completely regained my strength, and it would be
remiss, not to say ungracious of me, to absent myself
when my friends and neighbors gather round to wish us
well. I have already decided that today— Ah," he said
in satisfaction as the door opened to admit two footmen,
"here are the young men I sent for to assist me downstairs."

Diana perceived that one of the young men was her
brother, who dropped her a wink as he passed her. He
moved to the armchair and bent to assist his lordship,
who was attempting to rise unaided. Suddenly Marcus
straightened, a stupefied expression on his face. Following his gaze, Diana's eyes came to rest on Lissa. That
young beauty, all unaware, hovered over her grandfather
in pretty solicitude. Diana turned back to find Marcus
still staring at Lissa, and she was forced to administer a
surreptitious kick to bring him back to his surroundings.

The young man returned to his duties, but the expression of incredulous wonder stayed with him as his eyes strayed again to Lissa's fairylike countenance.

Lady Teague, meanwhile, had drawn herself up briskly.

"Papa, I must protest. You know very well the doctor said you might go downstairs, but only for an hour or so at a time. And you are not to allow yourself any excitement. We were hoping you might join us for dinner, but if you persist in overtiring yourself with visitors, you will deny us that pleasure. That would be too bad of you, Papa."

In the face of his daughter's gentle but implacable remonstrance, the old gentleman breathed a martyred sigh.

"Oh, very well, Amy. I shall compromise. To be honest, I have little desire to see the parcel of cloth heads that will no doubt be showing their faces. But if Tom Warfield should come, or Dandy Morris, bring them up here to see me."

Relieved at having won the major portion of the battle, Aunt Amabelle promised hastily that if these gentlemen or any other of the marquess's particular cronies appeared, they would be shown directly to his lordship's chambers. She dismissed the footmen, and Marcus, with some difficulty, wrenched his gaze from Lissa's elfin form. When the two young men had left the room, her ladyship rose, declaring she must be off.

"If I hurry," she said, "I should be back from my visit to Cook's mother by luncheon, and that is when, I should imagine, callers will begin to arrive."

She bustled out of the room, and Lissa drew close to Diana.

"Very well," she trilled, "I shall stay here with you. Very likely Patience and her parents will call here before long." She drew Diana to her feet, and with a smiling wave of farewell to her grandfather, she hurried the older girl out of the chamber.

Propelled into the corridor, Diana drifted like a storm-tossed leaf, without will or emotion.

Beside her, Lissa was chattering excitedly.

"You must tell me everything! How long have you and Jared been interested in one another? Had you become well acquainted before you came to visit? And why did you not tell me anything? I declare, I don't understand why you and Jared didn't simply come out with it when—''

Diana raised her hand. She must bring this to a halt right now.

"Lissa, this whole thing is a dreadful mistake. Your brother and I are not betrothed, and have no intention of becoming so. The announcement in the *Post* was inserted by your grandfather, who seems to have taken a notion in his head that—''

"But that's nonsense. You cannot make me believe that you are indifferent to one another—not with the two of you going about smelling of April and May!''

"What do you mean?'' exclaimed Diana.

"Just that a person can tell, that's all,'' replied Lissa with a knowing smile. "The way you look at each other, the way Jared goes out of his way to let his hand rest on your arm—that sort of thing. It's all been perfectly obvious to anyone of the least sensibility.'' A dreamy expression settled on her exquisite features. "A person can tell when someone is attracted to someone.''

Ninian! thought Diana. Of all the young men upon whom Lissa might have bestowed her youthful affection, why did it have to be Ninian Crowne?

But there was no time for that now. She thrust the problem from her mind, returning to the matter at hand. Here she found herself at a standstill. She could not explain to Lissa that Jared's gestures of affection were pure artifice, because that would mean revealing the betrothal scheme, which would, in turn, lead to a most uncomfortable discussion of how she and Jared had come to meet in the first place.

Oh, what a tangled web, she reflected dismally.

She faced Lissa and tried again.

"You are quite mistaken,'' she said in a firm voice. "Lord Burnleigh has been most courteous, and I am grateful, but that is all there is to our—our relationship.''

Lissa grinned skeptically.

"I don't know what game you're playing at, Diana, but I shan't tease you anymore. I'll simply say that if Grandpapa considers you betrothed, you might as well start getting your bride clothes together. In the meantime, prepare yourself to accept the congratulations of the world.''

Diana turned to her, startled.

"Do you really think Lord Burnleigh's betrothal will create such a stir?"

"But, my dear," drawled Lissa, essaying the role of sophisticate, "Lord Burnleigh is the most notable catch in the marriage mart. The announcement that he has at last fallen into parson's mousetrap will set the *ton* on its ear!"

"Oh," replied Diana hollowly.

"And I will wager my best pearls that right this minute everyone within thirty miles is making preparations for a visit, hoping to be the first to do the proper."

"Oh."

Events soon proved Lissa to be eminently correct, for the ladies had just risen from luncheon when the first caller arrived at the front door.

The visitor was Ninian Crowne.

20

Diana stood near the fireplace in the Gold Saloon, where
the ladies of the house had gathered after leaving the
luncheon table. She felt the blood drain from her face
when she heard the name of the spurious viscount announced, but by a strong effort of will she kept her face
composed. When her enemy's graceful form stepped into
the room, she greeted him with a semblance of cordial-
ity.

Good manners dictated that he make his first pleasantries to Lady Teague, and he accomplished this with his
characteristic polish. Lissa then came in for several fulsome compliments, under which she blushed adorably.

He turned a flat, unreadable stare on Diana, but his
smile, as usual, was blinding in its vivacious charm.

"Miss Diana," he bubbled, "I feel I must scold you.
'S truth! Though our acquaintance is of short duration, I
very much count you my friend—yet you said nothing to
me of your, ah, understanding with Lord Burnleigh.
However, I quite forgive you. I can only be happy for
your good fortune. Tell me, how long has this felicitous
relationship existed between you and his lordship?"

Diana, eyeing him shrewdly, realized that behind his
artless prattle, Ninian Crowne was profoundly disturbed.
His slim white fingers plucked at the seals that dangled
at his waist, and his speech was high-pitched and breathless.

She moved to seat herself beside Aunt Amabelle, thus
reinforcing her status as honored guest in this noble
home, and bestowed a guileless smile on Ninian.

"My lord, you must know we have all been put into
such a taking by that ridiculous item! It was put into the
paper all unknown to us by—well, someone who acted
out of misguided benevolence. Lady Teague and I have

just been discussing the best way to counter the news. We shall have a retraction printed, of course.''

Ninian was standing very still, his sapphire eyes suddenly alert.

''The statement is untrue, then? You and Lord Burnleigh are not betrothed?''

''As to that, sir, I can hardly—''

''Of course the statement is true, Stedford,'' a deep, quiet voice said from the doorway. Diana whirled at the sound, the blood rushing to her face. Jared entered the room and strode swiftly to Diana's side, smiling warmly into her eyes. Gently grasping her hands, he pulled her to her feet and bestowed a light kiss on her cheek.

''Good afternoon, my love. How ungentlemanly of me to have been away from home when that wretched piece appeared. If Grandfather has not already raked down his secretary for sending it out before he was told, I promise you I shall.''

Observing that his fiancée was totally bereft of speech, Jared turned to greet his aunt and Mrs. Sample, and gestured briefly at a beaming Lissa.

Ninian stood motionless, an odd metallic glint in his eyes. To Jared, he said, ''So it is true!'' He ran his hand over his hair in a characteristic gesture. As though this had somehow reassured him, he bowed with his usual grace, and, if his smile seemed a trifle rigid, his words indicated nothing but pleased sincerity.

''It seems as though I must wish you happy, my lord.''

Jared accepted his congratulations with a becoming modesty that infuriated Diana. When Ninian bowed over her hand with another simpering speech, she was again swept by the feeling of unreality that had been with her since the appearance of the betrothal notice. Blinking, she returned Ninian's pretty sentiments with murmured courtesies.

It appeared the merest chance that after unburdening himself of these pleasantries, Ninian found himself near the settee upon which Lissa disported herself. Bowing again, he pressed a kiss on her small hand, and seated himself beside her.

At this point Mallow entered the room, ushering in three servants bearing trays laden with assorted refreshments. One of the footmen separated himself from the main body and headed unerringly for the settee and Lissa.

Diana watched intently as Marcus hovered with tea and cakes. He presented a plate of macaroons to Lissa, which she absently spurned without even glancing at her worshiper.

"And when is the happy event to take place?" Ninian asked, his eyes darting from Diana to Jared.

The earl answered before Diana could respond.

"We have not yet set a date. Miss Bavister's mother is not well at the moment, and we are not sure when she will be able to make the journey from Wales to Kent."

"And, of course," continued Diana, determined to carry this lunatic charade to its conclusion, "we cannot begin to make bridal preparations until then. We have not even decided where the wedding is to take place. Jared leans toward St. George's in Hanover Square, while Lord Chamford is in favor of the Stonebury village church. I must say, however, that I am partial to my own church—in the tiny village where I was raised—in Wales."

She gazed soulfully at Ninian.

"Of course," agreed the false viscount after a moment's hesitation. "Dear me, there are so many things to consider when one marries. It quite frightens me away from the whole idea of matrimony. Of course," he added, bestowing a significant smile on Lissa, "the right person could change my mind."

The appalled silence that greeted this sally was broken by a howl of anguish from Ninian as a cascade of steaming tea poured into his lap. He leapt to his feet to face a stolidly unrepentant Marcus, who said in a voice void of expression, "Terribly sorry, my lord. How clumsy of me."

Ninian, fairly gabbling with rage and pain, turned on the supposed footman in fury. He raised his fist, and for a moment Diana thought he meant to strike Marcus. But he stilled himself abruptly, his mouth open and his eyes fairly bulging in astonishment.

He stood thus for several seconds, simply gaping at the servant, who handed him a cloth and smiled back at him in bland unconcern. He took the cloth absently, then stared at the hand that had proffered it, on which a silver ring winked in the light. The others stared at the scene in varying degrees of consternation, except for Jared, who smiled broadly.

At a gesture from Lady Teague, servants ran to minister to the sodden guest with napkins, but Ninian waved them off in irritation. With a not wholly successful attempt at *sang froid* he made his good-byes, assuring his hostess stiffly that no harm was done, and that he had planned to make an early departure, anyway.

Jared moved to stand next to Diana.

"Marco the Magnificent strikes again," he murmured in her ear.

Diana was in no mood for his lordship's wit.

"What on earth," she whispered furiously, "did you think you were about to declare to that wretched creature—that we are really betrothed? We cannot continue . . ."

Her incensed splutterings were halted as a neighboring squire and his wife were announced.

Feeling as though the room were reeling about her, Diana forced a smile to her lips. It became necessary to keep it in place for many hours to come, as all during an interminable afternoon the best county families processed through the Gold Saloon, avid curiosity showing through polite expressions of good will. Diana smiled and smiled, and murmured courteous responses to all the wishes for a long and happy marriage, blessed with a nursery full of children. Her feeling of nightmarish unreality increased, and as the hours passed, she was sure that her face must be permanently frozen in a blank simper.

The long afternoon finally lurched to a close, and Diana allowed the smile to curl in on itself as visitors began to make their farewells. She bent her head attentively as a bejeweled dowager twittered a last pleasantry and moved majestically toward the door.

The lady was stayed in her stately progress by the entrance of Mallow, who announced the imminent advent of two latecomers: Their Graces, the Duke and Duchess of Barnstaple. Diana, standing beside Jared, felt him stiffen. She watched curiously as the pair made their way into the room, causing a breathless hush to blanket the saloon.

The duchess, though not in the first bloom of youth,

was strikingly beautiful. Raven hair waved luxuriantly above an alabaster forehead, and brilliant green eyes flashed a smile at the assemblage. Behind her trailed the duke, an elderly unobtrusive gentleman whose eyes never left the vision of feminine splendor preceding him.

Every other gaze seemed to be fastened on the duchess as well, as she glided to where Aunt Amabelle sat in a damask-covered armchair.

"Lady Teague," trilled the dark-haired beauty in dramatic accents, "so naughty of us to be the last ones to arrive, the last to offer our congratulations at your news. What a happy time for you, to be sure!"

Aunt Amabelle opened her mouth to deliver what promised to be one of her more incoherent replies, but the duchess, after squeezing the older woman's hand, turned away and searched the room with restless eyes. Almost immediately her gaze fluttered to Jared, and with another sinuous movement, she crossed the room.

"And you, Jared, how naughty of you to keep your glad intentions from your dearest friends."

She extended a graceful arm, and after a moment's hesitation, Jared grasped her hand and brushed her gloved fingertips with his lips.

"Serena," he murmured, "how very nice of you to make the trip all the way from Berkeley Square—and in such haste."

Her grace's answering trill was a shade less musical than before, but her lips curved enchantingly.

"But of course we came. The announcement fairly leaped at us this morning from the paper, and Barney agreed with me that we must simply fly to Kent to be among the first to wish you happy." She turned to Diana. "And this must be the lucky miss."

Again the throaty laughter sounded, but when Diana met the woman's eyes, she found herself the target of two shafts of pure emerald venom. She almost stepped back under the unexpected onslaught, and her murmured response was disjointed. She glanced swiftly at Jared, who had moved to stand very close to her.

"Yes, indeed," he was replying smoothly, "I am indeed fortunate to have found a true pearl. They are so hard to find, don't you agree?"

The duchess paled, and it could be seen that the delicate bloom suffusing her cheeks owed its existence solely to cosmetics. Diana, feeling as though she were being tossed like a toy boat on the unseen currents that swirled about her, addressed a word of greeting to the duke, who stood a little behind his wife, smiling uncomprehendingly. Her grace retrieved the charming smile that had slipped so perceptibly, and leaned forward to bestow a kiss on the cheek of the newly affianced bride. Diana's nostrils were filled with an exotic, musky scent, as familiar to her now as it was hated.

The next moment the ducal couple had moved on to converse with others in the saloon. Shaken, Diana watched the beauty's progress. So this was Jared's current love, the author of the pink billets-doux. Had he sent for her? Had she come, with compliant husband in tow, to ease the discomfort of his present awkward situation? Good heavens, she must have spurred her little duke to a demoniac pace to have reached Stonefield on the same day that the announcement appeared in the London papers.

Not that she cared, Diana reminded herself yet again. The wretched earl could stuff Stonefield Court to the rafters with his mistresses, and she simply *did not care*. He was, after all, nothing to her. Less than nothing.

However, her fingers curled into rakes when, a few moments later, the duchess returned to speak again to Jared. Diana pointedly turned her back in order to converse with the vicar's wife, so that her betrothed could speak more privately to his inamorata. She resolutely ignored the murmur of their voices, and it was only after some minutes that words, uttered sharply, reached her ears.

"Jared, you cannot mean this. You know you cannot!"

The duchess's voice quieted then, but a few minutes later she spoke again, this time with a trembling edge to her voice.

"Come, Barney, it is time we were on our way."

Then she was gone, her husband trailing after her like an obedient shadow.

Finally the last of the callers departed sedately from the entrance portico, and the family made their way to their respective chambers to change for dinner. Jared held the door for his aunt and Mrs. Sample, and for Lissa, who was still flown with the romance of the coming nuptials and Ninian's inflated compliments.

"To think that it will all take place in my very first Season!" were the last words to be heard as she wafted through the door, an ethereal smile on her lips.

Jared shook his head ruefully at his sister. Then, still holding the door, he turned to usher Diana into the corridor.

That young woman, however, had other ideas. The events of the day had taken their toll, and her mood could only be described as ominous.

"One moment, if you please, my lord." The quietly spoken words were belied by the storm signals plainly displayed in her cloudy eyes. Thus, Jared was undeceived by her seemingly courteous words. He closed the door and advanced toward her.

"Yes, my love?" he inquired innocently.

The tempest broke.

"How *dare* you address me in such a fashion!" The words burst from Diana in an outraged torrent. "And how dare you allow this absolutely scandalous situation to continue. You know your grandfather inserted that wretched announcement without anyone's knowledge. Now that he has, you must realize that your precious scheme has fallen apart, and if you possessed a grain of propriety you would bring the whole preposterous project to a halt right now. For heaven's sake, my lord, go to Lord Chamford now. Tell him—"

"Tell him that the betrothal is a monumental hoax? That you are not Diana Bavister? That there never was a Diana Bavister, and that I have no fiancée? What do you think that would do to him?"

Diana's gaze faltered for a moment, then lifted to meet his.

"His health is vastly improved. He is bound to find out the truth eventually, and in postponing the inevitable you have exposed him and the rest of your family to the gossip and ridicule of the fashionable world. When all the high-born personages who today bestowed their best wishes on us discover the fraud that has been perpetrated on them, I shudder to think what the consequences will be."

"Nonsense. In a few days they will have a new subject

to chew over—the appearance of the rightful Viscount of Stedford, for example—and the affairs at Stonefield will be forgotten.''

Diana could only stare at him.

''I know I have said this before,'' she said, ''but now I really believe it to be true. You are absolutely and irredeemably mad! Have you stopped to consider my particular circumstances, and those of Marcus? It is no longer possible for Diana Bavister to disappear unobtrusively to reappear as Diana Crowne. The people who were here today will be my neighbors. I had hoped they might be my friends as well, but you have effectively destroyed that possibility.''

Somewhere, deep inside her unhappiness, Diana knew she was not being fair. Jared's motive in fashioning his deception had taken root in his love for his grandfather, and he could not be wholly blamed for the disastrous events that had resulted.

Nerves stretched to screaming point, however, do not lend themselves to logical thought, and it was only through a strong effort of will that Diana did not burst into a flood of tears on the spot.

For a moment Jared said nothing. He had suddenly gone very pale, and an odd, desperate expression flared in his eyes. His voice, when he spoke, was choked and barely recognizable.

''Then perhaps the best course would be for us to marry.''

In the profound silence that fell between them, Diana felt that she might, for the first time in her life, simply sink to the floor in a faint. Gazing up into Jared's face, she read an expression of shock and incredulity there, as though he were as much astounded by his words as she.

''Sir!'' she gasped. ''What kind of monstrous joke are you trying to perpetrate now?''

Jared made no reply for a moment, but stood for a long moment staring blindly at her. Then, slowly, as though against his will, he moved to her and put his hands on her shoulders. Looking down into her white face, he spoke with an awkward urgency.

''But it is the perfect solution after all, is it not? You will soon become the Honorable Diana Crowne of Silverwell, sister of the Viscount Stedford. You are the grandchild of Grandfather's dearest friend in the world. He will be ecstatic at this turn of events. You, of course, will benefit by aligning yourself with one of the oldest, noblest, and wealthiest families in the country.''

Diana could only gape at him. A feeling of terrible cold that seemed to penetrate the center of her soul crept over her.

She said in a frozen whisper, ''And you, Lord Burnleigh, what benefit will you derive from this—this union?''

For an instant Diana thought she saw in Jared's eyes a pinpoint of flame, such as she had beheld that day in the meadow, but the next moment he stepped away from her, his face cold and distant.

''I shall gain a wife of beauty and breeding, of course.'' His tone was dry and prosaic. ''You have described yourself truly as a woman of sense and practicality, and as you have proved in the time I have known you, possessed of an innate dignity. These are, of course, the qualities my family has urged me to seek in a bride, and it is obvious that they have perceived them in you. You have won all their hearts.''

''That is most gratifying, my lord.'' Diana was vaguely pleased that her voice gave no hint of the churning in the pit of her stomach. The Schoolmistress was once more firmly in charge. ''However, though I am greatly honored by your condescension, I must beg to refuse. As you have pointed out, you have a large selection of prospective brides to choose from, and I wish you and your wife and your mistresses all the happiness in the world. Now, if you will excuse me.''

Diana attempted to sweep past him, sensing that her hard-won control over her emotions was slipping away, but Jared's grasp tightened.

''Please, Diana. What happened with Serena today was—regrettable, but I assure you there would be no repetition. . . .''

''No, of course not,'' replied Diana through gritted teeth. ''Such an aberration would never occur again in a well-run household. After all, how often is one's paramour likely to invade one's drawing room?''

''You don't understand. She is nothing. Please—just

consider what I offer you. I know that our relationship did not get off to a very cordial start, but . . .''

"Cordial?'' Diana essayed a small smile. It was not a success.

If only she were not so cold, she reflected irrelevantly. She could not think properly. She must get out of this room, away from Jared and his eminently reasonable arguments.

He continued in a more temperate tone. "I do not mean to distress you, nor do I wish to be importunate. I ask only that you think over what I have said, and we will discuss the matter again when you have had a chance to do so.''

"Yes, my lord. Thank you.'' Diana sensed her control tremble, like a length of overstretched piano wire. She moved rigidly and carefully toward the door, feeling that she might at any moment shatter into great, icy shards. "I shall indeed think over your proposal. We will speak again later.''

She made her exit and for an instant, leaned against the other side of the closed door, utterly drained of energy and emotion. Slowly she made her way to the music room and sat down at the piano. This time, however, the great instrument provided no solace. She felt as though her hands were carved from marble and the music had fled from her spirit.

Why, she mused dismally, was the idea of a marriage of convenience so abhorrent to her? The heroines of Mrs. Radcliffe's novels, of which she had perused a great number, would shudder at the very idea, but life could not be lived between the pages of a romance novel. She had already, for all intents and purposes, left behind the life of a humble schoolmistress. Her brother was a nobleman, and would soon take up his duties as the head of a family of power and privilege. She was about to enter the world of arranged unions and calculated dowries. In all probability, if she did not marry Jared, she would eventually find herself wed to another like him, with little to say in the matter.

No, not like him. That was the crux of the matter, wasn't it—the reason for all her maidenly flutterings. Jared's proposal had nearly broken her heart, because she was in love with him. She had been aware of that fact since that single soul-shattering kiss in the meadow. She knew now that she had been attracted to him almost from their first meeting. Despite his arrogance, beyond the insults, she had been drawn to the man beneath the haughty exterior.

He pretended to be cold and uncaring, yet the love he felt for those who dwelt in Stonefield Court was readily apparent. His attitude was one of bored cynicism, but his wit was lively and challenging. His absorption in the land surrounding his ancient home belied the image of the Corinthian man about town he so carefully cultivated, and more than once she had caught a glimpse of the vulnerability that lay behind his facade of weary indifference.

This was the man she had come to love against her will, although she had thought her heart untouched until that day his lips had possessed hers by a laughing stream.

But he did not love her.

Diana let her fingers trail over the keys, producing a ripple of mournful chords.

Yet, if she must be married, why not to Jared? She would at least share his life, if not his heart. She thought ahead to days and years of being Jared's wife. She pictured his cool lack of interest, and listened in her mind to an eternity of indifferent courtesies and meaningless civilities. He had apparently bid farewell to his current light o' love this afternoon, but he would no doubt find a replacement soon. She envisioned nights alone in a great, cold home in London, waiting for the sound of her husband's footsteps as he returned from a cozy rendezvous with his latest mistress.

No. Dear God, no.

21

Diana was outwardly composed as she entered the breakfast room at an early hour the next morning. She found Jared there before her, alone at a meager repast of coffee and toast. He looked up, startled, and rose as she stepped into the room.

"Good morning, my lord," she began in a carefully controlled tone. "I trust I do not disturb your breakfast?"

"Not at all, Miss Crowne," was the courteous reply. "Shall I ring for coffee? Or chocolate, perhaps?"

Lord Burnleigh, Diana noted with some irritation, did not appear to be suffering from any residual awkwardness after their interview of the previous night.

"No, thank you." Only the extreme paleness of her face indicated her nervousness. "I have something to say to you, and I would prefer that no servants be present."

Jared started toward her, then stopped. His eyes were two chips of impenetrable black granite, as they had been on their first meeting.

"Perhaps," he said, "we should go into the library, where we need not fear interruption."

"No!" She must get this over with as quickly as possible. "That will not be necessary. What I have to say will take only a moment." She took a deep breath, hoping that the beating of her heart was not apparent through the thin muslin that covered her breast.

"Yesterday you made me a proposal of marriage." Her lifted brows made almost a question of the statement.

"Yes," replied the earl sardonically. "I recall it quite clearly. I also recall that, though you refused me, you promised to think the matter over and discuss it with me again."

"That is what I wish to speak to you about," continued Diana, her pulse thundering in her ears. "I have thought over all that you said, and my position remains the same, so there is really no need for further discussion."

She was aware that she sounded more like an intransigent head of state than a gently bred maiden refusing her first marriage proposal. The main thing, however, was that she had gotten the words out. She had said them.

It was a short speech, but it had taken her nearly all night to compose. The rest of the small hours had been spent in surmising Jared's reaction to it. She did not in the least expect what actually occurred.

Jared merely raised his brows slightly and said, "Why not?"

Diana stiffened. She longed to blurt out, "Because I love you!" Instead, she took refuge in tradition. Inclining her head, she responded in coldly measured tones, "Because I fear we will not suit, my lord."

Jared apparently remained unfazed. His brows lifted again almost imperceptibly.

"Then there remains no more to be said," he declared, "at the moment, anyway. I do not promise to give up, however. I am considered remarkably persistent in gaining my ends, you know."

Diana experienced a flutter of desperation.

"My lord, why do you *wish* to persist?"

A sudden thought struck her.

"That night in the music room, with Marc, you mentioned atonement. Can it be—is this your idea of restitution for your abominable behavior in the first days of our acquaintance? Please know, my lord, that the idea of a marriage of convenience is abhorrent to me. Chalk it up to my lamentably plebeian upbringing, but I believe the union of two people should be based on love, not duty."

Jared, at last stung to a reaction, whirled on her.

"Good God, Diana, is that what you think? Do you believe I would ask a woman to marry me as an apology for past misdeeds?"

Diana, her earlier composure deserting her, faced Jared, her eyes bright with unshed tears.

"Then why? Why are you so adamant in your wish to

marry a person for whom you feel nothing but common civility—if that?''

For an instant there was silence in the room, and the space between them was charged with an emotion Diana dared not interpret.

The moment was abruptly shattered by the entrance of Marcus, who almost skidded into the room in his distracted rush. His satin coat was unbuttoned, and his peruke wildly askew as he blurted out his news.

"Jared! Danny! Thank God I found you together. You cannot conceive what has just happened. Someone has been in my room—ransacked it—the papers are gone!"

Jared and Diana sprang apart, but such was the tension that stretched between them that for an instant their eyes remained locked in an almost physical embrace. Then Diana shuddered slightly, and turned blindly to her brother.

"It happened," panted Marcus, "sometime after I left my room to take up my duties, about two hours ago. I was just setting out from the kitchen with a tray for Lord Chamford when Welles, the steward, pointed out that a buckle had come off one of my shoes.

" 'Can't go into his lordship's presence like that, lad,' he said. 'Give your tray to young Phelps here, and you hot-foot it back up to your room and get on your second-best pair.' When I got upstairs, I found someone had been there before me."

Jared took an urgent step toward him.

"Did you see anyone in the area who might have—"

Marcus shook his head.

"No. I looked all up and down the corridor, and saw no one."

"But," interjected Diana, "how could Ninian, or even Churte, have—"

Again Marcus interrupted.

"Don't be a widgeon, Danny. Of course it wasn't precious Ninian or his handy helper. It was someone living right here that did this. By God, Jared, you were right. That bastard has someone inside the house working for him."

Jared stood for a moment, deep in thought.

"You're right, Marcus. I should have thought to secure those papers in our safe. Of course, when Ninian discovered that his intended kidnap victim had taken up residence in a neighboring house, he would have lost no time in acquiring an accomplice who could move easily throughout Stonefield.

"And there is no doubt," he continued, "that Ninian recognized you yesterday, Marcus, when you unobtrusively poured hot tea down his trousers."

Marcus flushed.

"Yes," he growled, "I suppose that was a cloth-headed thing to do, but when I saw that toad breathing his foul flummery into the ears of an angel like Lady Felicity, I could not just stand by. Besides, how was I to know he would recognize me?" He looked at Jared and said grudgingly, "I suppose it was the portrait."

Despite themselves, Jared and Diana exchanged amused glances.

"Yes," replied Jared gravely, "I should imagine that was it. Dressed in your satin knee britches and peruke, you could hardly have better emulated the portrait of Charles Crowne had you set out to do so. If an additional clue were necessary, you neatly provided it by wearing the talisman ring into his presence."

"All right," said Marcus in haste, ready to abandon the subject. "But why do we just stand here? We must—"

At this moment, Aunt Amabelle bustled into the room. Her bracelets and necklets chattered agitatedly, and her already plump blossom swelled in indignation. Without preamble, she addressed herself to the earl.

"Really, Jared, that girl must be taken in hand. Do you know what she has done?"

Her harassed nephew turned to her in some irritation.

"Really, Aunt, can't this wait? Miss Bavister and Mar—this young man and I were discussing a matter of—of business."

Aunt Amabelle shot a disapproving glance at Marcus.

"Whatever you have to take up with the staff will have to wait, Jared. And you, young sir"—this to Marcus—"will have the goodness to return to the servants' quarters and repair yourself. I'm sure Welles will have something to say to you."

Scarcely pausing for breath, she swung back to Jared and resumed her monologue.

"Lissa has left to go riding with that dreadful young

man—at the crack of dawn—without permission. How *could* she? With Lord Stedford, of all people.''

"Ninian!" exclaimed three voices in unison.

"Yes, Ninian. She virtually crept out of the house this morning without so much as a by-your-leave.''

Jared approached Lady Teague with a soothing gesture.

"Slow down, Aunt. How do you know all this? Just because she is not in her room?''

Aunt Amabelle clicked her tongue in exasperation.

"Really, Jared, as though I would take alarm without reason. No, it was my maid who told me when she brought up my breakfast. She said she had bumped into Odile, coming from the garret. And that was most peculiar, because the maids are quartered in the west wing—as far away from the footmen as possible,'' she finished severely.

"Wait a minute, Aunt,'' interrupted Jared, suddenly alert. "How long ago was this, did your maid say?''

"Um, well, from what Blodgett told me—let's see— oh, I suppose perhaps an hour gone. She said Odile was dressed to go out, and when Blodgett asked her where she was going, she said she was to accompany her mistress on an early-morning ride with a gentleman. Well, of course, Blodgett asked what gentleman, and Odile told her that it was the Viscount Stedford. Now, really, Jared, you know that sort of behavior . . . Jared! What on earth . . ?''

But she spoke to the empty air. Jared had already run out of the room in the direction of the stables, followed closely by Marcus and Diana.

As they ran, Marcus's lips moved in a silent litany of curses and threats against the person of the false viscount. Diana caught at Jared's sleeve.

"Do you think it was Odile who stole the documents?''

"I think it a most likely possibility. She must be Ninian's accomplice. After he left here yesterday, having discovered Marcus's presence, his idea must have been to search his room. Ninian knew that Odile's best opportunity for this would be early in the morning, when the staff is busy elsewhere with breakfast chores. However, that would also be a difficult time for her to leave the house afterwards, since at that time of day her mistress might call for her at any moment. Hence the invitation to Lissa for a delightful morning excursion with my lord—properly accompanied, of course, by her maid.''

They had now reached the stables, where Briggs, the head groom, hurried to meet them.

''I knew it was trouble, my lord,'' he said, shaking his head. ''I knew Lady Lissa had no business setting off like that.''

''Then why did you not send to me immediately?'' Jared asked harshly.

''Well, my lord, it's not up to me to judge Lady Lissa's doings—and she did have that Frenchie maid with her, and his lordship's man. All the same, it didn't look right. I had just about decided to send a message to you when you come a runnin' out.''

Jared and Diana exchanged glances, while Marcus ran directly into the stables.

''Do you think that they are going to Silverwell?'' Diana asked. ''They have a considerable start on us, but— Marcus!'' This to her brother, who had emerged from the stable with Jared's gray, Thor. ''What are you doing?''

''I'm going after them, of course. My God, when I get my hands on that blackguard! To think of him, for all intents and purposes alone with that pure little flower . . .''

Briggs, observing in some fascination the sight of a footman in full livery saddling my lord's favorite mount, apparently with the intention of appropriating the animal for his own use, turned to the earl.

''I have another horse already saddled, my lord. I was just going to take that tricksey bay—the one you bought last month—out for exercise.''

''Good man!'' Jared clapped the man's shoulder, then went to assist Marcus in saddling Thor. When this was accomplished, he directed Marcus to the rangy bay being hurried out of the stable by the head groom.

As soon as Briggs had handed over the bay, he stepped to Jared and raised a gnarled hand.

''Beggin' your pardon, my lord. When the boys was saddling Lady Lissa's mare, his lordship was natterin' with that makebait, Churte. They kept their voices low, but I caught something about the old oast house. Do you think. . . ?''

Jared nodded abruptly.

"Yes, Briggs, I do, and I think you may have saved the day.''

He spoke rapidly to Diana and Marcus.

"I doubt they would go to Silverwell. It is too obvious a target of pursuit. Ninian must find someplace where he can retrieve the papers from Odile. Someplace where he can examine and then destroy them at his leisure.''

"But what of Lissa?'' Marcus grated.

Jared's face was a mask of cold rage.

"I believe she is in no immediate danger. Ninian has no reason to harm her; indeed, it is to his advantage to keep her safe. After all, unless I very much mistake the matter, Ninian foresees a marriage between the Viscount Stedford and the youngest granddaughter of the Marquess of Chamford.''

Marcus uttered an inarticulate cry and ran across the stable yard, where he vaulted onto the back of the bay being held by Briggs. Jared prepared to mount Thor, but Diana placed a restraining hand on his arm.

"No,'' replied Jared curtly, in answer to the question in her eyes. "I do not want you involved in this. There may be danger.''

From somewhere Diana produced a shaky smile.

"I will match you two stalwarts against Ninian and Churte any day. When you catch up with them, Lissa may find the presence of another woman comforting. Then, too, there is the possibility that Odile might create a problem for you.''

Jared hesitated a moment. Then, without a word, he put down his hand to Diana and swung her up before him in the saddle.

"Follow me!'' he called to Marcus, and a moment later the two horses hurtled in file along a faint path leading from the stable yard.

22

Jared spoke to Diana in brief salvos, his words caught by the wind that tore at her hair and stung her eyes to tears.

"An oast house is a building which contains ovens for the drying of hops. The one to which Briggs referred lies on Crowne land, and is the only place for miles around that could serve as a perfect hiding place for Ninian. It has not been used for years, having been abandoned long before Simon and I played there with the Crowne children. It served us as pirate lair, poop deck, and haunted castle, among other things."

Diana shivered against Jared's breast. She had come out of the house without so much as a shawl, and she curled gratefully into the warmth of his body. Gathering her more tightly into his arms, Jared continued.

"There is a shortcut to the oast house, which I fancy is unknown to Ninian. With any luck, we shall arrive at approximately the same time as his lordship. Hang on, for we'll be traveling through rough country."

He spurred his mount to even greater speed, and Diana heard only the wind in her ears, the thudding of hoofbeats, and the steady beat of Jared's heart against her cheek. The path soon took a course away from the open fields of the Home Farm, through patches of gorse and overgrown briar. Fences were vaulted and hedges breasted, and still the great horse galloped on. Diana was at once terrified and exhilarated. Part of her, reveling in the strength of Jared's body pressed against hers, wished the ride would never end.

Finally, however, he slowed the animal's pace, and in another few moments reined in and came to a stop. Almost immediately, Marcus drew up behind them. Diana raised her head, but did not free herself from Jared's hold. She observed that they had come to rest in a sort of spinney on a slight rise overlooking an odd little structure some two hundred yards away.

"The oast house," explained Jared. "And see, we have come in good time."

He pointed to a small cavalcade approaching the oast house from another direction. Though they were at some distance, the figures could be clearly discerned. Ninian and Lissa were on horseback, while Churte followed, driving a small gig, with Odile as his passenger. Lissa did not appear to be under constraint, yet a certain rigidity in her carriage indicated her uneasiness.

Marcus drew in a sharp breath and lifted his reins as though to urge his mount forward, but Jared halted him with a gesture.

"No!" he commanded. "If we are to ensure Lissa's safety and regain your papers intact, the element of surprise is absolutely critical."

His gaze hardened.

"Do you understand me, Marc? This is not the time for buffle-headed heroics. Believe me, the opportunity will come for you to vent your outrage, but first we must gain the upper hand."

Marcus stiffened, his mouth a thin white line that set at variance with his youthful features. He said nothing, but allowed the reins to slacken as his fists slowly unclenched.

"Right," said Jared. "Now, the ovens are located at the back of the building, so there are no windows there. We should be able to walk up without being seen. At that point, we will make our grand entrance. Do you feel yourself able to deal with the estimable Churte, Marco?"

Marcus's assenting growl was largely unintelligible.

"Excellent. Here we go, then."

All went according to plan. After tethering the horses, the three silently made their way on foot to the oast house. When they reached its single entrance, Jared signaled a halt, and turned to scan the surrounding landscape. For a moment his gaze rested speculatively on a nearby clump of bushes, and then he lifted his brows at his cohorts. Marcus nodded, while Diana, expelling the breath she realized she had been holding for some time, also indicated that she was ready for the assault.

They burst into the small area that served as the building's main chamber. Ninian and Odile stood at a small hearth at the far end of the room, where a fire blazed high in the grate.

Lissa had taken up a position near a plank table in the center of the room, where Churte was clumsily trying to push her into a broken-backed chair.

At the entrance of the three, those in the room swung toward the door. Lissa sprang forward, bursting into tears as she saw her brother on the threshold.

"Oh, Jared," she sobbed, "I am so glad you have come! These people are just beastly. Lord Stedford insisted we come here, and this dreadful person . . ." She indicated Churte.

Marcus hurtled into the room with a roar, and sprang at Churte, who immediately released Lissa. With a swift motion, Ninian's burly confederate drew a knife from within his coat. Diana observed in horror that the blade was long and eminently serviceable, and it looked as though Marcus's furious momentum would thrust him onto its wickedly gleaming point.

Instead Marcus, without slowing, veered to one side and, in a lithe motion, sprang atop the plank table. In a blur of speed, he pivoted on one foot, and raised the other to deliver a vicious kick that sent the knife spinning from the hand of the astonished Churte. In the next instant, Marcus leaped to the floor and landed a powerful right to the center of Churte's face, followed by a left to his midsection. Before anyone could draw breath, the man lay stretched out on the dusty floor at the feet of the white-faced Lissa.

She swayed in a half-swoon and Marcus sprang to catch her, reverently lowering her into the broken chair. For an instant Lissa remained still against his breast; then, with a flutter of dark lashes, she lifted her eyes in wonder to the face of her rescuer.

Diana stood rooted at this Homeric display on the part of her brother. Jared murmured with a grin, "Well done, Marco," and strode directly to where Ninian still stood by the fireplace, his eyes the color of gun metal against the paleness of his face.

With a cry Odile, still wearing her cloak, attempted to run from the house, but was blocked by Diana, who moved to stand in her path.

"Burnleigh!" Ninian's voice was a mere croak. "May I ask what is the meaning of this intrusion? We interrupted a pleasant ride because Lady Felicity complained of a headache. We took shelter here so that her maid could, er, prepare a posset. Her ladyship, I fear, has displayed a surfeit of sensibility, but I see no reason why—"

"Shut up, Crowne," said Jared conversationally, cutting off Ninian's flow of high-pitched chatter. "It's all over, so you may return the papers."

There was an instant's pause as Ninian's eyes darted from Jared to Diana, and then to Marcus, who was still kneeling beside a delicately flushed Lissa.

"My dear fellow, I'm afraid I have no idea what you are talking about."

Jared's demeanor did not alter, but his voice was now chilled steel.

"Let me be plain, then. I am speaking of the documents which establish the identity of the real heir to Silverwell—the true Viscount Stedford. You have stolen those documents, and their owner"—he indicated Marcus, who had risen and now took a menacing step forward—"would like them back."

Ninian licked his lips, but his narrowed eyes did not falter.

"I begin to see," he said, his mouth jerking into a parody of an enlightened smile. "I had heard rumors of a pretender to the title having come into the neighborhood. This"—he gestured to Marcus—"is evidently the very person. He and his accomplice"—here he waved a hand toward Diana—"have evidently managed to pull the wool over your eyes, Burnleigh, with their ludicrous story."

Jared shrugged as though Ninian had not spoken.

"You are beginning to bore me, Crowne. The papers, if you please."

Ninian's voice took on an edge. "What are these papers you keep talking about? I have no papers. Would you have me turn out my pockets?"

At this, Jared moved toward Ninian, but was halted by a cry from Diana.

"No! Jared, wait! Look at Odile."

The maid stood alone, her cloak drawn tightly about her. Beneath the voluminous garment, something protruded, something that Odile tried to hide with trembling hands.

"Open your cloak, girl," Jared commanded.

Odile stood unmoving, her eyes wide and terrified.

"I don't think she understands much English," Diana interjected, and turning to Odile, she said quietly, *"Ouvres ton manteau, ma p'tite."*

Odile hesitated, glancing at Ninian as though for instruction. For a moment, Ninian's returning gaze was filled with unspoken menace. Another few seconds of thought, however, apparently brought him to the realization that Odile was no longer under his control. To Diana it seemed that behind Ninian's sky-blue stare, a change in strategy clicked almost audibly into place.

The false viscount folded his arms and leaned against the mantel, a bland smile on his lips, as though the events of the moment concerned him not in the slightest.

"Do you suspect Lady Felicity's maid of having stolen something?" He paused. "But how disturbing."

He watched disinterestedly as Odile moaned, then fumbled at the strings of her cloak. Opening it wide, she produced a thick packet, wrapped in faded brown paper and tied with a worn tape.

Jared took the packet from her and unwrapped it. He looked at the papers contained in it, then thrust them at Marcus, who glimpsed them briefly and nodded. Jared thumbed through them, and raised his head to look at Ninian.

"Yes," he said softly, "they're all here, all the documents necessary to prove that Marcus Crowne is the legitimate son of William Crowne, and the grandson and heir of Charles Crowne, the Viscount Stedford."

He turned menacingly to Ninian, who remained seemingly unperturbed.

"Dear me," said that gentleman, wide-eyed, "it would appear that the maid did indeed steal something! I'm sure it has nothing to do with me. You see," he went on, gesturing contemptuously at the trembling Odile, "she does not deny it."

Odile stared wildly at the men standing before her, then turned helplessly to Diana.

Diana spoke to Odile in rapid French, and was rewarded with a torrent of words in reply. Diana turned in triumph to Ninian.

"She admits everything, Mr. Crowne. She says that she became acquainted with Churte some time ago while on an errand in the village. On the day that you saw me in the road with Miss Bledsoe, she was given money by him to spy on me and report my movements to him. Soon after, she hurried to you with the news that I had left the Court to visit the vicarage with Lady Felicity, and yesterday Churte offered her more money to slip into a certain footman's room and search for a packet of documents. She found the papers, and was just about to give them to you when we arrived."

At this point Marcus, who could no longer control his rage, lunged at Ninian. Jared tossed the packet to Diana, then threw himself at Marcus, who had grasped Ninian by the throat, lifting him quite off the floor.

"Enough, young Marco," panted Jarred, settling the young man as he would a mettlesome colt. "It will do you precious little good to assume your title if you end up in the hangman's noose."

Marcus abruptly released his quarry, who sank to the floor, choking and clutching his throat.

Diana returned the packet to Jared, who continued perusing its contents. A few moments later, a sound from the fireplace drew his attention back to where Ninian lay, gasping. He blinked his eyes frantically, apparently unable to regain his breath.

Jared hurried to him, dropping the packet as he bent over the stricken man. With an exclamation, he grasped at it, but Ninian was quicker. His assumed indisposition vanished, and in a frantic lunge, he scooped up the envelope and flung it into the fire, where it was instantly consumed in the hungry flames.

A profound silence fell over the room. Diana and Marcus stared at the small conflagration in horror. Ninian drew a long, shuddering sigh. Odile still sobbed quietly into her apron, while Lissa gazed at them all, uncomprehending. Nearby, Churte stirred into consciousness. Only Jared appeared unmoved by the tragedy he had been unable to prevent.

Ninian, in a characteristic gesture, brushed his hand

over his disarranged curls. He moved to Jared, a broad smile spreading over his features.

"Now, then, my lord, what was it you were saying about papers? You know," he continued meditatively, "it is a strange thing about courts; one may make claims, even produce witnesses, but in the absence of physical evidence, the law invariably allows the status quo to prevail. And now I really must ask all of you to vacate this place, which, if I am not mistaken, lies on my land."

Marcus, a snarl sounding in his throat, advanced toward Ninian.

"You sneaking little worm! You know you have no right to so much as an inch of this land."

Ninian did not retreat, but lifted a languid white hand.

"Burnleigh, I must request that you take this overheated servant of yours in hand. I see that Churte is reviving, and he looks quite murderous. I would not like to see him involved in a rematch with a person of such a low order. I really do think it would be quite the best thing if you were all to simply leave."

Marcus raised both hands as he lunged at Ninian.

"Marcus!"

Something in Jared's tone caused the young man to halt abruptly, and he swung toward the earl in puzzlement.

Diana, too, turned toward Jared.

"My lord," she began hotly, "I realize that the affairs of two strangers cannot mean much to you, but this usurper has stolen my brother's birthright." Her voice broke. "All our hopes for the future went up in the flames that destroyed those documents. You cannot expect us to just turn about and walk away."

She searched Jared's face, and to her surprise and anger, could find only amusement and a gentle warmth.

He said, barely above a whisper, "Bravo, little hornet—well spoken!" Then he raised his voice. "I believe the time has come, gentlemen."

To Diana's utter astonishment, a stranger entered the little building in response to Jared's words. He wore a frieze coat, and was as bulky as the now recovered Churte, but of a much more cheerful mien.

"Right, gov'ner," he said briskly, bowing slightly to the earl. He strode into the room and planted himself directly in front of Ninian, arms akimbo. Behind him, a second stranger appeared in the doorway. This man did not enter, but stood watchfully at the threshold.

"Mr. Ninian Crowne," declared the man in the frieze coat, "I am Tobias P. Lightfoot of The Bow Street Runners, and this here"—he jerked a stubby thumb at the man behind him—"is my personally deputed assistant, Jasper Coombs. I am placing you under arrest for the fraud you've been tryin' to perpetrate—and for kidnappin' as well."

Ninian backed away from the man until he stood against the wall, so near to Diana that she could have touched him. His gaze seemed to turn inward in a moment of azure self-communion. Then his eyes darted about the room, stabbing, as if probing for an escape. He licked his lips once, then became calm.

"I'm afraid," he declared in a bewildered voice, "that I don't know what you're talking about, my good man. If you want to arrest someone, I suggest you start with this person here." He indicated Marcus with disdain. "He just attacked me in the most appalling manner, and if it were not for Lord Burnleigh's intervention, I shudder to think what would have happened."

His listeners could only stare, and Ninian continued gently.

"As for this fraud business, I would very much appreciate it if you would endeavor to straighten it all out. Lord Burnleigh maintains that I have stolen some papers, but I cannot think what he is talking about. There are, as you can see, no papers to be seen."

"Not now, there ain't," retorted Mr. Lightfoot. "We stood right there at the window, cully, and watched you shove 'em into the fire. No, no, never mind. You might as well know that me and my assistant have been following you and your precious henchman here"—he shot a look of intense disfavor at the unfortunate Churte—"since his lordship came to us to lay information against you early yesterday."

"But—the papers!" Ninian was so pale now that Diana could see a tracery of veins against his temple. "You have no proof. My good man"—he made a pitiful attempt to draw himself up into a stance of authority—"I am Ninian Crowne, the Viscount Stedford. If you do not leave immediately, and take these persons with you, I shall have something to say to your superiors.''

Mr. Lightfoot's only response was a mirthless bark of laughter. Jared moved forward and fixed Ninian with a pitiless stare.

"Don't you understand, Crowne? By throwing those papers into the fire, you snapped your own trap. You see, until you actually tried to destroy the documents, you had done nothing criminal in front of witnesses. Now, you have implicated yourself beyond hope.''

Jared sighed.

"One must give you credit for persistence, but there is not the slightest doubt you knew the packet contained the papers you had gone to such lengths to obtain.

"As for the documents themselves, I took them to the magistrate yesterday and he certified their validity, and recorded copies of them with the clerk's office. So, you see, your efforts were quite wasted. And, by the by, a messenger was sent to the village of Bythorne yesterday, and he discovered there the record of William Crowne's marriage.''

At last Ninian appeared to have no more to say. Once more he stared around the room with eyes lifeless as lake pebbles. He shot a glance at Churte, but that burly individual merely shook his head and shrank as far as he could into the shadows in the corner of the room.

When Ninian finally spoke, it was in a dry, despairing whisper.

"You have ruined it all, Burnleigh,'' he said. With shaking hands he removed a handkerchief from inside his coat pocket and passed it across his brow. Suddenly he straightened. With a quick motion, he grasped Diana by the shoulder and pulled her to him. It was then perceived by the others in the room that, under cover of the handkerchief, he had drawn from his pocket a small pistol.

He pressed the pistol against Diana's throat.

23

For Diana the universe shrank to the small, cold circle of metal pressed against her flesh. In the position she was held she could not see Ninian, but she could hear the labored rattle of his breath. The rancid smell of his fear seemed to have physical substance. Her gaze flew to Jared, and she saw the agony of her terror mirrored in his eyes.

The room was very still, and time lurched as in interminable fragments. Now that Ninian held the power of life and death in his hands, he seemed uncertain as to how to proceed. Finally, he cleared his throat and took a shaky breath.

"What I'm going to do now," he rasped in a grotesque effort to assert his mastery of the situation, "is leave this place. I'm going to take Miss Diana with me. We will go on horseback, and if she is very good, I will drop her off when it suits me. In the meantime, if I see so much as a glimpse of pursuit on the horizon, I will put a bullet through her lovely slender neck."

During this little speech he had gained confidence, and now he swept the company with a contemptuous glare. "Do I make myself clear?"

There was another moment's silence; then Jared spoke in a slow, taunting drawl.

"Perfectly clear, Crowne. After all, it is just what one might expect of a sniveling, cringing dog like you."

Ninian gasped as though he had been struck. His head swung toward the earl, but he held the pistol steady. Jared took a small, casual step forward, and continued to speak.

"I knew you for a weakling the moment I first saw you, and it does not surprise me in the slightest that you would hide behind the skirts of a female in a last, desperate, and I might add, futile effort to escape the thrashing you so richly deserve.''

''Jared!''

Marcus's voice came in a hoarse whisper of warning, but the earl continued as though he had not spoken. Ninian, too, seemed unaware of the interruption, staring almost mesmerized as the earl spoke again.

''Yes, I said futile, for now I shall make it my business to find you in whatever sewer you crawl into for shelter.'' He laughed softly. ''You stupid little toad, you would have done better to take me hostage. None of the others here, after all, has the power, as I do, to hunt you down like the vermin you are.''

As he spoke, he maintained a slow but steady advance toward Ninian, upon whose face had crept a flush of anger.

''Indeed,'' continued Jared, the sneer in his tone pronounced, ''I'm surprised you did not perceive that it is I who am your enemy here, not this woman or her brother. It was I, after all, who foiled your ill-conceived plan to assume the Stedford title. If it had not been for my efforts, you would have had no difficulty in obtaining and destroying those documents.''

Diana felt the little steel circle waver ever so slightly, and from the depth of her nightmare, allowed herself to hope.

Ninian's voice screeched in her ear.

''Shut up, Burnleigh! I—I don't have to listen to you. Just shut up!''

''No,'' responded Jared, his deep, calm voice contrasting sharply with Ninian's hysterical bleating, ''you don't have to listen to me, but what are you going to do about it? Creep away with your tail between your legs, I suppose. You surprise me, Crowne, you really do—to have let the opportunity of dealing with me slip through your fingers. Did you not realize it was I who caused your precious plot to fail?''

Closer and closer he moved, as Ninian's rage became apparent. In the background Marcus tensed, ready to spring.

''And it was I,'' Jared's insistent voice continued, ''who provided the final blow to your whole ludicrous scheme. You know, I was hard-pressed as to how I was going to maneuver you into taking possession of the papers, but you arranged it for me with your crafty little charade. I suppose you thought I really believed you to be choking. Actually, I could hardly keep from laughing as I pushed the packet into your greedy hands, thus springing the trap that brought down the whole wretched scheme around your ears."

Diana felt the convulsive shudder that shook Ninian. With a howl of rage, he thrust her from him. Now she could see the full force of the madness that contorted his face, and she lunged desperately. With a strength she did not know she possessed, she grasped his arm and bore it down and to one side.

The earl flung himself forward, ducking his head to avoid the pistol aimed directly at him. The sound of a report filled Diana's ears, and it seemed to her that the whole world exploded in a burst of deafening flame. She caught her breath in terror as the widening of Jared's dark eyes indicated to her that, in spite of her efforts, the bullet had found its mark.

Jared halted for an instant, then continued forward. He swung his fist in a blow that caught Ninian squarely on his chin and sent him spinning into a crumpled heap against the wall. Jared stood over him for a moment, an expression of satisfaction in his eyes. Then he swayed and sank to the floor, a small, bright stain appearing on the front of his coat.

To Diana the events of the next few seconds would forever remain a chaotic blur of blood and screams and trampling feet. Her only concern was for the still form that lay amid the dust and clutter on the floor. She was dimly aware that Lissa, too, had reached Jared's side and was sobbing uncontrollably.

Of Marcus and the Runners, who pushed past her to where Ninian lay sprawled, she knew nothing. She knelt and lifted Jared's head to her breast. To her shuddering relief, she noted the pulse that throbbed erratically in his throat, and curtly directing Lissa to procure some water and a cloth, she opened his coat and blood-stained shirt.

"Jared!" She cried the word again and then again. "Please open your eyes. Oh, my dearest love, look at me. Please be all right. You *have* to be all right!"

Somewhere in the recesses of her consciousness, she

realized that her words were senseless and of absolutely no help at all, but she remained beside him, crooning his name as her fingers struggled with buttons and cravat. He appeared to have been hit high in the shoulder, and she allowed herself to hope that the wound was not as serious as she had first feared.

In a moment Lissa reappeared, carrying a pan of water obtained from the well outside. Odile drew near and began to tear strips from her apron to form a makeshift bandage.

Jared stirred in Diana's arms and muttered thickly. His eyes opened and focused blearily on her face. He attempted to rise, then sank back against her shoulder, wincing.

Diana forced herself to a calm she was far from feeling.

"Gently, my lord." She eased him to the ground, pillowing his head on Odile's cloak. "You have been injured, and you must lie still until we can ascertain the extent of your wound."

"I think," gasped Jared, his eyes glittering darkly against his white face, "that it is only a scratch. I was so close to him, you see—and the bullet is of a very small caliber. I believe it merely tore through the flesh of my shoulder, instead of imbedding itself in the—the tissue."

"Merely tore through . . ." Diana repeated in a faint voice. Recovering, she replied as prosaically as she could "I hope that will prove to be the case, my lord. In the meantime, please remain still until we remove your coat."

She turned to observe, almost without interest, that Ninian had regained consciousness and knelt cowering on the floor, his hands manacled behind him. Those incredible sapphire eyes were now merely a muddy blue, and they were lowered in an unseeing stare. Diana beckoned to Marcus, who stood menacingly over the fallen villain.

The next few moments proved the earl correct. The wound, though ugly and raw-looking, was not large, and it was clean. From a capacious greatcoat, one of the Runners (the personally deputized assistant, Jasper Coombs) produced a flask of brandy, which, he averred, he always carried in case of emergency. Thus fortified, Jared was assisted to the little broken-backed chair.

To Diana's vast relief, it was not long before a tinge of color returned to the earl's lean features. Outside, the Runners were making arrangements to transport their prisoners. Churte, now also in handcuffs, stood near Ninian, glaring resentfully at him. A subdued Odile stared about her in a dazed fashion.

Marcus, his apprehension over Jared's condition relieved, returned to Lissa's side. That young lady, bewildered by the morning's events, turned a questioning gaze upon the young viscount, and a dawning wonder appeared in her eyes.

Jared looked about him with gratification, then, over Diana's protests, rose to his feet. Lissa, her bemused gaze drifting away from the handsome young man hovering over her, saw him rise, and hurried over to him.

"Oh, Jared!" she cried. "Can you ever forgive me? I—I almost got you killed! I did not mean to—truly I did not. I only wanted to visit Silverwell, and when Lord—that is when that dreadful wretch suggested an early-morning ride, it seemed like the very thing. I knew very well that Aunt would not approve, or you either for that matter, but it seemed like such a delightful lark. And, after all, I thought since I had my maid with me"—she shot a fulminating glance at Odile—"it would be quite unexceptionable. Then that awful person veered off from the road, and when we neared the oast house, he said—if you would believe!—that I looked as though I had the headache, and should stop to rest. Nothing I said would dissuade him, and—and I began to feel quite frightened. Oh, Jared, I'm so very, very sorry!"

So saying, she flung herself dramatically on her brother's bandaged bosom and dissolved in a flood of tears.

Jared flinched and shot an anguished glance at Diana, who hurried to extricate him from his sister's remorseful clutches.

The earl patted Lissa's shoulder in a harassed manner, assuring her that all was forgiven, and she scurried back to the warmth of Marcus's beaming adoration.

The next person to claim Jared's attention was Mr. Lightfoot, who bustled up to report that his prisoners were safely secured.

"I have a carriage standing by a few hundred yards away, yer lordship, all amongst the trees. I brought it as a contingency, you might say, thinking if we was successful we'd be needing to transport the miscreants. And as it turns out," he continued, greatly pleased at his foresight, "that's perzackly what's needed at the moment. Do you and yer party wish to be taken someplace first, yer lordship?"

"Thank you, Officer," responded Jared with appropriate gravity. "However, we will avail ourselves of the transportation already at hand."

He turned to Marcus.

"I believe we can all fit into the gig in which Churte and Odile arrived. I'll send someone back to collect the horses."

Jared moved toward the vehicle, and Diana hastened to intercept him.

"An excellent idea, my lord," she declared. "I am sure Marcus will be more than happy to drive."

"Nonsense, I am perfectly capable . . ."

In answer to an unspoken message from his sister, Marcus strode forward.

"You've been given your orders, Jared. You may as well submit gracefully."

He turned to a blushing Lissa and, taking her hand, carefully lifted her into the front seat of the gig.

With a laugh, Jared admitted defeat and moved toward Diana. As he reached her side, he moaned artistically and slumped against her.

"Alas," he said in a faint voice, "I fear you are right. I am weak as a cat, and must ask for your support, Nurse."

He placed his arm about her shoulder and drew her toward him, and as he smiled down into her face, Diana uttered a flustered gasp. It was only when they reached the gig that the earl straightened and put out a hand to assist her. As she climbed into the vehicle, she said lightly, in an attempt to cover her confusion, "Really, my lord, I quite feel that I should be mounting a snow-white palfrey."

Jared's brows rose in a mute question, and Diana lowered her eyes, suddenly shy.

"I believe that is the requisite form of transportation

for damsels who are rescued by knights in shining armor,'' she said. ''If you had not taunted Ninian into turning his pistol on you, I don't know what—''

The earl laughed softly. ''You are unkind, my dear. I have been endeavoring to forget the clumsiness with which I accomplished that maneuver. It was not at all in my plan to be on the receiving end of that gun. My intent was to move more quickly than Ninian, but the villainous Mr. Crowne proved to be a bit swifter off the mark than I bargained for. Indeed, if it weren't for your presence of mind in spoiling his aim, I fear I would now be lying back there with a bullet between my eyes.''

Diana shuddered, but before she could give utterance to her thoughts, Marcus, his passengers all in place, urged the horses forward, and the party moved on its way.

No sooner had they begun their journey than Lissa, whose youthful ebullience had already overcome the shock of the last hour's events, demanded an explanation of all that had happened.

Marcus and Jared launched on a somewhat chaotic exposition of the facts, but Diana said little. Her thoughts were still held suspended in that small eternity when first her life and then Jared's had been threatened.

Jared had risked his life for her. The words repeated themselves endlessly in her mind. Had he been impelled by an innate chivalry, or could it mean that he really cared for her?

She was intensely aware of the lean strength of his body, pressed against hers in the restricted confines of the gig's rear seat, and she was more than a little relieved when the vehicle swung into the stable yard at Stonefield.

24

When they reached the house, it became apparent that Aunt Amabelle had been watching for their return. As soon as they had made their way through the little side door and advanced into the corridor leading to the main part of the manor, they were met by her plump form, accompanied as usual by a dissonant chink of jewelry.

"Jared!" she cried breathlessly. "What in the world have you been—"

She stopped short as she absorbed the sight of the earl's bloodied garments.

"Jared! My dear boy, what has happened?"

She gazed accusingly at Marcus, recognizing him as the recalcitrant servant who had not only poured tea over a guest of the Court, but had appeared this morning at his duties in a completely unacceptable condition.

All the persons present broke into a loud but largely incomprehensible explanation, of which Aunt Amabelle caught only the word "gun" and "shot."

"Never mind!" She raised her hand for silence. Once more her personality seemed to change in the face of crisis. Her beads and bracelets stilled. She strode purposefully to Jared and deftly examined the bandage beneath his shirt. Then she drew him along the hall, ignoring his protests.

"Never mind," she repeated. "You do not seem in very bad case, so I daresay just a dusting of basilicum powder will be necessary. The rest of you," she said, glancing severely at the remainder of the group as if they were personally responsible for this outrage, "may wait upstairs. This will only take a moment."

The little party trooped obediently up a narrow flight of servants' stairs and gathered in the Crimson Saloon, where they again pored over the momentous events of the day.

It was not long before Jared joined them, dressed in a clean shirt, and with his coat draped over his freshly bandaged shoulder.

He moved first to Diana, grasping her hands in his. Then he turned to Marcus and Lissa, who stood side by side, looking very much as though they planned to stay that way through the remainder of their lives.

Marcus spoke first.

"Lord Burnleigh," he began diffidently, "I cannot begin to thank you for your efforts, but I believe now it is time for me to take up the reins of my own destiny. I must put into motion the steps that need to be taken for me to assume my inheritance."

Jared nodded in smiling agreement, and would have spoken but for an irascible voice that could be heard in the corridor, fast approaching the room in which they stood.

"Fishperk, unhand me! I have told you for the last time, I am sick of conducting my business from beneath a quilt. Amy, stop blithering. I will see my grandson, and I will see him now!"

The next moment the door flew open and Lord Chamford strode into the room, dressed in normal day wear, and walking very much under his own power.

"Hah!" he fairly bellowed on catching sight of Jared.

Irritatedly, he waved aside the efforts at assistance put forth by his daughter and his hovering valet.

"Come here, boy, and explain yourself. What is all this about a false viscount? And you were shot? Good God, I can't take to my bed for a few days without the entire family becoming embroiled in what sounds very much like brigandry."

Jared and Diana exchanged rueful glances, and the earl advanced to lead his grandfather to an armchair.

"Sir," he said, smiling, "you are indeed owed an explanation. I ask only one thing of you—your promise that you will refrain from comment until I have finished the whole." He sighed. "I only hope at that time I will not have sent you into a relapse, or prompted you to disown me entirely."

The marquess looked up at him, startled, and his eyes

sparked dangerously. The earl held his gaze, and after a moment, the old gentleman said simply, "Just give me a round tale, if you please, my boy. I will hear you out."

Jared looked again at Diana, and then, as though taking heart from her presence, drew a deep breath and began to speak.

"The whole thing started, Grandfather, with an unexpected encounter in a roadside inn. . . ."

The story took some time in the telling, but Jared's audience stayed with him, hanging on his every syllable. Lord Chamford, while keeping his promise to remain silent, rumbled ominously at several points during the narrative. At other times, however, his lips twitched suspiciously, and once or twice something very like a snort of laughter escaped him.

At long last the chronicle drew to a close, and Jared brought Marcus and Diana to Lord Chamford's side.

"And so, sir, I would like to present to you Marcus Crowne, the Viscount Stedford, and his sister Diana, the only surviving offspring of your friend Charles Crowne."

For a long moment, the old gentleman stared at them, his face working. He rose unsteadily and faced them, and in the next instant he opened his arms to engulf them in a shaking embrace.

"Welcome to Stonefield Court. Welcome to you both. I cannot tell you how it gladdens my heart to know that you have been found."

He stood back to inspect Marcus more fully. The young man had long since discarded the peruke with which he had started out the day, and his waving, cropped hair glinted pale in the shaft of sunlight that slanted through the room's long windows. He stood, tall and slender, a wide smile lighting his hazel eyes.

The marquess put a shaking hand to his eyes.

"You are very like him," he whispered. "I could almost believe I was a boy again, with Charlie standing before me, ready for any devilment."

He turned to Diana.

"And you, my dear—not Miss Bavister from Dhu-Rydd, Wales, but Diana Crowne. And I must tell you, this old man has fallen captive to both of you." He raised a thin hand to touch her hair. "I knew I recognized that crown of old gold. I should have thought of the explanation myself. And to tell a sick man such an outrageous faradiddle! But," he said, swinging to fix Jared with a fierce glare, "I know well that the fault for that lies elsewhere. Abducting innocent females! Telling baldfaced lies to me!"

Jared lifted his hand in placation.

"Grandfather, you have every reason to comb my hair with a joint stool. All I can say is that it seemed like a good idea at the time. I truly meant it for the best."

"Aye, lad. I know that—and it's all that's saving you from the rarest trimming I've ever given anyone in this family."

Diana smiled mistily at the two. She had been greatly concerned at what Lord Chamford would say when he learned of the deception that had been perpetrated on him. She might have known that the bond between the old gentleman and his grandchildren could not be broken even by such a trick, engendered as it had been by love.

Aunt Amabelle was no less astonished at the tale that fell from Jared's lips. She hurried now to draw Diana to her bosom.

"I knew it!" she cried, her jewelry chiming merrily. "I knew there was *something* about you! And now you will be close to us always."

She turned and held out a plump hand to Marcus.

"And welcome to you, dear boy." She sighed, bringing her handkerchief to her eyes. "Oh, what a happy day this has turned out to be."

Talk of the astonishing sequence of events that had taken place continued throughout the remainder of the day. It was not long before the entire household had been put in possession of the facts, and Mallow allowed himself a few appropriate words of welcome and congratulations, as did Fishperk, Mrs. Ingersoll the housekeeper, and several other selected denizens of the stewards' hall.

Well into dinner, the ramifications of the news that would soon spread among the *haut ton* were exhaustively discussed.

"Wait until Simon and Charlotte hear of this!" crowed Lissa.

"How soon will you be moving into Silverwell?" asked Aunt Amabelle. "Not," she added hastily, "that you both are not welcome to stay for as long as you like.''

Jared spoke quietly.

"I took the liberty of sending a message to the estate attorneys shortly after our arrival home this afternoon. I requested a meeting with them at Silverwell tomorrow afternoon. At that time, I should think, the business will be cleared up, and if I am not much mistaken, Marcus and Diana will be able to move into their home at their convenience.''

Marcus grinned in satisfaction, and in the flutter of conversation that followed, Jared sank back in his chair and gave himself up to thought. The marquess sat ensconced in his chair at the head of the board, beaming his happiness at the entire table. Lord, it was good to see him back in place. But why, Jared wondered, had the old gentleman nothing to say about the very crux of the deception? He had not once commented on the fact that his grandson was not now, and never had been, betrothed.

At the other end of the table, Lord Chamford kept his own counsel. If this aspect of the day's revelations had occurred to him, he gave no sign. No one noticed his shrewd old eyes glance first at Jared and then Diana, and back again. No one perceived the small smile that curved his lips.

After dinner a fatigued Lord Chamford retired to his chambers. During the conversation that followed in the music room, Diana, her senses intensely heightened as far as Jared was concerned, became aware that he was observing her surreptitiously from across the room. One by one the family members bade good night to those remaining, until Jared and Diana were the only two persons left by the flickering fire.

Abruptly becoming aware of this fact, Diana rose and addressed the earl.

"It is indeed growing late, my lord—and, and this has been—that is, it is time for me to seek my bed as well.''

Mentally castigating herself for her inability to form the most commonplace civilities, she moved toward the door, but was intercepted by the earl.

For a long moment he just gazed at her. Dark eyes

reached into gray ones, as though he were searching into the very center of her heart.

She stepped away from him and put her hands behind her back, desperately casting about in her mind for something to say. Anything to interrupt that penetrating gaze!

"My lord, before I retire, I would like to take this opportunity to thank you."

Jarred stiffened, and Diana continued in some haste.

"You have done so much for my brother and me, and we are well aware of what we owe you."

Jared's brows snapped together, but Diana ploughed ahead, undeterred.

"Not only did you save my life today, but it was through your efforts that the Runners were put on to Ninian, and—and contacting the magistrate—and the attorneys, and—and all that. . . ."

Her mind simply dried up at that point, and her voice trailed off in a strangled gasp. Jared, the spark of devil's fire once more showing itself in his eyes, moved close to her again and placed his hands gently on her shoulders.

"Very prettily said, Miss Crowne, but I think we have something else to discuss."

Despite herself, Diana trembled slightly.

"By the by," continued the earl, "I very much enjoyed hearing my first name on your lips today. As a reward for all those wonderful things I have accomplished on your behalf, may I ask that you drop that infernal 'my lord' for good? Please?"

"But it would not be proper, my—sir," she murmured shakily.

The very improper feelings that his touch sent surging through her made the words seem ludicrous.

"In any event—Miss Crowne—we have some unfinished business between us, you and I. Shall we return to the extremely interesting conversation we were having this morning when your tiresome brother so rudely interrupted us? I trust it has not slipped your mind in the turmoil of the day's events that yesterday I offered for you?"

Diana tried to step back. She could not think clearly with the scent of him filling her senses, or his breath brushing warm against her face, but she remained imprisoned in a grip that was powerful yet achingly tender.

With all the dignity she could muster, she replied, "I have not forgotten, my lord. I hope that you also remember that you agreed not to bring up the subject again."

"Mmm, yes." His mouth widened in that heart-stopping grin. "But that was before you told me you love me."

"Love you?" The words ended in a quavering squeak. Dear Lord, he had heard all she had babbled to him when she thought him dying!

"Yes, I heard you quite clearly," Jared responded, as though reading her mind. His voice quivered suspiciously, and a devil of amusement danced in his eyes. "And I must say I will think myself hardly used indeed if you now play me false."

"Sir!" She drew herself up in an effort to salvage the last rags of her pride. "It is ungentlemanly of you to throw in my face words that I spoke in the heat of—in—in the commotion of the moment."

"But as you pointed out early in our acquaintance, I only call myself a gentleman. In reality, I am—what was it? I forget precisely what the particular term was that you used to denigrate my character." He raised his hand to halt the reply he saw forming in her eyes. "Not that I did not deserve every word."

He bent his head closer, and Diana found that her trembling seemed to increase proportionately to the narrowing of the gap between his mouth and hers. She searched inside herself for help from the Schoolmistress, but that bulwark of propriety had apparently been transformed into a simpering idiot, lost in a pink cloud of sensation.

Jared stepped back suddenly. His eyes were serious now, and his grip on her shoulders tightened. Haltingly, as though groping for the right words, he began to speak.

"Diana, listen to me. The things I said to you when we first met were unforgivable, and I can offer no excuse for them except that I hardened myself so many years ago to the pleadings and deceptions of grasping females that I had forgotten there was any other kind. I—I had a rather unfortunate experience a long time ago. Perhaps one day I'll tell you about it, now that it doesn't matter anymore.

"I knew long before I discovered your identity that you are a lady in every sense of the word, only my stupid pride—and . . .'' He paused. ''All I can say is that all the reasons I gave for wanting to marry you were pure face-saving drivel. I couldn't admit to myself the real reason. It didn't occur to me that you might return my—that is, like a clunch, I thought a title and property and wealth and all the nonsense that goes with it might sway you, but—''

The pent-up words tumbled from his lips, until at last he caught himself and stopped short.

''Oh, God, Diana, I've made such a mull of it. The reason I offered for you is simply that the prospect of living the rest of my life without you is more than I can bear. I want you, Diana, and I need you—and I love you with all my heart.''

Diana moved toward him slowly. She lifted a hand that now, oddly, did not tremble in the slightest. Gently she traced the beloved line of his jaw with one slender finger. At last she smiled, all the warmth of the sun at midday breaking from behind the clouds in her gray eyes.

''In that case, my l—Jared, I had better accept your proposal. I should not like to be the cause of a life of misery for you. And—and I think you'd better kiss me. I like it very much when you kiss me. I do love you, Jared,'' she finished in a shaky gasp. ''I love you with everything that's in me!''

His eyes alight, Jared drew her into an embrace that threatened to crack her ribs. He drew back for an instant, looking into her face as though he could not get his fill of her. Then his mouth came down on hers.

They were thus occupied some minutes later when Diana suddenly pushed herself gently from his embrace.

''Jared! What about all those people who were here yesterday? Your friends and neighbors. What in the world are we going to tell them?''

''Never fear, my angel,'' responded her beloved. ''I have a plan.''

''No, don't tell me,'' responded Diana mischievously. ''You will tell them that Diana Bavister is, in reality, a scheming adventuress who bears a striking resemblance to Diana Crowne. Realizing this, she insinuated herself into your household, with the intention of—''

Here Jared interrupted in a tone of mock disapproval.

"But, my sweet life, that would be an untruth. I am dismayed by this penchant of yours for deception."

He paused to close Diana's lips with his own to forestall any reply she might be about to make. After some moments, he continued.

"No, what I had in mind was to tell the simple truth—more or less."

Catching her expression, he assumed an air of reproachful innocence.

"We shall invite them all here to a dinner party, at which we will announce our betrothal. At some time during the proceedings, I shall announce that I am about to let them into a mystery. I shall give them an expurgated version of the Stedford usurpation, explaining that you and your brother, upon becoming aware of Ninian Crowne's perfidy, came to me for assistance."

"In our hour of need, as it were," murmured his betrothed.

"Precisely. With my usual quickness of mind, I instantly devised a plot to unmask the villain, which involved your coming to Stonefield under an assumed name—a temporary measure, of course."

"Upon which," continued Diana smoothly, "you seized upon the opportunity to arrange a marriage of convenience between the Talent and Crowne progeny."

Jared drew her into an embrace that left her breathless.

"No one, my very dearest darling, on beholding you, would believe such nonsense."

Silence fell on the music room, until a moment later Diana again raised her head.

"Your grandfather!" she cried softly. "What will he say about this?"

"He will say," responded her beloved, before bending his head to hers again, " 'Hah! About time, don'tcher think?' "

Ⓞ SIGNET REGENCY ROMANCE

ROMANTIC ENCOUNTERS

☐	LADY OF QUALITY by Georgette Heyer	(173457—$4.99)
☐	REGENCY BUCK by Georgette Heyer	(171713—$4.99)
☐	DEVIL'S CUB by Georgette Heyer	(172116—$4.99)
☐	A BARONET'S WIFE by Laura Matthews	(171284—$3.99)
☐	ALICIA by Laura Matthews	(171977—$3.99)
☐	THE SEVENTH SUITOR by Laura Matthews	(170202—$3.99)
☐	LORD CLAYBORNE'S FANCY by Laura Matthews	(170652—$3.99)
☐	THE BARBAROUS SCOT by Dawn Lindsey	(170628—$3.99)
☐	DEVIL'S LADY by Dawn Lindsey	(169603—$3.99)
☐	DANGEROUS MASQUERADE by April Kihlstrom	(170806—$3.99)
☐	THE RECKLESS WAGER by April Kihlstrom	(170903—$3.99)
☐	THE NABOB'S WARD by Evelyn Richardson	(170881—$3.99)
☐	COUNTRY DANCE by Margaret Westhaven	(170180—$3.99)
☐	THE LADY IN QUESTION by Margaret Westhaven	(171039—$3.99)

Prices slightly higher in Canada

Buy them at your local bookstore or use this convenient coupon for ordering.

NEW AMERICAN LIBRARY
P.O. Box 999, Bergenfield, New Jersey 07621

Please send me the books I have checked above.
I am enclosing $_____ (please add $2.00 to cover postage and handling).
Send check or money order (no cash or C.O.D.'s) or charge by Mastercard or
VISA (with a $15.00 minimum). Prices and numbers are subject to change without
notice.

Card #_____ Exp. Date _____
Signature_____
Name_____
Address_____
City _____ State _____ Zip Code _____

For faster service when ordering by credit card call **1-800-253-6476**

Allow a minimum of 4-6 weeks for delivery. This offer is subject to change without notice.

⊘SIGNET REGENCY ROMANCE　　　　　　　　　　**(0451)**

LOVE IN THE HIGHEST CIRCLES

☐　**MISS GRIMSLEY'S OXFORD CAREER by Carla Kelly**　(171950—$3.99)
☐　**THE IMPROPER PLAYWRIGHT by Margaret Summerville**

　　　　　　　　　　　　　　　　　　　　　(171969—$3.99)
☐　**A DASHING WIDOW by Carol Proctor**　　　　　(170423—$3.99)
☐　**LORD BUCKINGHAM'S BRIDE by Sandra Heath**　(169573—$3.99)
☐　**A CHRISTMAS COURTSHIP by Sandra Heath**　　(167929—$3.95)
☐　**LORD KANE'S KEEPSAKE by Sandra Heath**　　(172264—$3.99)
☐　**TALK OF THE TOWN by Irene Saunders**　　　(170172—$3.99)
☐　**THE DOWAGER'S DILEMMA by Irene Saunders**　(169581—$3.99)
☐　**LADY ARDEN'S REDEMPTION by Marjorie Farrell**　(171942—$3.99)
☐　**AUTUMN ROSE by Marjorie Farrell.**　　　　　(168747—$3.95)
☐　**THE ROGUE'S RETURN by Anita Mills**　　　　(172582—$3.99)
☐　**MISS GORDON'S MISTAKE by Anita Mills**　　　(168518—$3.99)
☐　**THE UNOFFICIAL SUITOR by Charlotte Louise Dolan**　(173007—$3.99)
☐　**THREE LORDS FOR LADY ANNE by Charlotte Louise Dolan**

　　　　　　　　　　　　　　　　　　　　　(170644—$3.99)
☐　**THE RESOLUTE RUNAWAY by Charlotte Louise Dolan**　(171691—$3.99)

Prices slightly higher in Canada

Buy them at your local bookstore or use this convenient coupon for ordering.

NEW AMERICAN LIBRARY
P.O. Box 999, Bergenfield, New Jersey 07621

Please send me the books I have checked above.
I am enclosing $_____ (please add $2.00 to cover postage and handling).
Send check or money order (no cash or C.O.D.'s) or charge by Mastercard or
VISA (with a $15.00 minimum). Prices and numbers are subject to change without
notice.

Card #_____ Exp. Date _____
Signature_____
Name_____
Address_____
City _____ State _____ Zip Code _____

For faster service when ordering by credit card call **1-800-253-6476**

Allow a minimum of 4-6 weeks for delivery. This offer is subject to change without notice.

Ø SIGNET REGENCY ROMANCE   (0451)

ROMANTIC INTERLUDES

☐ **AN UNLIKELY ATTRACTION** by Melinda McRae (170636—$3.99)
☐ **IRISH EARL'S RUSE** by Emma Lange (172574—$3.99)
☐ **THE UNMANAGEABLE MISS MARLOWE** by Emma Lange (170458—$3.99)
☐ **THE HIDDEN HEART** by Gayle Buck (172353—$3.99)
☐ **MUTUAL CONSENT** by Gayle Buck (169395—$3.99)
☐ **THE WALTZING WIDOW** by Gayle Buck (167376—$3.99)
☐ **A CHANCE ENCOUNTER** by Gayle Buck (170873—$3.99)
☐ **THE MOCK MARRIAGE** by Dorothy Mack (170199—$3.99)
☐ **A WIFE FOR WARMINSTER** by Margaret Summerville (169751—$3.99)
☐ **THE WICKED PROPOSAL** by Emily Hendrickson (172345—$3.99)
☐ **A SCANDALOUS SUGGESTION** by Emily Hendrickson (169921—$3.99)
☐ **THE DASHING MISS FAIRCHILD** by Emily Hendrickson (171276—$3.99)
☐ **A PERFECT PERFORMANCE** by Emily Hendrickson (171047—$3.99)
☐ **THE BATH ECCENTRIC'S SON** by Amanda Scott (171705—$3.99)
☐ **BATH CHARADE** by Amanda Scott (169948—$3.99)
☐ **A LOVE MATCH** by Barbara Allister (169387—$3.99)

Buy them at your local bookstore or use this convenient coupon for ordering.

NEW AMERICAN LIBRARY
P.O. Box 999, Bergenfield, New Jersey 07621

Please send me the books I have checked above.
I am enclosing $_____ (please add $2.00 to cover postage and handling).
Send check or money order (no cash or C.O.D.'s) or charge by Mastercard or
VISA (with a $15.00 minimum). Prices and numbers are subject to change without
notice.

Card #_____ Exp. Date _____
Signature_____
Name_____
Address_____
City _____ State _____ Zip Code _____

For faster service when ordering by credit card call **1-800-253-6476**

Allow a minimum of 4-6 weeks for delivery. This offer is subject to change without notice.

Ⓢ SIGNET REGENCY ROMANCE (0451)

NOVELS OF LOVE AND DESIRE

☐ **A CERTAIN MAGIC by Mary Balogh.** It was only after Piers Westhaven asked another to be his bride that the lovely young widow Alice Penhallow found that the way she needed Piers went beyond friendship . . . beyond propriety . . . to the very very brink of scandal. . . .

(169166—$3.95)

☐ **THE SUBSTITUTE BRIDEGROOM by Charlotte Dolan.** Elizabeth Goldsborough was to wed the most handsome gentleman of the *ton*. But an accidental encounter with the arrogant Captain Darius St. John left her with no choice but to marry this man she barely knew . . . (168917—$3.95)

☐ **DOUBLE DECEIT by Emily Hendrickson.** Miss Caroline Beauchamp accepted the tricky task of seducing the handsome husband of her dearest friend to break the hold that an infamous beauty had on the vulnerable Viscount. But she also had to bedazzle the most renowned rake in the realm, Lord Rutledge, to keep him from making Mary his latest conquest.

(168534—$3.95)

☐ **A REGENCY VALENTINE.** The joys and passions that surround St. Valentine's Day are captured in an extraordinary collection of all-new stories by five of the most highly acclaimed Regency authors: Mary Balogh, Katherine Kingsley, Emma Lange, Patricia Rice, and Joan Wolf.

(168909—$4.50)

☐ **THE UNLIKELY CHAPERONE by Dorothy Mack.** Alexandra was supposed to be protecting her sister, Didi, from men. But now she was sorely tempted to protect men from Didi. One man, at least. the man whom Didi wanted as a victim . . . and whom Alexandra wanted in a very different way. (168933—$3.95)

Buy them at your local bookstore or use this convenient coupon for ordering.

NEW AMERICAN LIBRARY
P.O. Box 999, Bergenfield, New Jersey 07621

Please send me the books I have checked above.
I am enclosing $_____ (please add $2.00 to cover postage and handling).
Send check or money order (no cash or C.O.D.'s) or charge by Mastercard or VISA (with a $15.00 minimum). Prices and numbers are subject to change without notice.

Card #_____ Exp. Date _____
Signature_____
Name_____
Address_____
City _____ State _____ Zip Code _____

For faster service when ordering by credit card call **1-800-253-6476**

Allow a minimum of 4-6 weeks for delivery. This offer is subject to change without notice.